URSULA ORANGE
COMPANY IN THE EVENING

URSULA MARGUERITE DOROTHEA ORANGE was born in Simla in 1909, the daughter of the Director General of Education in India, Sir Hugh Orange. But when she was four the family returned to England. She was later 'finished' in Paris, and then went up to Lady Margaret Hall, Oxford in 1928. It was there that she and Tim Tindall met. They won a substantial sum of money on a horse, enough to provide the couple with the financial independence to marry, which they did in 1934.

Ursula Orange's first novel, *Begin Again*, was published with success in 1936, followed by *To Sea in a Sieve* in 1937. In 1938 her daughter, the writer Gillian Tindall, was born, and the next year the war changed their lives completely. Their London home was badly damaged and, as her husband left for the army, Ursula settled in the country with Gillian, where she had ample opportunity to observe the comic, occasionally tragic, effects of evacuation: the subject of her biggest success, *Tom Tiddler's Ground* (1941). Three more novels followed, continuing to deal with the indirect effects of war: conflicts of attitude, class and the generations, wherever disparate characters are thrown together.

The end of the war saw the family reunited and in 1947 the birth of her son Nicholas. But Ursula Orange's literary career foundered, and the years that followed saw her succumb to severe depression and periods of hospital treatment. In 1955 she died aged 46.

By Ursula Orange

Begin Again (1936)
To Sea in a Sieve (1937)
Tom Tiddler's Ground
(1941, published in the U.S. as *Ask Me No Questions*)
Have Your Cake (1942)
Company in the Evening (1944)
Portrait of Adrian (1945)

URSULA ORANGE

COMPANY IN THE EVENING

With an introduction
by Stacy Marking

DEAN STREET PRESS

A Furrowed Middlebrow Book
FM12

Published by Dean Street Press 2017

Copyright © 1944 Ursula Orange
Introduction copyright © 2017 Stacy Marking

All Rights Reserved

The right of Ursula Orange to be identified as the Author of the Work has been asserted by her estate in accordance with the Copyright, Designs and Patents Act 1988.

First published in 1944 by Michael Joseph

Cover by DSP
Cover illustration shows detail from
Searchlights (1916) by Christopher R.W. Nevinson

ISBN 978 1 911579 29 8

www.deanstreetpress.co.uk

INTRODUCTION

ON THE FIRST page of a notebook filled with carefully pasted press cuttings, Ursula Orange has inscribed, in touchingly school girlish handwriting: *Begin Again, Published February 13th 1936*. Later she adds: *American Publication Aug 7th 1936*, and then a pencilled note: *Total sales 1221*.

She was 26, a young married woman, and this was her first novel. There are plentiful reviews from major publications in Britain, Australia and America. *Begin Again* by Ursula Orange is included in the *Washington Herald*'s Bestsellers' list for August 1936, where it comes higher than *Whither France?* by Leon Trotsky. The *Daily Telegraph* praises her insight into "the strange ways of the New Young, their loves, their standards, their shibboleths, and their manners ... An unusually good first novel, in a decade of good first novels."

To be greeted as the voice of the new generation must have been thrilling for a young writer, and a year later her second novel was published. *To Sea in a Sieve* opens with the heroine Sandra being sent down from Lady Margaret Hall, Oxford, the college which Ursula herself had so recently left. Rebellious and in pursuit of freedom, Sandra rejects convention, marries an 'advanced' and penniless lover, and the novel lightheartedly recounts the consequences of her contrariness.

But despite her light tone, Ursula Orange takes on serious themes in all her work. She explores the conflicts between generations, between classes, between men and women. Her characters embrace new and modern attitudes to morality, sex and marriage, and take adultery and divorce with surprising frivolity. She understands young women's yearning for independence, their need to express themselves and to escape the limitations of domesticity – though she often mocks the results.

In 1938 she had her first child, Gillian, and by 1941 when her third and most successful novel, *Tom Tiddler's Ground*, was published, the chaos of war had overshadowed the brittle 'modern' world of her generation. With her husband now away in the army, Ursula and her small daughter left London to take refuge in the country, where she could observe firsthand the impact of evacuation on a small English village (just as her heroine Caroline does in the novel).

Tom Tiddler's Ground is set in 1939-40, the months later known as the "phoney war." The evacuation of London is under way, but the horrors of the Blitz have not yet begun. The clash between rustic villagers and London evacuees, the misunderstandings between upper and lower classes, differing approaches to love and children, the strains of war and separation on relationships and marriage: all these indirect effects of war provide great material for the novel. The *Sunday Times* describes it as "taking a delectably unusual course of its own, and for all the gas-masks hiding in the background, [it] is the gayest of comedies." It's a delightful read to this day, and includes an astonishing number of elements, ingeniously interwoven – bigamy, adultery, seduction, fraud, theft, embezzlement, the agonies of a childless marriage and the guilt of a frivolously undertaken love affair.

The book reveals a real talent for dialogue and structure. As Caroline arrives for the first time at her new home in a Kentish village, the scene, the plots and sub-plots, the major characters and the themes are all established on a single page, almost entirely in dialogue.

> "Red car," said Marguerite ecstatically as Lavinia's Hulton sports model, with Alfred in the driving seat, drew up alongside.
>
> "Excuse me," said Caroline, leaning out, "but can you tell me where a house called The Larches is?"
>
> "The Larches!" Alfred was out of his seat in a minute, and advancing with outstretched hand: "Have I the pleasure of addressing Mrs. Cameron?"
>
> "Good God!" said Caroline, taken aback. "So you're – are you Constance's husband by any chance, or what?" (It might be. About forty. Not bad-looking, I will say that for

Constance. That slick, smart, take-me-for-an-ex-public-schoolboy type. Eyes a bit close together.)

"Yes, I'm Captain Smith." (Caroline found her hand firmly taken and shaken.) "And Constance and I are very very pleased to welcome you to Chesterford."

"But that isn't Constance," said Caroline, feebly indicating Lavinia. Alfred gave an easy laugh.

"Oh no! Constance is home waiting for you." (Or I hope she is and not hanging round after that slum-mother and her brat, curse them.) "This is Miss Lavinia Conway," he said, taking her in a proprietary way by the elbow to help her out of the car.

"How do you do?" said Caroline, recovering herself. (.... Who is this girl? Good God even I didn't put it on quite so thick at her age. Can't be Alfred's little bit, surely?)

Part of the entertainment throughout the novel is the contrast between the perfect politeness of everything expressed aloud, and the bracketed thoughts that are left unsaid. Ursula Orange uses the device not to convey complex interior monologue, in the way of Virginia Woolf or Joyce, but as a comic, sometimes cynical, commentary on her characters' evasions and self-deception.

The notices and sales for *Tom Tiddler's Ground* were good, but Ursula must have been disconcerted to receive a personal letter from her new publisher, Michael Joseph himself. He had been away at the wars, he explains, and has been reading the novel in hospital. He writes that he was "immensely entertained" and predicts "that it is only a question of time – and the always necessary slice of good luck – before you become a really big seller ..." But then he adds: "The only criticism that I venture to offer is that Caroline's unorthodox behaviour ... may have prevented the book from having a bigger sale. I think it is still true, even in these days, that the public likes its heroines pure."

Whether influenced by Michael Joseph's strictures or no, in her next novel, *Have Your Cake*, the clashes of moral values, of hidden motives, of snobbery and class distinction, are not taken so lightly. Published in August 1942, it features an ex-Communist writer who (in the words of *The Times*) "is one of those devastating people who go through life pursuing laudable ends but breaking hearts and ruining lives at almost every turn." But lives and hearts are not ultimately broken: the notices are good; sales figures top 2500 – evidently "the Boots Family Public", and her publisher, were pleased.

By 1944 when *Company In the Evening* was published, Ursula Orange's crisp dialogue-driven style has altered. Told in the first person, with greater awareness and self-analysis, it is the story of Vicky, a divorcee whose marriage had been abandoned almost carelessly (and somehow without her ex-husband discovering that she's having their child). Vicky finds herself coping single handedly in a household of disparate and incompatible characters thrown together by war. Less engaging than Ursula Orange's earlier heroines, Vicky seems particularly hard on her very young and widowed sister-in-law, who is "just so hopelessly not my sort of person", in other words what her mother would have called common.

The novel is full of the taken-for-granted snobbery of the era – hard for the modern reader to stomach. In fact Vicky raises the issue, though somewhat equivocally, herself.

> "When I was about 19 and suffering from a terrific anti-snob complex (one had to make *some* protest against the extraordinary smugness and arrogance of the wealthy retired inhabitants ...) I practically forbade Mother to use the word 'common' ... "Don't you see, Mother, it isn't a question of phraseology, it's your whole *attitude* I object to."

But just as one starts to feel sympathetic, she adds:

> "Goodness, what mothers of semi-intellectual daughters of nineteen have to put up with!"

As the novel progresses, Vicky's faults are acknowledged, her mistakes rectified, her marriage repaired. She returns contentedly "to ordinary married life in the middle of the worst war ever known to history."

Perhaps this context is the point. The *New York Times* praises Ursula for her admirably stiff upper lip: "Ursula Orange, calmly ignoring as negligible all that Hitler has done, ... has written a novel that is a wet towel slapped nonchalantly across the face of the aggressor. " Her light and entertaining novels were indeed helping the nation to carry on.

At last in 1945 war came to an end. English life returned to a difficult peace of deprivation and scarcity. Tim Tindall, Ursula's husband, had been almost entirely absent for 5 years, a total stranger to their young daughter. He had had – in that odd English phrase – a 'good war', seeing action in North Africa, Salerno and France. After his return, the family opted for country life; Tim picked up the reins of the family's publishing firm, commuting daily to London and an independent existence, while Ursula passed her time in Sussex with Gillian and her new baby son. That year she published one more novel, *Portrait of Adrian*, which escapes to an earlier period and the happier existence of young girls sharing a flat together in London.

Ursula's horizons seem gradually to narrow. She had been the smart, modern voice of a young and careless generation that no longer existed, and she did not find a new place in the post-war world. Severe depression set in, leading to suicide attempts and hospital treatments. Her literary life had virtually come to an end. She undertook two projects but these were never realized, perhaps because they were well before their time: an illustrated anthology of poetry for teenagers, a category as yet unnamed; and a play about Shelley's as yet unheralded wives.

In *Footprints in Paris*, (2009) their daughter, the writer Gillian Tindall, describes her mother's decline as she becomes "someone who has failed at the enterprise of living.... London now began to figure on her mental map as the place she might find again her true self." But the hope of finding a fresh life when the family moved to a new house in Hampstead, proved illusory. "Six days later, having by the move severed further the ties that had held her to life ... she made another suicide attempt which, this time, was fatal. She was not found for two days."

But we cannot let this sad ending define the whole of Ursula Orange. It should not detract from our enjoyment of her work, which at its entertaining best, gives us a picture of a sparkling generation, of intelligent and audacious women surviving against the odds, with wit as well as stoicism, with courage in the face of deprivation and loss.

Stacy Marking

Chapter 1

IN THE EVENT OF AN AIR-RAID PASSENGERS ARE ADVISED TO ... ETC.

I DID NOT WANT to keep on idly reading and re-reading this notice, and yet, as I sat in my third-class railway carriage, travelling slowly and with frequent stops, not to mention two changes, towards my destination—Winterbury Green in Sussex—my eyes were constantly falling on it. There was, as always, a certain grim humour in the picture it conjured up. ("Excuse me if I lie on top of you, Madam." "Not at all, I believe it's safer underneath.") I remembered the mixture of horror and amusement with which I had first read such a notice in the early days of the war. Fantastic that such instructions should actually appear in a railway carriage on a branch line of the Southern Railway, a line that, moreover, I had known all my life! Yes, the instinctive "It *can't* happen here" reflex was pretty deeply-rooted in all of us, I suppose, even in those who, like myself, had been worrying about the impending war for a long time before it happened. Later, of course, during that first winter of the war, one had become so used to all the paraphernalia of A.R.P. and its faintly comic charade flavour (with jokes about 'casualties' due to falling over sandbags in the black-out) that one ceased to pay any attention to such notices.

But now it was August, 1940, and I did not need the newspaper that lay beside me on the seat of the railway carriage to remind me that the instructions to passengers in the event of an air-raid were no longer entirely a joking matter. Not, of course, that I had the slightest intention of taking the advice given. Like everybody else, I hung out of the window and saw and heard all I could. Already there had been three or four alerts, and, from my carriage window, I had seen patches of sky strangely patterned with wreaths and puffs of smoke. Now and again, when the train was stationary, I had heard the rattle of machine guns in the clouds above, and once I had caught a glimpse of a plane heeling over and diving drunkenly downwards, smoke pouring from it, plunging into the sunlit August woods beyond Redhill—whether one of Ours or one of Theirs I had no idea.

War in the air over a countryside I had known all my life! (Yes, the nerve of shocked incredulity was evidently not quite dead.) I could not help remembering, with a further shiver at the sheer incongruity of it, that it was along part of this same pleasant meandering railway line that the troops rescued from Dunkirk had travelled back from Dover. At every little stop the inhabitants of the villages had gathered to cheer, to cry, to press cups of tea, glasses of beer, packets of chocolate on the returning soldiers. I had never been able to make up my mind whether it was a fine outburst of spontaneous emotion or a rather regrettable display of mass hysteria. Perhaps the latter possibility only occurred to me because my brother Philip was one of the ones who didn't come back from Dunkirk.

Philip's death was really the reason why I was now travelling, only in the opposite direction, through these same villages that might once have welcomed him back as a returning hero. I was going to spend the week-end with my mother at Winterbury Green, and the object of my visit was to discuss the problem of Rene, Philip's widow. Mother had written me a long letter about it.

The letter was not entirely a cry for help, and yet I naturally interpreted it as such. It was, I felt, my turn to help Mother out now. Four years ago, at the time of my divorce, Mother had been a tower of strength to me. I had more or less collapsed on her shoulder and allowed her to take charge of me. Mother, being Mother, was, of course, only too ready to do so. And I, being I, had used her as a refuge while I was in need of a refuge, drawn strength and encouragement from her, and then, when I was restored again, had slipped back into being my old independent self. Not that Mother would ever hold this against me. Not that she would consider for a moment that I 'owed' her anything. Not that I would tell her, in so many words, that I thought I did. Nevertheless I felt that, if only to get the sensation for my own satisfaction of a sum coming out right, I ought now to relieve Mother of the responsibility of Rene.

Mother was sixty-six—just twice my age. It was only quite recently that I had begun to notice that she might strike one possibly as an 'old lady' rather than as a 'middle-aged woman.' I think the double shock of Father's death and my divorce, following close on each other, had aged her more than I, selfishly wrapped up in my own unhappiness, had noticed at the time.

Her letter to me was more of an appeal for help than I had ever received from her before. Was it (bless her!) meant to be a model of tactful suggestion? I did not have much difficulty in reading between the lines:

> FOURWAYS,
> WINTERBURY GREEN,
> *August 20th.*

DARLING VICKY,

Such an extraordinary thing has happened—two things really. I have got a very good offer for the house, and I must say I do feel very tempted. It has been so *much* too big for me since Daddy died and the young maid I have working for me now is a perfect *rabbit* about air-raids and I seem to spend all my time escorting her to the shelter and back—*such* nonsense, but of course I did promise her mother I'd send her to it (not that she needs sending, she simply scuttles), and then I do feel I ought to make Rene go too because of the baby, so the result is we pop in and out all day, and it's exactly like playing that idiotic game of rabbits that you and Philip used to love so when you were small, only really now I'm too old for that sort of thing. Well, the other thing is (and it's really extraordinary how it's happened at the same time!) I have had a long letter from Aunt Maud *urging* me to join forces with her in her cottage at Chipping Campden. Poor darling, she's very lonely since Uncle Hubert died, and although I know people always pretend sisters don't get on if they live together, she and I have always been the *greatest* friends, and we would prevent each other from being lonely. Not that

I mean I'm lonely, darling, because, of course, I'm luckier than poor Aunt Maud with no children, because I've still got you and your visits to look forward to and my darling grand-daughter to brag about, although it does make me *furious* that you can't bring her here any more, because of the raids, and that's another reason why it seems pointless keeping on the house.

Well, that's how it is, you see, and of course the only problem is Rene. I know I told her there'd always be a home for her with me, and for the baby too when it comes (I do *hope* all these sojourns in the shelter won't affect it mentally!), but the trouble is there just isn't room in Aunt Maud's cottage, and really I can't help thinking she'd be happier with people nearer her own age. She's only nineteen, poor child, and I'm afraid sometimes she pines a bit. There's nobody for her here among all us old people, except Mrs. Grantham's Sylvia, and I tried to make them chum up, but they tiresomely wouldn't. Have you any possible suggestion? I haven't breathed a *word* about all this to Rene yet, and of course the *last* thing I want is to make her feel she's not wanted, particularly as the poor child hasn't any parents of her own. Couldn't you come down for a week-end soon and we could talk it all over? I make Rene sleep under the stairs—I draw the line at the shelter at *night*!—so you could have your old room. A kiss to my darling Antonia and tell her I have nearly finished knitting the doll's frock. Let me know soon, darling, whether you can come, won't you?

Much love,
MOTHER.

Poor Rene! "The *last* thing I want is to make her feel she's not wanted." I knew my mother's tender heart well enough to know that this was absolutely sincere. I would even refrain from pointing out to her that the plain truth *was* that Rene was not wanted. Poor Rene! Newly widowed, expecting a baby, very little money, no relatives at all of her own. Could anything be more

5 | COMPANY IN THE EVENING

pathetic and more of a nuisance—the *nuisance* of it, of course, recoiling back on the pathos, and making *that* worse!

As for the girl herself, I hardly knew her. I had only seen her about twice, and nineteen and thirty-three rarely immediately find each other in sympathy. We had not known her at all until Philip had suddenly produced her while he was on leave in February and announced that he was getting married to her the next week. It was no use pretending that she hadn't been, at first acquaintance at any rate, a bit of a shock to Mother, although Mother with great dignity and good sense had refrained from all criticism, even to me. When I murmured something a little awkwardly to her about it being a democratic world these days, and probably how much better that it should be, she had agreed instantly. "In *any* case," Mother had added, "they're getting married next week, so there's nothing more to be said." Nothing more was said.

I could not help wondering how Mother and Rene had been getting on together during this summer. I had only seen them for one short week-end just after Philip's death, when an emotion common to all three of us had temporarily obscured any trivial difficulties of contact and relationship. Rene had just been obliged to give up her job (she was a shorthand typist) because of her pregnancy, and Mother had urged her to come and have the baby at Winterbury Green. She had settled in the following week.

No one knows better than myself that emotion, of whatever kind, dies down. Life just cannot be lived at a level of "darling Philip's poor widow" any more than a marriage can remain in the ecstatic honeymoon mood. I could not help suspecting that everyday difficulties were already beginning to make themselves apparent. The habit of ordinary life is deeply engrained in most of us. Even with the sirens wailing and the whole country facing the blackest crisis in its history, Mother had found time to mind about whether Rene 'chummed up' with Mrs. Grantham's Sylvia or not. 'Tiresomely' she hadn't. And now Mother was wondering whether she wouldn't be happier living with people nearer her own age. Wondering whether someone wouldn't be 'happier' somewhere else: we all know what *that* means.

Of course, I should have to ask Rene to come and live with me at Harminster.

Because it was Mother I was really bothering about and not Rene, I would not be grudging about it to Mother. I would say a lot of things that were true. I would say that Blakey (my old family retainer—she had been my grandmother's maid and was now half-cook, half-nurse to my child Antonia) and I were often hard put to it to get through the work. That, on days when I had to go up to the office, and everything had perforce to be left to Blakey, Rene could help me by doing the shopping. I would say that Blakey would be thrilled by the prospect of Rene's baby. I would say—and this was really, stretching a point when you visualize a baby in arms and a child of four—that it would be nice for the children to have each other. I would say that Rene could have the little room at the head of the stairs—and I would *not* say how my heart quailed at the prospect of clearing out the accumulation of lumber. I would not say myself, but I would allow Mother to say, that Rene would be "company for me in the evening."

I have never tried to make Mother understand that, of all the unhappiness my divorce has brought upon me, loneliness has never been in the least a part. A sense of failure—yes. A rather frightening feeling of being alone against the world—yes. Regret that Antonia should be brought up without a father—yes. Loneliness—no. Lack of "company in the evening" is to me an absolute luxury. During the day I am, generally speaking, working for the convenience of other people. Either I am at the office (three days a week) or, if I am at home I am working or looking after Antonia or trying to get well ahead of the shopping. In the evenings I please myself and nobody but myself—and if it suits me to have a bath at seven o'clock and retire to bed with the crossword, an anthology of poetry, a novel and a bit of knitting and have Blakey bring me a tray of liver sausage sandwiches and coffee, why on earth shouldn't I?

I made up my mind, there and then, that, if Rene was to live with me I would begin as I meant to go on.

7 | COMPANY IN THE EVENING

* * * * *

"Darling, it's a weight off my mind. I can't tell you what a weight off my mind it is," said Mother. She added happily, "I shall write to Maud this evening."

It was Sunday afternoon. Since my arrival on Friday, everything had been fixed up. Slightly to Mother's horror—she belongs very definitely to a generation which believes in "breaking the news gradually"—I had even insisted on tackling Rene on the subject. The atmosphere of Mother and me playing at Conspirators together was tiresome, and in any case there was a genuine need for decision and action. I pointed out to Mother that one could hardly sell the house over Rene's head without at least *telling* her. Mother looked relieved when I said *I* ought to be the one to approach Rene, and murmured that she was sure I'd do it very tactfully.

"I dare say I shall be quite tactful," I said cheerfully, "because you see I genuinely *shan't* be embarrassed and you undoubtedly would be."

With Rene I took the tone that I myself would have preferred had I been in her situation. I was business-like and got down to practical details as soon as possible. I didn't actually tell her in so many words about the liver-sausage sandwiches in bed, but I *did* say she should have a bed-sitting-room of her own with a fire in it, and left her to draw her own conclusions.

If there is one thing I can never bring myself to do it is to bemoan, either directly or indirectly, my divorced state. I suppose it was partly this that led me to eschew all sentiment in my conversation with Rene. I told her, I hope convincingly, that she would be welcome. I told her what I myself would have liked to hear in her place—that she could be a help. I tried to be cordial and not too take-it-or-leave-it. In point of fact, it wasn't even that for the poor girl. It was quite simply 'take-it.'

I think even at the time I had an inkling that what Rene would really have preferred would have been a good cry on my shoulder, and a sort of 'we're two lonely women without men to look after us, let's face it together' attitude.

Mother, however, subsequently reported, with decorously subdued glee, that Rene had spoken to her about the scheme and seemed "really to have taken to the idea." It was just after this that Mother made the remark about a weight being off her mind.

"Well, now that the weight *is* off," I said, a little naughtily, "would you mind telling me how much it weighed, so to speak? I mean, what *is* Rene like to live with?"

Mother has a very expressive face. I could see loyalty and a desire to confide having a lovely pitched battle in her mouth and eyebrows.

"Well, put it like this," I said hastily. "Just give me a little *advice* on how to treat her."

Mother saw through this, of course, but nevertheless could not resist the lure.

"Well, darling, she really *is* a bit . . ." Mother paused awkwardly, and I knew perfectly well what she was trying not to say.

When I was about nineteen and suffering from a terrific anti-snob complex (one had to make *some* protest against the really extraordinary smugness and arrogance of the wealthy retired upper-middle-class inhabitants of Winterbury Green), I practically forbade Mother to use the word 'common.' I said, with the delightful idealistic gusto of nineteen, that it made me feel sick. ("But Vicky, I don't *like* the word either, but what *am* I to say?" "Oh, don't you see, Mother, it isn't a question of phraseology, it's your whole *attitude* I object to." Goodness, what mothers of semi-intellectual daughters of nineteen have to put up with!)

On this occasion, being fourteen years older, I merely helped Mother out.

"Genteel?" I suggested.

"Exactly!" Mother looked relieved. "You know, darling, it's all very well to say the world's changed and nobody minds about that sort of thing nowadays, but all I can say is in Winterbury Green they just *do*. Perhaps they oughtn't to, but they just do."

"I'm sure they do," I agreed. "And even if they oughtn't to, one can hardly enter a room saying, 'This is Rene and the world's changed and nobody minds about this sort of thing nowadays.'"

Mother laughed. "You know, Vicky, people are such awful cats. One after another they all come up and ask me where Philip met her."

"Where did he?" I said, suddenly curious.

"Oh, she was a typist in his office. Her parents have been dead for ages. She lived with an aunt or something—who's now dead also."

"I wonder if she cried on Philip's shoulder and told him she was so lonely," I murmured.

"Why?"

"Oh, nothing. She just struck me as the type, that might be rather good at crying on people's shoulders. And you must admit that Philip's shoulder rather lent itself to that sort of thing."

"Poor Philip," sighed Mother. "He *was* too tender-hearted."

"He got that from you, darling. Whereas I'm brutal and bitter like Daddy."

"No, Vicky, I won't have you saying things like that about yourself. You've inherited your father's brains, of course, and made use of them, and you've led a different sort of life to anything *I* ever wanted. But that doesn't mean you're brutal and bitter or any such nonsense of the sort."

"Mother, you *are* sweet," I said, laughing. "Wonderful how the maternal instinct to defend one's child persists, isn't it?"

"Of *course* it persists," said Mother, and then added hastily, "but whether it persists or not it would be just silly to say you were brutal and bitter—although Heaven knows you *might* have become so, after all you've—" Mother broke off guiltily. She knows I hate her to talk like that.

"Oh Mother!" I said reproachfully. "*Can't* you—*won't* you once and for all accept the fact that I have no reason to feel bitter against Raymond? No more reason than he has to feel bitter against me."

Silence. If Mother hadn't really rather a sweet face, I should say she was looking as obstinate as a mule.

"*Can't* you?" I persisted.

"Vicky, there's one plain fact that *nobody* can get over. It was Raymond and not you who . . . who . . ."

"Pretend you're in church and say 'committed adultery,' " I suggested. (Not the sort of witticism that Mother likes, but she was annoying me.)

"Very well then," said Mother stoutly, "who committed adultery. Nobody can get over that, can they?" she repeated triumphantly.

"Nobody of your generation and upbringing, perhaps, Mother, I suppose it's incomprehensible to you if I say that to myself and, most of my friends, it's really rather irrelevant?"

"Well, Vicky, since you ask me straight out, I *do* find that incomprehensible. Yes, I do."

"Well, I think that makes it game, set and match to you," I said, getting up, rather thankful that the conversation could now be closed.

I went up to Philip's room because, before I left the next morning I had undertaken to perform the melancholy task of clearing and sorting his things—a job Mother had never had the resolution to make herself do until the prospect of selling the house had forced it upon her. I had found her that morning in his room gazing unhappily around at the infinitely pathetic accumulation of a boy's junk. Philip had never had a home of his own in London, only lodgings, and had continued until the end of his life to keep the majority of his possessions at home.

Ever since I had helped Mother after Father died I have thought the aftermath of death—the sorting, the clearing, the throwing away—most cruelly and unfairly poignant. Unfair, because why should inanimate objects, even though once handled and treasured by their owners, suddenly become imbued with such unbearable pathos, when, during their owner's lifetime they held no sentiment whatsoever for one? Philip's room was particularly calculated to disturb a healing grief, because it was stuffed full of a boy's treasures and redolent of the passing of the years—a Kate Greenaway picture inherited from the night-nursery, a cricket bat that he had had when he was twelve, a college blazer. Really, I had thought angrily that morning, as I stood in the doorway and watched Mother looking helplessly around, really it was unbearable that she should have to set about such a task. Almost angrily I had told her that I would see to all that, adding, unkindly perhaps (but I was cross with myself because tears were stinging my eyes), that it wouldn't be so bad for me as for her.

It wouldn't. Fond as I was of Philip, obviously one's grief at the loss of a brother is on an entirely different plane from one's feelings at the loss of a son. Moreover, Philip was five years my junior, so that we had not really shared our childhood together. To be quite honest, I doubt if we had ever known each other really well. Probably, had he lived, we should have discovered each other as real persons in the thirties when the distance in age would have dwindled to insignificance.

He was a gentle unassuming person, the sort of man whom one imagined living a nice ordinary undistinguished life, adequate in the office (he was a solicitor like my father), happiest in his own home. He would have adored his children, had a few very faithful friends, and no enemies at all, lived to a ripe old age and died, mourned quietly by all who had ever known him. That was, I felt, how it ought to have been for him—so much more appropriate and fitting somehow than a soldier's death on a foreign beach at the age of twenty-seven.

I had once remarked to Mother that I ought to have been the boy and Philip the girl, and she had almost agreed with me.

I caught sight of myself in the glass, and suddenly found myself wondering if I *did* look bitter. I came nearer to have a better look.

Thirty-three. Traces of the hag, of course. Plenty of bone in the face, thank God (I have always abhorred pudginess), but plenty of lines too. One begins stoutly to assert that they give character.

Raymond used to say I wasn't pretty but that I had a "smart" face. He liked me to use plenty of make-up, and it has become second nature now, so that I feel half-naked without lipstick or polish on my nails or my hair properly set. Of course, in London, my appearance was quite unremarkable, but in provincial Harminster it sometimes suddenly occurs to me that I don't look in the least like any other woman in the room.

Well! there I was, thirty-three, and I hadn't got a husband or much security or much money or the prospect of peaceful companionship in old age; but I *had* got a home and a child and a job, and, if I had known through and through what 'disillusionment' means, I had known passionate love too, and if I was sometimes frightened about the future, an apprehension usually shouldered by the man, I had known also the joy denied to many wives, the solid satisfaction of earning money. If you added it all up the answer honestly didn't seem to me to be 'bitterness,' and anyway, who the hell wants an unlined face?

There was a movement in the doorway and, turning, I saw Rene.

Nobody is pleased to be found looking at himself or herself in a mirror. My immediate instinct was to cover up my slight embarrassment by saying something quickly.

"This is all horribly Time-and-the-Conways, isn't it?" I said, gesturing vaguely round at the room.

Rene looked puzzled, and I had time to reflect that my remark was not happy. It was unnecessarily allusive and possibly a little flippant—not what I should have chosen for Rene as my opening comment on Philip's death. Well, she shouldn't have startled me.

"*Time and the Conways* was a play on in London by Priestley," I explained. "But perhaps you didn't see it?"

"No—no, I didn't," said Rene. A pause. "Are you—are you fond of going to the theatre?"

Oh dear, oh dear, I thought.

"Yes, very," I said, and then, since there seemed nothing else to say, "Are you?"

"Yes, sometimes," said Rene.

And that, I thought, closes that interesting discussion. Now let's try again.

"In Harminster—" I began, but Rene was quicker than I.

"Your mother said that when you were living in London, you used to know quite a lot of people on the stage," said Rene, with a distinct flicker of interest lighting up her face.

"Yes, I did know some," I said, and told her a few names.

"Oh! What were they like?"

"Like? Well, like other people, of course. No, to be quite honest, I think stage-people usually *are* a bit of a class apart."

"Oh. *Are* they? In what way?"

"Oh—a bit petty and childish and utterly absorbed in the gossip of their world and extraordinarily indifferent to everything outside it. Just a bit, you know," I added kindly, seeing the disappointment on Rene's face.

"You didn't *like* them then when you met them off the stage?" persisted Rene.

"Yes, some of them I liked very much. They're very easy to like. They have such beautiful manners."

"Oh," said Rene, and *that* topic dropped.

"You were going to say something just now when I interrupted you—I beg your pardon," said Rene.

(Good heavens! Had the word 'manners' set her off like that?)

"Oh, it was nothing. I was only going to tell you that we have a repertory theatre in Harminster, but I'm afraid it isn't very good."

"Do you like Harminster? Is it a nice place?"

"Nice? Well, it's a provincial town, of course. I can't pretend that I don't prefer London, but it has its points. It suits me because the good trains only take three-quarters of an hour to get to London—I go up three days a week, you know—and yet, so far at least, it hasn't had any bombs to speak of. The result is, of course, that it's horribly overcrowded. The river's quite nice in the summer, though, and there's nice country round—only I never seem to have time to get out to it."

"I expect there's good cinemas," said Rene hopefully.

"Oh heavens, yes!" I said heartily. "There's a terrific new Odeon with terrifically plush seats."

"Do you often go?" said Rene with another real flicker of interest.

"Practically never, I'm afraid." (I couldn't help it, I just *wasn't* going to raise false hopes in the girl.) "But, of course, *you'll* be able to go as much as you like," I added quickly.

"Well . . ." Rene blushed slightly. "Perhaps I'd better wait until after Baby is born. It's getting rather close now, you see—the beginning of November, and one doesn't want to go in crowds very much towards the end, do you think?"

And this, I thought, is where we ought to sit down together and have a cosy little chat about Baby. Only I *did* want to get on with the job of clearing Philip's room.

"Oh, you've got nearly another three months to play about in, haven't you?" I said encouragingly. And then, because *really* I was trying not to be horrid, in spite of my resolution to begin as I meant to go on, "Although I expect you're already very tired of lolloping about in a tactful smock, aren't you? I know I was."

To my horror Rene blushed an unmistakable pink and it occurred to me that once again I had put my foot in it. Good heavens, did the child really imagine, as the advertisements for maternity frocks say, that nobody would have an inkling that she was a little mother-to-be?

"Incidentally there's a very good maternity home at Harminster," I said. "I know the Matron quite well, so I'll just force her to squeeze you in somehow. It really is a good one. They're frightfully good with the babies and have nearly always got them trained to sleep all through the night by the time you come out."

"Poor little mites," said Rene vaguely. "I do hope Baby will be good and not disturb you too much when I get him home."

"That's all right," I said heartily. "Don't think me brutal if I assure you that somebody else's baby crying doesn't worry me at all. I shan't expect him to be a 'property child.' Antonia isn't."

"'Property child'?" said Rene in a puzzled voice.

"Oh, *you* know. Like children in books. One minute the mother adores it so much that she can't bear to let a nurse touch it. The next minute she's apparently forgotten all about it and is perfectly free to prance off unencumbered with Another Man—oh no, I forgot. She does usually rush in in evening dress and pick it up out of its cot after it's asleep and clasp it to her bosom and swear one day it will understand how she's suffering. And then she puts it back in its cot and it doesn't seem at all disturbed by all this procedure—I suppose property children get used to it—and it goes off to sleep again clasping a rose-leaf that has fallen from her corsage. It doesn't even eat the rose-leaf, as a real baby undoubtedly would. Oh, property children are *very* convenient."

"I don't think I've read that book," said Rene, politely bewildered.

Oh dear, oh dear, I thought again.

"No, nor have I," I explained patiently, "It's just the result of all the short stories I have to read in the office. I work in a literary agency, you know."

"Yes, your mother told me," said Rene politely, but I could see her attention was wandering and I suddenly realized why. During the course of our conversation I had been rather vaguely moving about, pulling drawers open, throwing things on the floor, and now just at Rene's feet was lying a large photograph of Raymond and myself on our wedding-day. Rene was obviously wondering whether to comment on it or not.

Well, some time or other some reference to Raymond had clearly got to be made. I took the bull by the horns, picked the photograph up and handed it to her.

"I think it was rather sweet of Philip to have kept that," I said.

"It's an awfully good likeness of you," commented Rene bravely.

"It's good of Raymond, too," I said, not without, I'm afraid, some malicious enjoyment in her embarrassment.

"Is it?" said Rene, and then added quickly, "Let's see, how old were you then?"

"Twenty-two." I tried to keep my voice casual. I felt casual myself. (I was long past the stage when such trivial reminders of the past as photographs could hold any power to wound me.) 'It was only Rene's evident embarrassment that made my indifference at all self-conscious. Indeed, the poor child looked so unhappy that I relieved her of the photograph and shut it quickly away into a drawer.

To somebody my own age I would have said outright, "Don't worry, don't bother to be tactful, I don't *mind*." To Rene, I just couldn't.

It occurred to me there and then that probably there were going to be a lot of things one just could not say to Rene. It did not augur very brilliantly for the future.

I had shut the photograph away in a drawer, but I evidently could not shut away her embarrassment with it. I did try—I was even willing to talk about films if that was any help—but after the episode of the photograph no topic seemed very successful. In the end I helped her out of the room (she was obviously dying to go, but didn't know how) by shoving a volume of old family snapshots at her and suggesting to her that she should look through them and take out any that she liked that had Philip in them.

Just as she turned at the door, on her way out, to thank me again (really rather prettily) for thinking of such a nice idea, I got my first hint of the appeal she might have had for Philip—nothing sparkling and edgy that you could catch on to. Not the sort of 'charm' that I personally like, not poised or self-confident or humorous, but nevertheless sweet of its kind, the soft, big-eyed appreciative sort. It suddenly occurred to me that Rene was only just twenty, and might well, some day, marry *again*.

Chapter 2

MOTHER'S PARTING WORDS to me on Monday morning were: "And don't forget, darling, when I'm at Chipping Campden we can *easily* meet in Oxford for the day, and perhaps you can bring Antonia sometimes? And I *do* hope you and Rene will get on nicely together. She's a sweet girl, really, and even if she is a bit *young* for you . . ."

"Oh well, we were all twenty once, God help us," I finished for her.

"Vicky dear, don't talk as if you were my age. It's absurd."

"Darling mother, I can't help feeling I'm nearer in age to you than to Rene, when all's said and done."

"What nonsense, darling! I never heard such nonsense."

The engine whistled, the guard started slamming the doors, the train began to move.

"Why, it seems no time at all since *you* were twenty," yelled Mother stoutly after me.

I fell back on my seat, laughing, and then found myself reflecting that really it was a good job for Rene that I *wasn't* twenty now. At thirty-three I might not be her sort of person, nor she mine, but at least we could put up some sort of a show of it between us. My twenty-year-old self she would quite rightly have found intolerable.

Twenty. In my last year at Oxford. Cocksure, arrogant, gloriously patronizing towards my parents and indeed towards almost everybody of an older generation. The sort of young woman who takes a pride in announcing at a tea-party in her parents' drawing-room that she is an agnostic. The sort of young woman who has affairs 'on principle' and tells you all about the principle. (Actually I hadn't. I meant to once, but baulked at the last minute to my secret shame.)

'Showing off' it is called in the nursery, and public opinion is very rightly against it. I can't think why public opinion wasn't more against me—or perhaps it was, and I just didn't notice, invulnerable in my shining armour of youthful idiocy. Or perhaps I got away with it just because I *was* twenty and rather striking-looking and popular in my own circle and attractive to men. If people take one, as is sometimes said, at one's own valuation I was certainly pretty expensive in those days.

How I wanted smacking and *how* I enjoyed those radiant, insolent, flaunting years, and *how* Raymond and I used to laugh and mock and prance gaily about all over other people's feelings and susceptibilities and reticences and prejudices. Because I was twenty and he was twenty-four and we were both on the crest of a wave and mutually in love we ourselves had no reticences or prejudices of our own at all. Those that we had been brought up on we had already discarded as painlessly as milk-teeth. We had had no time to acquire others, because nothing in our young lives had ever seriously hurt us.

Raymond had just been called to the Bar. His prospects were not bad, as he had what are called 'useful connections' (both his family and mine went in for the law), but meanwhile, of course, no one could call him overworked. He employed his spare time in writing a novel, and it actually got published and had a certain amount of success. It hit the taste of the time, being wittily cynical in a superficial Noel Cowardish kind of way. I thought it brilliant.

At this time I was working for my degree, but the terms at Oxford are only eight weeks long, and, in the vacations I used to stay with a married friend of mine in her London flat. When Raymond and I went out together in the evening I used to get the most exquisite intoxicating sensation that he and I between us owned London—lamp-lit streets, winking electric signs, the hooting jam of taxies in Shaftesbury Avenue after the theatres came out, the statue of Eros in the middle of Piccadilly and all.

We were married in 1932, and divorced in 1936.

* * * * *

And now I had got to break the news to Blakey. Rene was coming in a fortnight's time.

Antonia came running out to meet me at the gate, and, as always, I felt that absurd instinctive uprush of delight and relief at being once more reunited with her after a few days' separation. Bless her, what a satisfactory and exquisite thing a four-year-old daughter in a cotton frock with dangling sun-bonnet is! I packed her up and hugged her, revelling in the scent of her newly-washed hair, in the soft touch of her grubby little hands artlessly smearing earth on my brat travelling frock, loving the whole feel of her in my arms—a piquant mixture of solidity and fragility—luxuriating in her affectionate greeting of me and knowing perfectly well and not minding in the least that the real reason why she was so thrilled to see me again was because I had promised to bring back the doll's frock my mother had been knitting for her. The fact that, on Friday, I had been quite pleased at the prospect of three days' holiday from Antonia was not really in the least inconsistent with my delight at seeing her again, as every mother will realize.

"I've got the frock in my suitcase here," I said instantly.

"Oh Mummy, *where*? May I see? May I unpack for you?"

Bless her, she couldn't really be 'spoilt' if she was so thrilled over a tiny present of the sort. (If there's one thing that infuriates me it's the way people always imply that only children *must* be spoilt. I am uneasily conscious of the truth of this generalization and therefore furiously on the defensive about it.)

"Can you unpack for me really beautifully, darling—put everything in the right place—while I have a cup of tea and talk to Blakey?"

Antonia nodded self-importantly, lips pursed up.

Of all the extraordinary treats the child likes, 'unpacking' is about the favourite. God knows why I should have been honoured with a passionately tidy child—neither heredity nor example can have anything to do with it. When I first discovered it I was quite horrified. I think I felt if she was going to be *'tidy'* she couldn't be long for this world. Nowadays I have just accepted it and even make use of it on some occasions—although a little guiltily owing to a vague feeling that it would be 'better' somehow for her to be romping vaguely about and getting dirty.

"You'll find the frock in a piece of tissue-paper, and when you've unpacked everything perhaps you'd like to put it on Susie and bring her down to show me?" I suggested, calculating rapidly that all this would probably take her long enough to keep her well out of the way while I had my talk with Blakey. I badly wanted to get it off my chest, so that I could settle to some work that evening, and I also wanted to be interrupted *after* I had got it off my chest, so really Antonia was being delightfully useful.

I carried the suitcase up to my room, dumped it on the floor, opened it for her and left her to it.

I knew that, when I went up again, I should get my usual fond smile out of seeing my hair-brush, comb and jars of cosmetics ranged with absolutely military precision on the dressing-table.

Blakey was clearing away the tea-things from the dining-room as I went downstairs. She will not permit Antonia to have tea in the kitchen when I am away, although Antonia loves it, and it must be much less trouble for Blakey than carrying trays into the dining-room. When Blakey is out Antonia and I often treat ourselves to this luxury.

For sheer engrained snobbishness I do not think you can beat the 'old family retainer' type, like Blakey. I suppose she is about sixty now, and, ever since she was fourteen she has been in service, always, one understands, in the best families. After listening to her earlier reminiscences I sometimes wonder whether she didn't consider it a bit of a come-down to enter my grandmother's house, because, after all, my grandfather was only a K.B.E. However, I suppose she thought it better to be head-housemaid in a staff of five rather than one of the under-housemaids in a staff of twenty or so. In any case, she stayed with my grandmother for more than twenty years, and towards the end of my grandmother's life, when the old lady was something of an invalid, she rose to the position of a sort of mixture of housekeeper and personal maid. When Philip and I, as children, were brought to my grandmother's house, Blakey always used to carry us off to her special sanctum and give us 'squashed-fly' biscuits out of a tin covered with sea-shells. I thought the tin about the most beautiful thing I had ever seen in my life, and did not mind at all that it was not airtight, and the biscuits, in consequence, always tasted stale. One could not, I felt, have *everything*.

Grandmother died in 1937 at the fine old age of eighty-five. It was then that Blakey came to me. Antonia was one year old, and I was living in a flat in St. John's Wood with a nurse for Antonia and a 'daily woman' who was always being prevented from turning up. As a matter of fact, it was a rather more extravagant establishment than I could really afford, but Blakey, when she saw the squalor to which I was reduced, was absolutely horrified. I honestly do not think that, living all those years in Grandmother's house, she had noticed how the world around her was changing. Anyway, she came to tea and found me on my hands and knees scrubbing the kitchen floor, the daily woman having once more followed her usual routine of not turning up. Blakey was so shocked that she insisted on coming to me the next week.

I believe there were terrible battles between Blakey and Nanny in the flat, but really, all that year (the year before the war) I was too harassed by the strain of going back to work and my private unhappiness over my divorce and trying to be a good mother to Antonia in spite of everything, that I just hadn't the energy left to bother about their quarrels. When the war came and I had to move out of London, I let the nurse go without feeling much of a pang. I thought it probable that Blakey was the difficult and unreasonable one (she had never quite got over the fact that Nanny was out for a walk with Antonia while *I* was scrubbing the kitchen floor, although really one hardly engages a college-trained nurse to scrub the floor while one takes one's baby out oneself), but, on the whole, I preferred her about the place. She was a link with old times. She was a part of my childhood. In her own obstinate, loyal, rather maddening way, she was genuinely devoted to me and, much as, intellectually speaking, her attitude to life appalled me—"Miss Vicky, it's my opinion that Nurse sets herself up to be as good as you are." "Well, Blakey, why not? So she is." "There now, Miss Vicky, what a thing to say! How you do talk!"—I could not help finding it infinitely restful. I was glad that it was Blakey I was taking to Harminster with me on the outbreak of war. She was devoted to Antonia and Antonia to her, and the child was past the stage which nowadays necessitates playing about with veal broth and sieved vegetables. Blakey, I am sure, would think of giving a child food, not 'a diet sheet.'

The furnished lodge cottage I was lucky enough to find in the grounds of a big estate just on the outskirts of Harminster was even more of a come-down for Blakey than the flat. I told her it had 'character,' and she looked at me as if she thought I was crazy, and said she supposed it was meant for the gardener's wife or someone of the sort. I waited to see how much she would permit me to demean myself by helping her, and it turned out that I was to be allowed to do light dusting and make jam and cakes. I was a bit rebellious at first (I *hate* light dusting and rather like washing-up), but in the end I got to know my place and keep to it. I was, however, permitted to take charge of Antonia on the days when I was not at the office, and this, after two years of Proper Nannies I found refreshing—although, at first, of course, much more exhausting than making a dozen beds.

Infuriating, loyal old body! Sometimes I used to feel I really could not bear her 'Poor Miss Vicky, she's come down in the world and no mistake' attitude a moment longer. Then I imagined life without Blakey and my heart quailed.

Antonia, I believe, sees a different side of her. She has a wonderful stock of stories and old songs and, although she firmly believes that the great lesson children have to learn is that they can't always have their own way, she is not 'strict' in the sterilized, white-apron discipline-for-the-sake-of-discipline way some nurses seem to go in for. A biscuit at an unorthodox hour or a new toy taken to bed isn't an unthinkable crime to her, but a natural and unremarkable occurrence.

Having called me 'Miss Vicky' since I was a child, that is how she still continues to address me, except when company is present, when I am occasionally 'Madam.' I have never discussed with her my divorce, but somehow I have been given to understand that her attitude is that I have been badly let down by an unscrupulous man who was not worthy of me. Since this has never been put into words, I have never had an opportunity of denying it.

As I came downstairs I said, "Blakey, I've some news for you," and then, taking the bull by the horns, "Mrs. Sylvester—Mr. Philip's widow, I mean, not my mother, of course—is coming to live with me here."

Blakey's immediate reaction was, as I knew it would be, to fall back on her 'well-trained-servant' act, look non-committal and say, "Oh yes, Miss Vicky. I suppose you'd like me to get the little room ready for her?"

Yes, yes, Blakey, I wanted to say, yes, I *know*, it's my house, and I know I've a perfect right to invite anybody I like here, and I know your job is to take orders from me, but can't we pass all that over and talk about it as human beings? However, one just can't skip the preliminary stages with Blakey. She is a stickler for formality.

"Yes—the little room," I said. "We'll have to clear it out together next week-end."

"Yes, Miss Vicky," said Blakey formally.

Annoying old woman! Of course she was longing to hear all about the whys and wherefores, and, of course, she would be very hurt if I didn't tell her everything. Why couldn't she be natural and ask?

"Give me a cup of tea, Blakey—no, no, out of that pot will do—and I'll tell you all about it."

I did. Blakey received it all with great decorum. Badly as I wanted a little reassurance and encouragement, I obviously wasn't going to get it at this stage. Blakey, under cover of the well-trained-servant act, was holding her hand—an old trick of hers.

"... And the baby's due in November," I finished.

"Antonia will be ever so excited at finding a little baby in the house," said Blakey, unbending a little.

"Yes. Of course, I shall prepare her beforehand. Don't start talking about gooseberry bushes to her, will you, Blakey?"

I don't really think the whole of a child's development is twisted by an injudicious reference to a gooseberry bush at the age of four, and, as soon as I had said it, I wished I hadn't, for Blakey immediately froze again.

"It's for you to say, Miss Vicky."

Damn!

Conscious that I had put my foot in it, I made one last bid for friendliness and chattiness.

"I hope it will work, Blakey," I said, and I would not swear that my voice wasn't wistful. "Of course it's never very easy sharing one's house with someone but Mrs. Sylvester will—will be company for me in the evening."

Having embarked on that sentence, I could not, for the life of me, think how to finish it in any other way.

"Oh, by the way, Miss Vicky—Mr. Fortescue rang up and said were you expecting him to-morrow to supper? He wasn't sure."

"Oh, thanks, yes I am expecting him. I'll ring him," I said, hardly noticing what I was saying because, having had my joke with myself about 'company in the evening,' I was now anxious to get the bed-sitting-room-for-Rene idea across to Blakey at once to prevent future misconceptions. "Although, Blakey," I went on quickly, "I expect Mrs. Sylvester and I will both want to be pretty independent in some ways. I mean, we'll each have our own room and we shan't necessarily want to be always together."

Nicely put, I thought. I could not think why Blakey gave me such a very odd look. More of a comprehending look than the situation really warranted—and anyway, Blakey never really has understood that I genuinely like my own company.

However, Antonia came running in to show me Susie in her new frock, and it was only half an hour to her bedtime, and I hadn't seen her for three whole days. I gave her my whole attention. She was distressed because the frock was too big at the neck and, because I was feeling affectionate and maternal and cosy about her, I didn't think she was a bit of a nuisance to be so fussy, but got quite a mild kick instead out of being a Resourceful Mother and producing a bit of ribbon to pull it up with. Then we played snakes-and-ladders, revised version: the one who wriggles down the longest snake wins, because Antonia likes wriggling down snakes better than going up dull, straight ladders; and finally we topped up with three chapters of an appallingly dull and rather revoltingly instructive book about some priggish children who are of the greatest possible help to their parents on a farm.

It was a very cosy and 'only-childish' sort of play-hour, and, even if it would have been healthier for her to have been playing cricket in the garden with six brothers and sisters, and getting hard bumps and *not* making a fuss, it wasn't my fault that things were as they were, and I didn't see why both I and Antonia shouldn't take our pleasure where we could find it.

Later, when I was having my bath, my thoughts reverted to Blakey and the way she had taken my news, and I reflected that it was really very irritating of Blakey to put on the automaton act when it suited *her*, because, as I knew quite well from experience, she wouldn't necessarily put it on at all when it suited *me*. Behind the façade of a well-trained manner she was as human as the rest of us, and would find exceedingly human ways of showing me what she thought and felt. When it suited her she could play the 'privileged old family retainer who speaks her mind' rôle with equal exactitude.

Blakey wanted it both ways, I decided, yawning. Like most of us, I conceded, pulling out the plug by hooking my toes round the chain—a habit Raymond used to laugh at.

Raymond—marriage—Blakey. Out of the jumbled juxtaposition of these musings a sudden comprehension flashed across my mind, so that I could almost hear the click with which the links in the chain of thought joined up. I nearly laughed out loud.

Why had Blakey suddenly remembered about Barry Fortescue ringing up? Because I had just made that silly remark to her about 'company in the evening.' What had I gone on to say to her next? That nice little speech about Rene and me being 'independent' and each having our own room.

There was absolutely no connection in my mind between the two subjects. Obviously there had been in Blakey's, and that was the reason why she had suddenly given me that extraordinarily comprehending look.

Oh dear! Was that Blakey's little dream for me? Now I came to think of it, she did usually smirk a bit when she announced Barry. Oh dear, oh dear! Could I possibly, without being a swine to Barry, tell Blakey that I had most definitely refused Barry six months ago, and so prevent any further misplaced comprehension from her on the subject?

Oh dear, oh dear. Still giggling slightly, I trailed into the bedroom. On a table by my bed stood a nice little tray scrambled eggs on a hot-water plate marked 'Baby's Own' (Antonia gobbles and I don't, so I use it), a salad, coffee. Also on the table lay six short stories, of the would-be woman's magazine type, all of which I had resolved to read and write reports on before going to sleep. A typical evening.

My thoughts, however, were, for once, not entirely typical. I suddenly had one of my bad turns—by which I mean that for about five minutes I missed Raymond so badly that it was like a positive physical pain.

It was the giggling over Blakey that had done it, of course. Suddenly, excruciatingly, I wanted someone to tell the joke to, to giggle with. And the need, in such cases, was always for Raymond—or someone so like Raymond that you wouldn't know the difference.

He wasn't what you'd call the epitome of a Good Husband, with capital letters. He wasn't a rock of gentle integrity, like Barry. I could never rely on him to back me up at all costs (and this was not because he was fickle, but because his conception of me was always of a Person, never primarily of a Wife). But if, at the moment, you don't happen to be wanting a Good Husband and, in all honesty, nine-tenths of the time I don't—and do happen to be wanting someone to share a joke with, someone utterly companionable, someone restful because he's quick, not because he's slow, someone with whom you drop at once thankfully into a sort of allusive mental shorthand, then, to my mind at least, you want Raymond; and I very much doubt if, for me, there does exist anyone so like him you wouldn't know the difference.

* * * * *

Blakey had succeeded in getting a chicken for supper for Barry and me.

"What on earth are you doing?" enquired Barry.

After I had served helpings for us both, I had turned the chicken upside-down on the dish, and was rummaging about with the carving-knife.

"Getting out the oysters to keep for Antonia. If I don't they may get eaten by mistake."

The moment I had spoken, I saw of what appalling bad manners I was convicting myself. This is just the sort of trap that mothers of only children ought to take the greatest care to avoid. One becomes so used to keeping the brat bits for one's child that one begins to do it automatically. Perhaps this can't be helped—but I could have avoided being so rude as to tell a guest that he might eat something by mistake which he shouldn't.

I felt so shocked at myself that I dropped the carving-knife and fork as if they had been red-hot, and quickly offered Barry the bread-sauce.

Barry, however, was not looking shocked, but interested.

"Oysters? Whatever do you mean?" he said.

"Oh, don't you know? We always called them that in our family. Those two oyster-shaped meaty bits you find underneath. Philip always had one and I the other. What Mother would have done if she'd had three children, I can't imagine. Perhaps that's why she never did."

"Antonia is lucky and gets both," suggested Barry. "Do go on—please. I want to see these strange delicacies."

"No," I said obstinately. "It was very rude of me to set about doing such a thing, and I certainly won't go on. Not unless you'll eat them yourself when I find them."

"Me?" Barry looked horrified. "Good heavens, no! They're Antonia's."

"No, they're not. She'll grow up into a perfectly horrible little girl if everything's always kept for her."

"Vicky, you are absurd," said Barry laughing. "Fancy calling Antonia a horrible little girl."

"I didn't. I said she might be. Not that I'm not sure she isn't, sometimes, already."

"What nonsense," said Barry easily. "Why, you know you're devoted to the kiddy."

Well. I don't much mind what people look like and I don't much mind what clothes they wear, but I am, I'm afraid, absurdly fastidious about the words they use; and a phrase like 'devoted to the kiddy,' said in all seriousness, makes me writhe inwardly. Bad language doesn't. Inverted snobbery, I suppose, but I just can't help it.

I changed the subject hastily and began to talk about the office, I don't think Barry ever knew how often, in his company, I changed the subject for just such an absurd reason. I hope not, because, in all humility, it never has been a question of Barry not being good enough for me. I am not nearly good enough for him.

I had met him soon after I had come to Harminster. He was (and is) some ten years older than myself, unmarried, the head-master of a boys' preparatory school just outside the town. He comes, I understand, from one of those solid North Country Quaker families, the members of which run so curiously to type—good idealists and good educationalists, and good employers; men of the world, perhaps, and yet, at rock-bottom, out-and-out Puritans.

The way in which I had first made his acquaintance was characteristic of the man. I had travelled back from London by a late train, and a party of very noisy and drunken soldiers had invaded the carriage in which Barry and I were already decorously sitting. They didn't worry me particularly, but obviously Barry thought they did—or else, that such language *ought* to shock me. Anyway, he had gone exploring further up the train and come back firmly to extract me and show me another place he had found. I went without protest, and subsequently chatted to him politely. It was the only thing to do.

Barry afterwards told me that, after the first meeting, he hadn't been able to get me out of his head. However, characteristically, he made no attempt to see me until we met by chance at a Sunday afternoon tea-party, where we were formally introduced by our hostess.

He walked back with me to my cottage, and I asked him to tea the next week. After that, I saw him constantly. His school was only a quarter of a mile from where I lived.

I did not want Barry to fall in love with me, but I cannot pretend that I did not enjoy the sensation of having a man about the place again. I do not consider myself in the least the sort of woman who *must* have a man to lean on, but neither do I care for an undiluted feminine atmosphere. I like pipe-smoke and masculine voices and men's scarves in the hall and a good reason for getting out the drinks. Barry, on the other hand, I am certain, doesn't care a rap for smart frocks and painted finger-nails and high-heeled shoes and the chatter and laughter of women in general. He fell in love with me, I'm sure, in spite of my appearance, not because of it.

When I turned him down (as nicely as I could, because, although I did not feel any pain myself, I *did* feel his pain), he only said one bitter thing:

"You know, Vicky, you can't be surprised I fell in love with you. You did give me every chance."

I ready was a little taken a back. Ever since I had begun to suspect he was getting serious about me, I had tried to show him tacitly it was no good. A man more used to women would have understood at once.

"Chance? In what way—beyond just seeing me?" I enquired.

Barry looked uncomfortable.

"Well, I mean—oh, *you* know."

"I don't. I honestly don't."

"Well—telling me to drop in whenever I liked in the evenings and so on. Letting me be alone with you for hours sometimes. I thought—I rather hoped—you wouldn't be quite so . . ." (he fumbled for a word and finally brought out a rather gallant choice). . . "so hospitable to anyone."

"Oh Barry! I would be just as 'hospitable' to anyone I liked as much as I like you. I'm sorry. But I would be, really."

"Do you think that's wise?" said Barry gravely, and, much as I liked and admired him, I felt an awful nervous giggle welling up inside me.

"Wise? I'm terribly sorry if I misled you."

"I meant wise for you," explained Barry gently.

"Are you trying to tell me that 'some men are pretty good cads'?" I said, and the giggle burst its way out and exploded in an awful sort of strangled snort (and *that* was caddish, if you like. However, Barry didn't know that 'some men are pretty good cads' was one of the many stock phrases Raymond and I used to bandy about between ourselves, and I hope he just thought I was overwrought.)

"Well—yes," said Barry stoutly. "I mean, without being melodramatic or anything, there is your reputation to think of, isn't there?"

"You can't talk about a woman's reputation without being melodramatic. That's one of the rules," I said. "Besides; believe it or not, I just honestly don't mind 'what the neighbours say.' "

"But you ought to," said Barry.

"You mean I'm not so far sunk in the world already that I haven't a right to hold up my head and boast I keep myself respectable?" I said naughtily.

"Oh Vicky—you turn everything into a joke," said Barry reproachfully.

"No, I don't. No I don't, Barry, *really*," I said quickly penitent. "Only—only in many things you and I just don't talk the same language, you know. We really don't."

"On the face of it, perhaps not," conceded Barry, "but I know—and you must know too, surely—that because you talk about things jokingly it doesn't mean that you're a flippant person underneath. Does it?"

I was serious then. I did want to make him understand.

"It's like this, Barry," I said. "Of *course* what people are really like underneath matters infinitely more than how they talk and the things they laugh about. I couldn't possibly deny that. And obviously if you're passionately in love, such trifles don't matter at all. Only one doesn't spend the greater part of one's life being passionately in love. It always seems to be Monday morning much more often than Saturday night and most of life *is* made up of small things and consequently non-essentials *do* matter by sheer bulk. To me, at least, they do. I can quite see that to you they probably don't."

"Thank you, Vicky. That's honest, at least—even if I don't agree."

"Barry, darling, it isn't a question of agreeing. It's just the way I am. Put it another way, if you like. It's often said that if the bedroom's wrong in a married couple's house, all the other rooms are wrong too." (I saw him flinch and hastened quickly on—I did not want him to think for a moment that the blow was coming from *that* quarter.) "Well, to me, Barry, if the jokes—the manner of speech—the language, whatever you like to call it—between a married couple are wrong, don't fit—well then, nothing else would really go right either."

"But the converse isn't necessarily true?" said Barry.

I wondered if this was a shot in the dark. I have barely mentioned Raymond to him. If he were curious, I would not blame him.

"Oh no, no," I said definitely, "the converse isn't true. If I thought that, Barry, I *would* be a superficial person and no mistake."

"And *that* you certainly are not," said Barry gravely.

It was when he said that, that I felt for the first time a real pang of regret that I could not possibly feel differently about his proposal. I do respect a man who can *make* me be serious. I do respect a man who can take a knock and pay it back with a compliment.

However, all that was six months before our conversation on this particular evening. We had, as Barry wanted, gone on seeing each other, although not quite so frequently as formerly. We always had plenty to talk about. When it's a case of serious discussion, of something concrete, Barry is an excellent person to talk to. I used to tell him about the office, and he used to tell me about his school. We discussed the war too, of course, but in this book I am taking such conversations for granted. They are not worth recording, so swiftly out-dated were all our feeble comments by the grim march of events.

On this occasion I told Barry all about some trouble we were having at the office with one of our authors. Unless you are an avid reader of women's magazines you would not know her name, but even if you had happened to notice it somewhere, you would be surprised to hear what a large and steady income she makes for herself from her writing. The woman's magazine short story market may be a footling one, from the point of view of literature, but it's an extremely lucrative one for the skilful craftsman. Ten per cent of this author's earnings (the agency's share) was well worth bothering about.

The agency's share only, of course, if we had 'placed' the stories for her and that was just our trouble now. For years we had placed all her stuff and, in all honesty, we had done much better for her than she could have done for herself. (It isn't a matter of lunching with editors and pulling strings, as many people seem to think. It's a matter of persistence and special knowledge.) Doubtless had this woman—let us call her pen-name Dorothy Harper—worked entirely on her own she would have succeeded in selling a story or two, but she would never have built up such useful connections for herself as we had done. She would never have sold her stuff in the U.S.A. or got so many contracts for series of articles or probably even heard of 'second serial rights,' which sounds abstruse and mathematical but really only means selling a story twice over. As a matter of fact, she would probably never have persevered as we made her persevere. Psychologically, an agent is important as a good shoulderer of disappointments. An agent is hardened to refusals and doesn't find it necessary to tell the author about every one.

Well, for many years—since before I went to work in the agency, which was immediately after I came down from Oxford—Miss Dorothy Harper had been a loyal and amenable client of ours. Not only had we placed her stories but we had advised her as to the sort of stories she might write that we could most easily place. We had worked splendidly as a team.

All this I rapidly recapitulated for Barry, and, with quick interested nods, he took it all in. He knew already, from me, a good deal about the workings of a literary agency.

"So what's the trouble now?" he asked sympathetically.

"Well, it all started some time back. She wrote a story quite out of her usual line—a sort of highbrow, trailing off into dots, reader-no-wiser-at-the-end style of story—and sent it to us saying she had an idea that this was the sort of thing she was really *meant* to write. We weren't enchanted, of course. There's not much money in that sort of thing."

"Was it—well, you know about writing and all that and I don't—but was it 'better' than her usual stories?" asked Barry.'

"Better? God knows. It was a different class of thing altogether. Not so awful in some ways, I suppose, I'll grant you that."

"Well. Go on."

"Well, this is where we made a mistake: she happened to drop into the office one day shortly after and, all bubbling over with enthusiasm, she asked Mrs. Hitchcock—she's the head and owns the place, as you know—what she thought of it, and Mrs. Hitchcock more or less showed her. Our Dorothy went off in something of a huff. Extraordinarily touchy creatures, authors. What are you grinning at?"

"I feel a bit sorry for Dorothy. I mean, probably to her the story meant quite a bit—a fresh development and so on."

"Quite. That's just what Mrs. Hitchcock was afraid of. God help us when one of our competent hacks starts 'developing,' after all the trouble we've taken to standardize her. Now don't start grinning again, Barry. I'm talking money and business, not literature."

"I can see that, Vicky."

"Yes. Well, hold on to that then, and don't get an attack of chivalry about Dorothy, because it's quite misplaced. Incidentally she's a woman of forty-five and quite hard-boiled in most ways."

"All right. Go on. What happened next?"

"Dorothy said if we didn't *like* the story, please give it back to her. No, no, we said, we'll try it for you. No, no, said she (all grand), I didn't want you to handle my work if you don't *appreciate* it. Great *fun* to say, of course, but absolute rot. Because for years we'd been talking honest commercial sense to each other."

"This was a different sort of honesty, in a way," suggested Barry.

"Yes, quite. Only this conversation took place in an office, not in a debating society. Well, she took the story away and she did actually sell it to some new, slightly highbrow paper. I suppose you'll say 'Good for her!'?"

"Yes," said Barry, laughing.

"Well, yes and no, really. The paper went smash after very few issues, and I very much doubt if she ever got her money. Then, shortly afterwards, *we* had a sudden patch of luck with one or two of her stories that we already had on our hands, and, anyway, our Dorothy graciously gave us to understand that she had forgiven and forgotten all, and turned out two splendid new stories about mother-love and the straying wife who sees the error of her ways. A bit on the hot side, but not too hot for the shilling magazines—the best market of all. I will say this for our Dorothy, she *is* a worker."

"I know you're not really so cynical about your wretched authors as you pretend to be," said Barry.

"I'm not at all cynical about the money side, Barry darling. Do you know what our Dorothy's doing now?"

"No. What? Has she left you?"

"No. It's more annoying than that in a way. If she left us outright and went elsewhere we'd be sorry, of course, but that would be that. No, she's playing a really rather dirty game. She's selling her best stuff herself and letting us handle the less hopeful chances, and that *really* is not fair."

"Best? Do you mean her more highbrow stories?"

"Oh Lord, no," I said scornfully. "She's welcome to handle those herself. She'll never really break into *that* market, and, anyway, there's comparatively little money in it. No, Barry, this is *not* a story about idealism justified. Our Dorothy may have spasms of the creative urge, but she's also got a sound head for business—we've *taught* her that, don't you see? That's what's so aggravating. I can't pretend she needs us quite as much as she used to, but she does still find us useful. She doesn't want to break with us altogether, so she just sends us her less good stuff."

"Has she told you so outright?"

"No, the mean skunk. We're just beginning to guess it—but I bet we're right. We saw one of her stories published that we hadn't handled—a real good Dorothy Harper one that was almost certain to sell. I expect there are others—stories aren't published immediately they're sold, you know. And then Mrs. Hitchcock met an editor of one of the women's papers who let drop something that pointed to our Dorothy having submitted a thing to the magazine directly, I won't go into all that mixture of gossip and etiquette, but what she's doing is pretty clear."

"Have you any remedy?"

"No legal remedy whatsoever, Barry. We've no contract with her. There just aren't any contracts in our business."

"Well, you can't do anything then, Vicky?"

"Mrs. Hitchcock wants me to have a talk with her; that's what's on my mind, and the reason why I've been pouring out all this rigmarole to you. I wanted Mrs. Hitchcock to talk to her herself, but she wants me to do it. She says she thinks I'll be more tactful than her."

"That's a tribute to you, Vicky."

"Not really," I said grimly. "Really, Mrs. Hitchcock's a bit annoyed with me because I hinted it was her fault all the trouble started over that ridiculous highbrow story. Of *course*, Mrs. Hitchcock shouldn't have offended Dorothy over it. I more or less told her so, and her retort was to the effect that if I was such a wonderfully tactful person *I* had better be the one to talk to Dorothy. There's a certain coolness between me and Mrs. Hitchcock now, I can tell you. *That's* why I've got this talk with our Dorothy more on my mind than ordinarily I would have. I can't help worrying about it."

"Poor old Vicky," said Barry, patting my hand, "it does seem a shame..."

He was being sweet, of course. But it wasn't the reaction I wanted.

"What's a shame?" I said suspiciously.

"That you should have to... oh, I don't know... cope with all this and be worried about things like this when—"

I got up hastily. We had, by this time, finished dinner.

"No, no, Barry," I said quickly. "It *isn't* a shame, and it's not that at all. I *like* it, I tell you."

"*Like* it? You said a moment ago you were worrying about it," said Barry, reproachful as a man checked in mid-sympathy naturally is.

"Yes. I mean I *like* being worried," I retorted absurdly. "At least, I mean I'm all for a nice change of worry, and if I had to stay at home all day with nothing to worry about except Antonia and Blakey—I expect I should put in some good strong worrying about them, being disengaged otherwise, so to speak—well, I should go absolutely crazy."

"Well, if you don't want sympathy, what do you want, Vicky?" (Barry can say that sort of thing without sounding peevish—I do admire him for it.) "You can hardly want my advice. I know nothing of literary agencies, except what you've told me."

"Oh, I think the plain truth is, Barry, I don't want anything, except just to *tell* you, which is a certain relief in itself. Although why the hell I should use you in this way I really don't know. I wouldn't stand it, if I were you."

"Oh, please Vicky! I like it. I value your confidence immensely. You know that."

"You're far too nice to me, Barry," I said penitently, "I ask you to dinner, I bore you with a long rigmarole about the office, I snub you when you sympathise, and then finally you pay me a compliment. What a man! Incidentally, all this story *is* in confidence in the strictest professional sense. I had no business to tell you a word of it really."

"Of course I shall treat it as absolutely confidential, Vicky. In the unlikely event of anybody mentioning the name 'Dorothy Harper' to me, I shan't bat an eyelid."

"Nobody ever will mention Dorothy Harper to you," I said cheerfully, "because, as far as I know, no such author exists. The facts are exactly as I told you, but I did alter the name."

"I expect that was a wise precaution," said Barry politely. But he did, I am afraid, look a little hurt nevertheless.

Chapter 3

THERE IS, as I remarked to Barry, a great deal to be said for a change of worry. During the weeks that followed, sirens and bombs formed an excellent counter-irritant to private difficulties. London, during the time of those autumn air-raids has been too often described for me to go over that ground again. It affected me, as it affected many people, with a most terrible sense of wrathful impotence. Also, for the first time, I knew what it was to feel really vindictive against the Germans, and was quite shocked at the intensity of my hatred.

On the whole, I was lucky enough to be angry nearly all the time, and that meant that I escaped being consciously frightened.

Not, of course, that, living in Harminster as I did, I went through anything really bad. It was mostly just a matter of setting my teeth and determining that I *would* carry on with my ordinary life whatever the difficulties. Mrs. Hitchcock felt the same, and we never closed the office, although for a week or two there was practically no business to be done. I got quite used to glancing quickly towards the building in which the agency is when I turned the corner of the road, just to see whether it was still there or not, after the previous night's raid. The moment I saw it was, I heaved a sigh of relief and dismissed the matter from my mind. Ordinary life is a tough plant, as I observed once before, and minor affairs and interests *did* continue to matter even though the skies were raining death and the British Empire was fighting with its back to the wall.

I may say at once that the office survived the blitz with only one quite minor 'blasting.' As for Harminster, it was lucky enough to escape with only a comparatively few stray bombs, mid none of those near my cottage. I can quite imagine that, had Antonia ever been exposed to real danger, I should have been in a pitiable state of terror.

By November it was apparent that, bad as the night-raids still sometimes were, the intensity of the enemy's attack had reached and passed its zenith. I felt that I could turn round, breathe again, and take stock of my position.

Rene's arrival had coincided with the beginning of the bad London raids. In the circumstances I did not notice the consequent domestic upheaval and reorganization quite as much as I might otherwise have done. Most people's houses were crammed full of evacuées, paying or otherwise. Everything everywhere was at sixes and sevens.

Rene was evidently determined to be as little trouble as possible. She had, I think, hopes of 'helping Blakey,' but Blakey ruthlessly treated her as 'Mr. Philip's widow,' and Mr. Philip's widow in a certain condition, at that. I'm afraid poor Rene's only occupation at this time *was* her condition. She treated it as a full-time job, but I can't really blame her, as-what else *was* there for her to do?

Sometimes I used to think that I really must bestir myself and prod her into making some sort of life for herself somehow—ask a few people in to meet her, introduce her to the head woman at the W.V.S. office, and so on—but I always ended by deciding that I could not really do much until after the baby was born. Rene was unnecessarily conscious of her appearance. She was even coy of shopping and travelling in buses. So, rather thankfully, I shelved *that* responsibility and, for the time being, just mentally placed her on a sofa with her feet up.

Some time I meant to do what Mother wanted and have a little talk with her about my divorce, but I hadn't even got round to that yet.

It was a letter from Mother that had made me feel I ought to tell Rene a little bit more about myself. It had arrived after Rene had been with me about a week. The first part was chitchat, the second Mother had evidently steeled herself to write:

> '. . . I *do* hope you and Rene are settling down all right together. Now, Vicky, don't be cross with me if I tell you that Rene *is* a little bit frightened of you. She told me so, although of course she never meant me to tell you. I'm only doing so because I think if you realize that you may be a little alarming sometimes to people who don't know you well, you and she will get on better. Heavens knows I don't want a daughter of your age to be as childish (in some ways) as Rene is, but I am afraid Rene has got a little bit the impression that you're too sophisticated altogether for her ever to be a real companion to you. I think your divorce worries her a lot. You know people . . .'

(Here something was vigorously scratched out, and I had some difficulty in deciphering it. I grinned when I saw at last that it was 'of that class.')

> '. . . people like Rene don't take that sort of thing easily in their stride.'

(Here there was an omission mark, and Mother had scribbled in: 'I don't myself' between the lines.)

> 'So think me an interfering old busybody if you like, but *do* just have a little talk with Rene some time and just tell her, quite simply, the bare facts. She tried to pump me, but

I *knew* you wouldn't like what I'd say, so I shut her up. I'm sure what's worrying her is the fact that you were divorcing. Raymond during the time Antonia was on the way. I didn't tell her so, but evidently she's worked the dates out for herself—because that's what she began to ask me about.'

More chit-chat followed. It was a rather sweet motherish sort of letter—so characteristic that I couldn't possibly really be annoyed.

Well. I didn't, as a matter of fact, *want* Rene to be a 'real companion' to me, but I did see that in the circumstances, she had the right to know at least some things about me.

The facts of the case were actually very simple. At the time I instituted divorce proceedings against Raymond I did not know I was going to have a child. Later, when I did know, I went obstinate. Nothing would have induced me to withdraw the case and attempt a reconciliation.

Fortune favoured me in that I was lucky enough, to have my case come on without the long delay that so often occurs, and consequently very few people had the opportunity of urging me to abandon it. I never disclosed the fact that I was going to have a child to my solicitors, and certainly Raymond never had an inkling. I made things as safe as I could for myself during the early months by burying myself in the country and seeing none of my London friends. I stayed with Betty Attenborough, the married friend with whom I had so often stayed during my Oxford vacations. She had a house in Berkshire as well as a London flat. She and her husband knew, of course, but they also knew it was useless to argue with me.

Antonia was five months on the way when I got my *decree nisi*, and I do not think anyone in court suspected anything. Raymond would have guessed in an instant I am sure, but the case was undefended, and he was not present.

It was not until after I had got my *decree nisi* that I did what I had secretly been longing to do—ran home to Mother and burst into tears on her shoulder. The news of the baby was of course a terrible shock to her, but nevertheless she behaved (as I knew she would) like the proper mother she is—by which I mean that she was utterly horrified and not entirely comprehending, but resolved at all costs to stand by me. She said that she and I would go right away somewhere into the country and she would stay with me until after the baby was born. When I protested that I didn't want her to put herself out for me, that I had got myself into this mess and would see it through myself, she said she'd never heard such nonsense in her life. It wasn't I who'd got myself into a mess; it was Raymond who had let me down, and in any case (she hurried on, as she saw I was making a gesture of protest), in any case there was nothing she'd like better than to go away with me for a bit. She'd been so lonely and miserable in the house since Daddy died and had been beginning to feel that nobody really needed her any more. Now (in a brisker tone) that was enough crying, Vicky darling. Crying wasn't good for the baby, was it now?

I believe she even produced her handkerchief to wipe my eyes. I felt about two years old.

I accepted Mother's offer on one condition. (Poor mothers! We neglect them when we're happy and successful, we collapse on their shoulders when we're miserable, we accept their help and solace and then have the nerve to make 'conditions' about accepting it. I expect I shall go through the same old hoops with Antonia in my turn.) I said very well, provided that Mother wouldn't ever try to persuade me, even at this late stage, to approach Raymond. I didn't even want him to hear about the baby until the latest possible moment. The baby was *my* affair, *my* responsibility. Did she understand?

"Darling," said mother uneasily, "you do realize what this attitude of yours about the baby will lead malicious people to say, don't you?"

"That the child isn't Raymond's? I daresay they will, but I can't help that. The baby's *my fault*, I tell you. I wouldn't have one when Raymond wanted one, and it isn't his fault that I'm having one now. I *won't* blackmail him back with a baby. I just won't ... Actually, it *is* Raymond's child, Mother."

"Darling!" Mother looked utterly horrified. "As if you needed to tell *me* that!"

"Well, it does look fishy, I'll admit—how fishy you don't know, Mother, because I never told you Raymond wasn't living at home then, did I? Things between us had got so bad that he'd taken a room somewhere else."

"Oh Vicky! Why didn't you ever tell me?"

"Oh Mother, I *couldn't* bother you with my troubles so soon after Daddy's death. I thought if it *did* all come right again you might never need to know. Only then it obviously wasn't going to come right and I asked Raymond to come and see me about a divorce, and he did and—I believe it's called 'condoning' or something, but honestly I was in such a state at the time that I was absolutely reckless, and—oh, I can't really explain how it happened, because I don't understand myself."

"Vicky, darling!" Mother got up. "Don't tell me any more. That sort of thing" (she blushed slightly) "isn't meant to be told—not to *anyone*. I doubt if I should understand if you *did* tell me."

I looked up, faintly surprised.

"Oh, of course I know what you *mean*, Vicky. You mean that it was you who was ... was careless about possibly having a baby on that occasion?"

I nodded. "Raymond always left all that to me. I had no business not to be careful. We'd *agreed* to divorce."

"Yes, well—exactly, Vicky. However much you explained all that to me, I doubt if I'd ever really understand. You know babies, children—to your father and myself—they're not, they never *could* be merely 'somebody's fault.' "

"You mean they're 'gifts from God' or something of the sort?" I hazarded.

"I expect that phrase sounds ridiculous to you, Vicky? You say it as if you thought it was ridiculous."

"Well—frankly yes, it does, Mother."

"Very well. Now to me *your* way of talking about marriage as merely a sort of contract sounds just as ridiculous. I'm not preaching to you, darling. I'm just telling you there are some things I'd just never understand. And"—with a change of tone—

"of course I don't mean for a *moment*, darling, that it's not Raymond who's really to blame. You can't prevent me thinking that, although if you don't want to talk about it, I promise I won't."

"Yes. Let's leave it at that," I said thankfully.

We did.

All that (thank God) took place more than four years ago.

* * * * *

In the end the subject cropped up fairly naturally between Rene and myself.

Rene's baby was due any day, indeed it was slightly overdue. She seemed upset and astonished about this, and I comforted her by telling her that I knew of heaps of babies who had been a fortnight late and, I added heartily and with no scientific justification whatever, all the better for it.

"Really, Vicky?" said Rene trustingly. "Oh well, if it's better for the baby, I'll stop worrying. Only I am so *longing* to see him."

"Or her," I said unnecessarily.

"Of course, or her," said Rene hastily (but there was not the same capital letter effect in her tone). "Oh Vicky, I can't help hoping and hoping it's a boy, you know. I think the suspense just at the end when I know he's actually coming will be awful."

"Don't worry." I said with an unkind grin, "you'll find you'll quite quickly reach a point when you won't care if you're giving birth to a boy or girl or a grand piano as long as you get it over."

"Oh Vicky!" Rene looked appalled. "Is it so very awful?"

"No, no," I said hastily. "Or rather, yes, yes, possibly, but what *does* that matter once it's over? Physical pain—particularly that sort of natural physical pain—can't really hurt you, you know. I mean" (for Rene was looking bewildered and I don't wonder), "I mean it can't get at your mind and hurt *that* and so leave any sort of mental scar behind. You'll forget all about it the moment it's over, like everybody else. And then" (for Rene was looking as if this was rather tough consolation, as indeed it was), "and then when it *is* over and you've got your baby, well then, you *will* get your thrill and no mistake."

"I keep on wondering and wondering what he'll look like," said Rene.

"You think of him as a real person already, don't you, Rene?" I said, interested.

"Oh yes," said Rene, and then added a little shyly: "Didn't you when Antonia was coming?"

"No, I'm afraid I didn't," I said.

"I expect it's silly of me," said Rene, instantly a little wistful and deprecating.

That was the worst of Rene. One couldn't disagree with her without her immediately becoming apologetic. Or at least, *I* couldn't. I remembered Mother's hint about her being a little frightened of me, and then it suddenly occurred to me that now was a good opportunity to take her just a very little way into my confidence.

"Not a bit silly, Rene," I said. "Natural and right, I'm sure, and as it's meant to be. *I* was the silly one, but then you see the circumstances of Antonia's birth weren't very happy for me. I couldn't help feeling that she was sort of illegitimate."

"But she *wasn't*, was she?" cried Rene, looking so utterly scandalized, so thoroughly jolted out of all wistfulness and sentimentality, and, at the same time so avidly interested, that I nearly giggled.

"No, no, of course not. Look Rene, this was how it was—there's no real mystery or skeleton-in-the-cupboard business about it—it was like this . . ."

I told her, very briefly, of course, and in dry unemotional language. Her eyes never left my face, but I could see very little glimmer of comprehension in them—which was not to be wondered at, considering I left out of the story not only all sentiment, but all feeling whatsoever. It made a very bald and distinctly sordid little tale.

"So you see," I ended up, "I never worried at all about it being a pity Antonia shouldn't have a father. That point of view didn't even occur to me until well after she was born. As I said just now, I didn't think of her as a real person at that time. Funny, when you think how now I'd do almost anything for her sake," I added, more to myself than to Rene.

"My baby won't ever know his father either," said Rene.

I felt convicted of slight tactlessness.

"No, Rene, but, sad as that is, that's through no fault of your own, is it? However, don't let's brood on the past. Antonia seems to have got along all right with only a mother, so far. The mother is the *most* important, I don't think anyone could deny that."

"Oh no, I'm sure they couldn't—and besides, Vicky . . ."

"Yes. What?"

"Well—if, if Ray—if your husband was really so—so unkind—perhaps it's better—better for Antonia, I mean—that she should be brought tip without him. I mean—"

I suppose she saw me glaring at her. Anyway, her stumbling attempt at consolation trailed off.

"Who told you Raymond was unkind to me?" I shot out accusingly.

"Nobody . . . I mean, I just got the impression that—that—"

"You didn't get that impression from anything *I* said just now, did you?" I demanded.

"Oh no, no," said poor Rene hastily. "Vicky, I thought *you* spoke about him most frightfully sort of unvindictively."

"Unvindictive! I should hope so. What I want to know is, who's given you the idea that I had anything to be vindictive about? Was it Mother?"

I see now that it was unpardonable of me to cross-examine Rene in this way. My only excuse is that I was really annoyed. Rene had evidently already got the one idea in her head that I was determined to keep out.

"Mother? Oh no! She hardly said anything to me about it."

"Well, who on earth was it then? Philip?"

"No, oh no. *He* never said much, either. Oh Vicky, if you *must* know, it was simply something Blakey let drop once, and I'm terribly sorry if—if you're upset about it. I oughtn't to have listened, I see I oughtn't now."

I suddenly woke up to the fact that poor Rene was almost in tears.

"That's all right, Rene," I said. "It was very naughty of Blakey to say anything, but I'm sure it wasn't *your* fault she did."

Even as I spoke I wondered for an instant whether this was true. What was Mother's phrase—Rene trying to 'pump her' about my divorce, wasn't it? Had Rene encouraged Blakey to talk? Well, if she had, probably it was my fault for not telling Rene myself sooner.

I think it flashed across my mind then that you *cannot* really live with someone in circumstances of intimacy and continue to avoid being really intimate with them. The conclusion was so unpalatable that I pushed it hastily from my mind.

"Only I must tell you, Rene," I said, "that Blakey never in her life laid eyes on Raymond, let alone ever seeing us together, and so anything that *she* lets drop isn't, even gossip or hearsay—it's pure imagination. *And* absolutely none of her business."

The telephone rang in the hall. I opened the door to answer it. There, on the mat, was Blakey with Rene's evening cup of Ovaltine.

I carried off the situation better than Rene, but then I had something to do. I simply swept past Blakey and answered the telephone. Rene, as I saw out of the corner of my eye, looked horribly guilty. Blakey wore her automaton look.

"Do you suppose she heard?" asked Rene nervously, when I came back.

"I don't know and I don't care," I answered grandly.

"I hope she won't think I've been telling tales about her and getting her into trouble with you," said Rene.

"She can think what she likes. I certainly shan't ever make any reference to it," I retorted sharply.

I honestly did not see at the time that it was poor Rene who was going to reap a whole harvest of minor unpleasantnesses from this unfortunate *contretemps*. Very unfair, considering that, it was *my* voice that was injudiciously loud, and I who had anyway forced the information out of Rene. Later on, when I could not help noticing how nasty Blakey was making herself to

Rene, I dated back the trouble to that evening. Rene's guess was right: Blakey evidently *had* heard the tail-end of our conversation and *had* therefore jumped to the conclusion that Rene had been 'telling tales about her.'

So ended my first attempt to make Rene stop being a 'little bit frightened' of me and to take her more into my confidence.

Chapter 4

SOMETIMES, DURING the first year after my divorce from Raymond, when I was still subject to waves of bitterness about him—moods which descended on me with no warning and passed for no reason, for all the world as though they had been physical attacks of some disorder to which I was prone—I had imagined to myself circumstances in which we might possibly accidentally meet again. Needless to say, I preferred to picture a setting in which I appeared in a slightly glamorous light—say, in evening dress in the foyer of a theatre, perhaps, on a first night. Escorted, of course, by somebody very distinguished-looking and possibly even well known in some world or other. (Famous writer? Politician? Doctor?) Myself looking my best and talking my wittiest. (Perhaps I was even the author of the play being performed? No, just a little too incredible, that.) A touch on my shoulder, a diffident touch.

"Vicky?"

"Raymond! Why, how lovely to see you again!" (Very gracious, very gay, very self-composed.)

How this promising conversation developed I never quite bothered to arrange. Artistic feeling would seem to demand that if I was gracious, gay and self-composed, Raymond should be deferential, wistful and nervous, and, as a matter of fact, I could not possibly imagine him being any of those things in any circumstances whatever. Slurring over all this, therefore, I passed on to the final fade-out.

The Other Man: "Vicky, excuse me, but we ought to . . . The others are waiting for us at the Savoy."

Me: "Yes, I'm afraid so. Well, Raymond . . ." (An afterthought.) "But won't you come along too? We're only going to the grill-room. It doesn't really matter about you not being dressed."

Raymond: "Thank you, Vicky, but I don't think I can. I promised my—er—Sandra, I'd be back and she doesn't like . . ." (looking henpecked), "I'm afraid I can't."

Highly satisfactory fade-out with me being reverentially handed into a taxi, and Raymond standing looking after me with a look of deep yearning and regret on his face.

At that time, of course, I still thought Raymond would probably marry Sandra, in due course, and therefore, since I refused to flinch away from that fact, I was obliged to imagine him married and regretting it. As I only knew Sandra very slightly, I was fairly free to imagine her offensive in any way I liked. I suppose I chose to imagine her domineering and pettily possessive because, whatever I had been like while I was married to Raymond, I had never been either of those things.

Raymond, however, did not marry Sandra; and when I did accidentally meet him again, it was in circumstances distinctly unusual, but totally free from glamour.

I was putting Antonia to bed one Sunday evening about a week after the conversation with Rene about my divorce. Blakey was out, and Rene had retired to her room after tea. The baby was now about ten days overdue, and the doctor had assured Rene that she would not have much longer to wait.

I could hear Rene moving about in her room, and all the time I was bathing Antonia it was at the back of my mind that I must go and fuss after Rene a little, when Antonia was in bed. I had hardly seen Rene all day, and, judging by the sounds from her room, she was dragging suitcases up and down.

"You're not very good at thinking of things this evening, are you, Mummy?" said Antonia eventually.

We were playing—or rather, Antonia was trying to make me play—the game called 'Horrid Mummies.' I do not really approve of this game, which was invented by Antonia and consists of thinking out unkind jokes to play on an imaginary child.

"When I have a little girl, Mummy, I'll tell her it's Christmas the next day and she'll hang up her stocking and the next morning she'll think it's going to be full of toys and it won't have anything in it at all." Peals of rapturous heartless laughter. "Now *you* think of something, Mummy."

And, although, as I have said, I do not really approve of the game at all, I cannot resist thinking out some rather more subtle and intricate form of disappointment and embellishing it with appropriate details, if only for the pleasure of watching Antonia's face as I come to my *dénouement*.

I was just drying behind Antonia's ears and saying, "No, let's play Nice Mummies for a change, and think of treats to give your little girl instead," when Rene put her head round the door and said, "Oh . . . Vicky, I think I'd better . . . what about that taxi . . . can you?"

"Yes certainly, Rene," I said briskly, reaching out meanwhile for Antonia's toothbrush.

I was matter-of-fact both for Rene's sake and for Antonia's.

"I can't find the number or I'd ring up," said Rene.

"Don't worry, there's loads of time," I said firmly. "I'll just plonk Antonia into bed and then I'll be entirely at your service."

"You said you'd tell me a story in bed," said Antonia.

"Oh darling, I'm so sorry. I'm afraid I can't to-night. I'm playing at 'Horrid Mummies' in real life, aren't I, darling? I'm so sorry."

"Where's Auntie Rene going?"

"To the nursing-home to have her baby," I answered without hesitation.

Rene, flinching from this bald statement, shot out of the bathroom, and I hurried Antonia into bed.

When I came downstairs Rene was hovering anxiously by the telephone.

I took off the receiver and waited for the usual dialling note. Greatly to my disgust I heard nothing but a few dead-sounding clicks.

I did all the things that one always does on such occasions—shouted "Hello," replaced the receiver and took it off again several times, dialled o, and so on, but the wretched instrument refused to respond.

"I'm sorry, Rene," I said, "but the damn thing seems to be out of order. Now will you mind if I leave you here, alone while I just run along to the garage and bring the taxi back with me? It won't take me more than ten minutes and is quicker than anything else I can think of."

"Oh *dear*," said Rene, looking utterly aghast.

It *was* irritating for her, but irritating was all it could possibly be. I refrained, however, from pointing this out to her again.

"I really won't be long," I said, snatching at an old coat that hung in the hall. "Make yourself a cup of tea or something."

Without further ado, I plunged into the rather nasty November evening. It was not a very dark night, and I could see my way sufficiently to run. I was by this time myself infected by a slight sense of drama and urgency, and the mere fact of running enhanced this sensation.

I arrived with my hair on end, my stockings splashed and my coat flying open.

The first person I saw was Raymond. I rounded the corner of the road, where the garage stands, and practically fell into his arms.

"Hello! Steady! Why, it's *Vicky*! What an unexpected pleasure! Splendid!" said an oh! so well-remembered voice.

Self-control in a difficult situation is a quality I admire enormously—and a mocking casualness is perhaps the best form self-control can take in circumstances where sentiment might be unbearable. I knew from the nervous tension in his fingers as he steadied me by the shoulders that his casualness was assumed, not real.

One of the garage cars complete with driver, was standing beside Raymond at the kerbside. It was no moment for chitchat and enquiries.

"Raymond! Are you just getting out of that taxi or just getting in?" I asked breathlessly.

"Just getting in, I hoped. Why? Do you want it? Can I offer you a lift anywhere?"

There was, in his light formal voice, a strong undercurrent of interest and—was it excitement?—but I do not think the chauffeur would have realized this. It was no new thing for Raymond and me to be communicating feelings to each other in public with no one the wiser.

"Well . . ." I recognized the chauffeur, a man who had often driven me. "Oh Wilkins! I expect there's another taxi I can have, isn't there?"

"Not just at the moment, there isn't, I'm afraid, Mrs. Heron. Sunday evening, there's some of us off-duty you know. If you care to wait a bit there should be one of the cars coming back soon."

"Oh well—I suppose I'll have to do that then."

I spoke calmly. Raymond hates fluster.

I did not fool him, of course.

"Oh—please, Vicky! Take this taxi, by all means. I'm in no hurry, at all."

"Oh Raymond! Well, thank you enormously. But what will you do?"

"Wait here till another comes back. I don't mind at all."

"No, don't do that. Come and wait at my house," I said on impulse, "and they can send one round there when it comes. Will you, Wilkins?"

"Certainly, Madam. I'll just leave instructions." He opened the door and Raymond and I climbed in. Wilkins disappeared into the office.

"Vicky, this situation interests me strangely," said Raymond. "I am not quite clear why I've got into this taxi with you, for instance. You're going somewhere in a tremendous hurry, passing your house on the way, for me to be dropped to wait. Is that it?"

I laughed.

"My hurry, if you can believe it, Raymond, is entirely for another. Rene is starting her baby and the telephone was suddenly out of order. The taxi is to take her to the maternity home. Yes, Wilkins, to the Lodge first to pick up someone."

"I hope nothing untoward will happen to Rene in the taxi with which you won't be able to cope, Vicky," said Raymond.

"Oh—I shan't go with her."

"My dear girl! In common humanity . . ." (Sub-mocking, of course.)

"I can't help it, Raymond. Blakey's out and I can't leave Antonia alone in the house. Besides, there isn't really any hurry at all."

I felt, rather than saw, Raymond's grin at this cool admission, but all he said was, "Vicky, I need a little help with the *dramatis persona* of this scene. Who, for instance, are Rene and Blakey? Antonia"—he paused and the amusement died out of his voice—"Antonia's name I know."

"Rene is Philip's widow. You heard about his death, perhaps?"

"Yes. I'm sorry—very sorry. I didn't know he was married."

"No, it was all very sudden. Well, Rene's living with me now. Blakey was Grandmother's maid, who's been with me some time now. She's the only other member of our household, but, as I say, she's out to-night. And this is the house. Wait just a minute, Wilkins."

Rene was still hovering in the hall. Her face, on seeing me accompanied by a strange man, was a study.

"Rene, this is a friend of mine whom I met by chance and who's kindly giving up his taxi to you," I said hastily.

I did not think that, in her present state of mind, Rene would recognize Raymond from the photograph she had once seen, and I guessed right. She glanced at him in a slightly scandalized way, but with no trace of recognition. I do not know quite why I did not want Rene to realize who Raymond was, but certainly I did not.

"Let me help you with your suitcases," said Raymond, tactfully taking to action.

"I'm sorry I can't come with you, Rene, as Blakey's out," I said, "but you'll be there in no time at all and you'll be perfectly all right. I'll ring up later to hear how you're getting on. Now good-bye"—(I kissed her, I think for the first time)—"and the very best of luck. To-morrow morning you'll be feeling marvellous. . . . To Harrington Maternity Home, Wilkins."

"She looks rather forlorn and agitated," said Raymond, as the taxi, with Wilkins at the wheel registering polite imperturbability, disappeared.

"I'm afraid she thought it execrable taste on my part to reappear with a strange man," I said. "Strange men are rather Strange Men with capital letters to Rene."

"Do you two get on well together?" asked Raymond.

"I'm not quite sure yet," I said cautiously.

"I wondered if I ought to offer to guard the house while you accompanied her," said Raymond.

"Oh really, darling!" (The 'darling' slipped out before I noticed it.) "Surely pinching your taxi is enough for one, evening without making use of you as a watchdog as well."

"What does a watchdog do? Prevent the house going on fire? Or rush to the cot-side if there are screams from upstairs?"

"Both. Neither ever happens, of course. But both undoubtedly would repeatedly if one went out."

"Of course, I quite understand. Probably I'd have been better qualified as a fire-fighter than as a cot-watcher."

"A piquant situation," I agreed. "'Don't be frightened, darling, I'm your Daddy.' Redoubled screams."

"Yes . . . yes," said Raymond, taking out his cigarette-case. (So familiar the tone, the gesture. That way of saying 'Yes . . . yes,' half-pondering, half-agreeing. That flat gold case, a twenty-first birthday present.)

"Have a drink, Raymond? Gin? Whisky?"

"Thank you, Vicky. Would you have any objection to my seeing Antonia—asleep, I mean?" He snapped his case shut and replaced it in his pocket.

All Raymond's gestures, all his words, are precise without being finicky. It makes him a curiously easy and at the same time satisfying companion. I had almost forgotten that restful feeling of the situation being under control—under his control—which one always gets in Raymond's company.

"No objection at all, Raymond. I'd rather wait half an hour or so, though, until she's really sound asleep, if you don't mind. Can you wait?"

"Thank you, Vicky. Yes, I can wait."

"What about some food? I can easily produce some sort of a meal."

"How one thing does lead to another, doesn't it, Vicky?" said Raymond easily. "Once again—thank you. Can I help?"

"No. Your rôle in this highly domestic little scene is to mend the telephone. It's in the hall."

Raymond went out into the hall and lifted the receiver.

"I've mended it," he said instantly. "Listen."

Sure enough, the dialling tone appeared to be functioning normally.

"Nevertheless, I think we'll test it," said Raymond, dialling rapidly. "This is a number I happen to know. Hello? Whiteway's Garage? . . . I'm speaking for Mrs. Heron. When she does want a taxi this evening she will ring you. You need not trouble to send one round . . . Thank you."

He came back into the sitting-room with perfect composure.

"I see you know this district," I said.

"Yes. Yes, well. How long have you been here, Vicky? It's very nice, your house." Raymond cast a quick appraising glance round the room. Some of the ornaments and cushions must, of course, have been entirely familiar to him. One would not have guessed so from his manner.

"About a year. Since the beginning of the war. And you?"

"About the same time."

"It's funny we never bumped into each other before, Raymond."

"The first six months I wasn't often let out."

"From the Army, you mean?" He was not in uniform, and, for the first time that evening I had time to wonder what he was doing in Harminster.

"No. From the sanatorium."

"Sanatorium . . . Raymond! How . . ."

". . . How I startle you?" finished Raymond dryly. "Yes. I startled myself at the time. T.B. is one of those many things that only really happen to other people, isn't it?"

"Are you—all right—now?"

As I spoke I looked at him anxiously. I had already found time that evening to wonder if Raymond was noticing much of a change in my appearance. I did, I knew, look older than when he had last seen me. But, curiously enough, I had hardly studied his face closely at all. From the first moment of our meeting he had seemed so utterly himself, the same Raymond in every particular, that it had never crossed my mind that his life might have altered too as radically as mine had done.

As a matter of fact I could, now I really looked at him, see little trace of what one would be careful *not* to refer to as 'the ravages of the disease.' He was thin, of course, but then he had always had that whip cord greyhound look. He was pale, but so he had always been.

"Don't look so aghast, Vicky. I assure you I'm not infectious."

"Oh, Raymond!" I cried, too hurt to hide the fact. "As if I was thinking of that! I'm just so—so *sorry*."

"That's sweet of you, Vicky, and I beg your pardon. One gets a bit on the defensive, you know. The ordinary reaction to T.B., as I have had every chance of finding out, is a horrified shudder."

"I'm not horrified, Raymond," I said quickly. "At least, I am—shocked—on your account, but I'm interested too. Tell me all about it. Only *do* sit down and look comfortable."

Raymond grinned. "It's not necessary for me to put my feet up on every occasion, you know. I can, thank God, lead a moderately normal man's life."

"You are—all right—then now, Raymond?"

"One's never precisely cured, Vicky. The disease is—one hopes—'completely arrested.' A nice phrase, that!"

"Are you?"

"I hope so. Actually that remains to be seen. I went to the sanatorium to-day to be X-rayed. The doctors have hopes that the plates will show a completely healed lung. I think they will, because when I was 'screened,' everything looked all right. This final X-raying is just to make absolutely sure."

"So then you *will* be cured, Raymond?"

"In so far as one *is* cured, yes. There's always a scar left on the lung, of course—it was only one lung affected in my case. One is supposed to take a certain amount of care—no violent exercise or sudden exertion and that sort of proviso. Otherwise, lead a healthy happy life, my dear, and never brood on your condition."

"Sounds like advice to an expectant mother," I said.

"Very like. By the way, Vicky, in common decency, I should now ask *you* about your operation."

"My operation? Oh, you mean Antonia being born? No, Raymond, I'll spare you all details. Everything was most uninterestingly normal. But anyway, Raymond, you haven't *finished* about your operation yet. I've heard the end of the story, not the beginning."

"Oh, that too was uninterestingly normal, Vicky. The only quaint detail is that it was an Army doctor who discovered it at a medical examination, thus shattering one of my oldest illusions."

"So you were in the Army for a bit?"

"For one glorious month, during which time the fighting was in Poland and absolutely nowhere else."

"You must have had the disease when you joined up then?"

"Yes. Undoubtedly. Would it surprise you to hear, Vicky, as we barristers so unfairly say, that most people contract T.B. at some time or other in their lives and recover again without knowing?"

"Well, since you put it to me, Raymond, yes, it would."

"Nevertheless, it's true. I don't know at all when I actually picked up the germ, but not, I think, very long before it was discovered."

"You didn't have it when we were—were together—then?"

The question was prompted by a belated quiver of maternal instinct towards Raymond. I do not blame him for misunderstanding its import. He had, after all, never known me in the rôle of solicitous wife.

"No. Certainly not, I should say. You need not worry at all about Antonia, Vicky. There's absolutely no reason why she should even have the slightest tendency towards it."

"Actually I wasn't even thinking of Antonia, Raymond."

"I'm sorry—I answered something you didn't ask. I thought— you are, I suppose, very fond of Antonia, aren't you, Vicky?"

Well! This was a new thing! Raymond and I at cross-purposes, actually groping for each other's meanings! We must both have changed more fundamentally than I had realized.

"Fond of her! Good heavens!" I laughed. "*You* need not worry on *that* account, Raymond. I never understood how mothers *do* love their children, until I *was* a mother with a child. It's quite extraordinary, I assure you. Nobody was more surprised than myself."

"Once again I beg your pardon, Vicky. It's quite monotonous how I keep on doing it this evening. My only explanation for my stupidity is that there are some things about which I am still—in the dark, so to speak."

I did not know whether I wanted to follow this up or not, and I had the feeling that Raymond was tacitly offering me the choice and that he would accept whatever course I followed. On the one hand I passionately wanted this odd conversation between, us to be carried through with grace and dignity, and laughter, and all my deep-rooted love for style and gesture and control in human relationships urged me to pass lightly over the past that lay between us. On the other hand I thought that if, perhaps, a few things were said, quickly and briefly, now, some vaguely-visualized pattern would be finally completed, and could then be allowed to drop from our fingers with all its interwoven strands of suffering and happiness neatly blending into a completed—and dead—whole.

"Raymond, I don't want to talk about the past any more than you do," I said finally, "but—like you, again—I hate loose ends. If there's anything that you're in the dark about, I'll give you quick, brief answers, and then get the supper."

"Fortunately, I'm practised in putting what are really personal observations into question form, Vicky. I put it to you, then, that you did not know that you were going to have a baby when you instituted divorce proceedings against me?"

"No. Yes. I mean, you're right."

"Quite. (You're not the first witness, Vicky, to find that form a confusing One.) I suggest to you that, when you *did* become aware of this fact, a sense of chivalry deterred you from communicating the knowledge to me?"

"Right again. You might prefer to call it obstinacy."

"I prefer chivalry, myself," said Raymond gravely. "There's only one more question, but it's a nasty one. Would you say that, generally speaking, a man had a right to know that his wife was going to bear him a child?"

"Generally speaking, yes. In the circumstances—I mean, I didn't think—it was ages before I even realized Antonia was going to be a real person—you see..."

"—In the circumstances that point of view, rather naturally perhaps, escaped your consideration," finished Raymond suavely, and then—with a complete change of tone—"Vicky, it's sweet to see you behaving and talking like, every witness under cross-examination always behaves and talks. And, incidentally, I do apologize for cross-examining you at all. I won't ever again, I promise you. There is this to be said for legal language—it helps one over an awkward patch, don't you think?"

"It makes everything sound less miserable and awful and more dignified," I agreed. "But Raymond, there's one question you haven't asked me, which I shouldn't exactly blame you for asking in the circumstances."

I meant, of course, that he might have wanted an outright assurance from me that he was Antonia's father. I could see by the quick glance he gave me that he understood what was in my mind. All he said, however, was, "No, no, Vicky, The cross-examination's over, Your Counsel is perfectly satisfied on every point—*every* point."

"Well then! If that's so, witness will go and get the supper. Do you—you aren't on a diet or anything, are you, Raymond?"

"No, no. Just give me *all* your ration of butter, milk, cheese and eggs for the week, and I'll be perfectly satisfied. May I go up and have a glance at Antonia now?"

I was glad that the atmosphere had lightened back to joking-level before he again made this request. I did nevertheless feel that, with the weight of things just said (and unsaid, too) still lying on us, I would prefer not to accompany him. Had we gone up to see Antonia the minute he arrived, I would have treated the episode with ironic amusement, mocked a little perhaps at its obvious sentimental appeal.

"Yes, certainly. I'll just point out the room to you and then start getting the supper. The light's just inside the door and you can switch it on. She's certain to be sound asleep by now, so it won't wake her. Look—up the stairs, that door on the left. See?"

Raymond nodded, and I left him to it.

I was in the kitchen when he came down.

"Tray in front of the fire, I think, don't you, Raymond?"

"Yes—delightful. Vicky, there was a teddy-bear which seemed to be in difficulties. Antonia was fast asleep all over it, I rescued it and tucked it in more neatly beside her. She never stirred. That was a permissible thing to do, I hope?"

"Yes, certainly, thank you, Raymond. I should have done the same myself later. I practically always have to."

"She's very alluring, Vicky. I like that white hair. It is white, isn't it?"

"Practically. Her eyes, however, I hasten to assure you, are not pink."

"Blue?"

"No—hazel, just to trick you."

"H'm. Altogether rather fun. Let me help you with that tray, Vicky."

Neither Raymond nor I made any further reference to Antonia or to our past that evening. During supper I learnt more about Raymond's course of treatment at the Sanatorium just outside Harminster—how they had performed on him operations which he alluded to as A.P.'s. A.P., I learnt, stood for 'artificial pneumothorax.' ("Come, Vicky, you must learn the jargon.") How, although he had left the Sanatorium five months ago, he had been going back regularly for 'refills.' ("'Refills, Raymond?'" "There now, I knew I should have to take to paper and pencil and drawing diagrams before I was through. No, let's be a little more ingenious. Look, that pepper-pot's my lung, and the toast-rack will do beautifully for my ribs. Now this knife is the needle that the surgeon sticks through the toast rack to blow in air—hand me the bellows, Vicky—between the toast-rack and the pleura, thus collapsing the pepper-pot—I'm laying it flat, you see—so that it has a rest and a chance to heal. You have to keep on repeating the operation because the lung expands itself again.")

I must confess that I found it all very interesting. If anybody had ever told me that T.B. and teddy-bears would be two of the topics Raymond and I would discuss at our first reencounter, I should have laughed heartily at such an impossible absurdity.

I was quite startled when I heard Blakey's step in the hall. I had no idea it was so late.

"And now I must be going, Vicky," said Raymond, rising to his feet.

"Where are you living? I never asked you?"

"I'm staying in a small hotel over the other side of the town. I've been able to find a certain amount of work to do here—legal army work. Funnily enough, I haven't been positively invalided out of the army yet. I even hope (with the aid of the Colonel, who's a friend of mine) to get a War Office job, if this last X-raying is satisfactory."

"I'm so glad," I said vaguely. "Well, Raymond—"

I paused, groping uncertainly for some suitable formula of farewell.

"'It's been so nice meeting you again?'" suggested Raymond, with a glint of amusement in his eye. "Or 'May I ring for a taxi for you?'"

"Well—may I?" I said, smiling.

"No, thank you, Vicky. I'll walk round to the garage and pick one up or else find a bus. No . . . I don't think we shall find anything very suitable to say, so I'd better be going quickly. Which, is not to say that I haven't enjoyed myself very much this evening. My coat I left in the hall, I think."

I followed him out. The situation was, once again, entirely under his control.

"Thank you for having me, Vicky," said Raymond, gravely shaking hands.

"Raymond—you'll let me know the result of the X-ray, will you? I can't help being—interested."

"Bless you, Vicky. That's a very nice note to end on. Yes—I'll let you know."

The front door slammed, and he was gone.

To end on? Well, of course to end on. Had I happened to meet Raymond in the ordinary Way, we should undoubtedly have merely exchanged a few words and passed on.

Chapter 5

RENE'S BABY was a boy, and she called him Philip, after his father.

Rene's three weeks in the nursing-home seemed to pass very quickly. In a flash, it seemed, she was back again, and Philip became very much a member of our household.

I think it natural and even right that mothers should be utterly absorbed in their babies while they are tiny. Nevertheless, the fact remains that mothers at this stage are irritating companions. Who first said that "to understand all is to forgive all?" Personally I have always found this an optimistic observation.

I *did* understand that it was quite natural for Rene to think that there had never been such a baby before. I *did* understand that Philip's death had centred her whole life on the child even more than would have anyway occurred. I *did* understand that it was sad for her that she had no home of her own to hear the baby triumphantly back to, and that the very fact that it was my house, not hers, made her even more passionately on the defensive on the baby's account than she need have been. I understood all this well, and yet I could not help finding Rene's attitude very trying.

The fact that I personally happen to prefer children to babies did not assist matters. It was over Antonia that I had my most direct battle with Rene.

Philip, was about six weeks old at the time and was allowed, by way of a treat, a short kick on the sofa before his six o'clock feed. Rene left us one evening to go and get Philip's night-things ready. On this occasion Philip did not seem to be appreciating his 'play-hour.' He was cross and whimpery.

"Mummy, could I hold him a minute?" said Antonia hopefully.

I really did not see why she shouldn't. I arranged her on a footstool, showed her how to put her arms, and lifted Philip carefully into them. Antonia sat very still, evidently enjoying her responsibility. Philip stopped crying and stared up at her with unwinking gaze.

I thought it was rather amusing to see them together.

Rene came into the room, saw this pretty scene, and immediately looked utterly horrified.

"Oh Vicky! She'll drop him!" she said, and snatched Philip instantly out of Antonia's grasp. Philip (greatly to my secret delight) burst into tears again. Antonia, whom Rene had pushed quite roughly, fell backwards off the footstool on to the floor, and looked thoroughly nonplussed and puzzled, and rather as if she might cry too.

"How *could* you, Vicky," said Rene reproachfully.

"Nonsense, Rene," I said briskly. "He was perfectly safe. I was standing close by and in any case Antonia was taking the greatest care."

"She might so easily have toppled over and then what would have happened to poor little Philly? She *has* toppled over now, you see."

"Only because you startled her and pushed her. Oh well, for God's sake let's consider the episode closed. I won't do it again if you don't like it—you've a perfect right to say so. Only presumably one *wants* to encourage the children to take an interest in each other."

This incident was typical, not so much of many others (for we seldom argued directly), but of the friction that arose between us after Philip's birth. Often and often I reminded myself that I, being by nature of things in the stronger position, ought to be the one to put myself out, if necessary, to make Rene feel that Philip was welcome. He *was* welcome, but there was really no chance to show it, so passionately, so almost aggressively, did Rene stand between him and the world. When he cried in the early hours of the morning I assured Rene (a little untruthfully) that be hadn't disturbed me at all. Had I been her, I should have been enormously relieved at this casual acceptance of what is, after all, generally considered part of the nuisance a young baby may cause in a house. But Rene looked at me as if I was a perfect brute not to be worried on Philip's account.

Blakey, although not, by profession, a children's nurse, was a perfectly responsible person, and might well have been left sometimes to keep an eye on the pram when Philip was asleep in the garden, but Rene, if she wanted to go to the shops, always solemnly wheeled the pram with her. Blakey, I knew, was a little hurt about this ("Does Mrs. Sylvester think I haven't got eyes in my head that I couldn't see if it was raining and bring the pram in?"), and eventually I did suggest to Rene that it was really healthier for Philip to finish his sleep, unjolted, in the garden.

"I know it's silly of me," said Rene wistfully, "but somehow I don't feel happy unless I can have a peep at him whenever I want to. Do you think that's very silly of me, Vicky?"

"I can understand it," I said cautiously, "but frankly, I do think it's silly—yes."

"I suppose it's just the way I'm made and I can't help it," said Rene, deprecating and yet with an undercurrent of complacency.

This was one of the many times when I could have smacked her.

Oh, these petty little feminine bickerings! How sordid and trivial and ridiculous they are, and how passionately I feel one should rise superior to that sort of thing, and how infuriatingly difficult it is to do so. Funnily enough, I think it was I who was much more anxious to avoid anything of the sort than Rene. I disliked it more, thought it more degrading. Rene, more placid by nature than I, I thinly assumed that minor little games of taking umbrage and making it up again were the natural fabric of a woman's life. I suspect she was one of the many people who think there's something rather cosy about a little domestic bicker. I never asked her, but I would not be at all surprised to hear that she really began to feel more at home with me when we started these silly little rows.

My marriage with Raymond had given me no practice in learning how to manage close-quarter domestic friction. I suppose we were unusual in never quarrelling about who was to have the bath first, or whether dinner was late or not, but anyway, we never did, or wanted to. At surface-level we had no disagreements whatsoever.

Well! There I was, and there Rene and Philip were, and there was nothing on earth to be done about it except to pretend to the outer world and especially to Mother that we were getting on splendidly. Mother, at any rate, was happily installed at Chipping Campden with Aunt Maud.

As for Raymond, he was presumably back in London. He had kept his promise and written me a short note to tell me that the results of the X-ray examination had proved to be entirely satisfactory, and that he hoped very much to get this legal job in the War Office. I tore up the letter with the feeling that I had tidied up the last loose end between us.

Domestic affairs being a little strained, and my future seeming more than a trifle dreary, I was quite glad of a sudden recrudescence of work at the office. London was in a more normal state by this time. Round about Christmas-time there was a lull in the raids, and, by the middle of January, the town was perceptibly filling up again.

The Dorothy Harper situation, which I had discussed with Barry, had been allowed to stand over for a while. Dorothy Harper had evacuated herself with all speed at the beginning of the blitz to her Cornish cottage. Not that I blame her—there was no reason why she should stay to be bombed. Only I couldn't help smiling a little when she came prancing back into the office in the middle of January with two nice new short stories, one about the heroism of an old woman in the blitz, the other about a crotchety spinster in Gloucestershire, whose whole life and outlook was radically changed (for the better of course) by her child evacuee. Miss Dorothy Harper herself was loud in her complaints against the billeting officer who had tried to push a schoolboy on to her. ("'But my dear man,' I said—I know him well, he used to be dear Lord Portarlington's right-hand man and was always about the place when one dropped in there—'My dear man, how can I? *Nobody* is readier than myself to help, but it would not be *fair* on the child to billet it in a place where it could not stay. I am not here permanently myself, alas, only for a very very little time.'") Mrs. Hitchcock caught my eye and gave me a wry grin. Dorothy Harper wafted herself out of the office, all pearls, fur-coat and scent, I am sure that she always pictured herself as bringing just a little colour and romance—a breath of the outside world—into our drab lives. As neither of us ever did anything but listen patiently while she talked her society prattle, perhaps we encouraged her in this conception. I was 'Miss Sylvester' to her, as I was to all our clients. I am sure that had she known that I was (like her) a divorcée, she would have been deeply shocked. Little typists in offices (she would think) have no business to be also divorced women with private lives of their own.

"It didn't seem the moment to say anything to her about her behaviour towards us recently," I said apologetically to Mrs. Hitchcock, as the door closed behind her. "There seemed to be such an accumulation of patronage for her to get off her chest to-day. I suppose it's because she hasn't seen us recently."

"There certainly was," said Mrs. Hitchcock grimly, "If that woman wasn't such a gold-mine, *what* pleasure I should have in telling her what I thought of her!"

Generally speaking, Mrs. Hitchcock and I get on splendidly together. She is as hard as nails, and I respect her for it. She could never have built up the Agency and kept it going had she not put business always first in her life. She has no objection to the people she employs having private lives of their own—indeed, as a feminist, she rather likes to employ married women—but she has every objection to private lives being allotted to intrude in the very slightest into business hours. Men do not ask for time off from the office if their wives are ill or their children in need of an escort to somewhere or other. Why should women? Such is her ruthless and logical viewpoint. She did not re-engage me after my divorce, and Antonia's birth out of sentiment and a desire to help—she merely knew I was a useful person in the office. She did not arrange for my benefit that I should only attend the office three days a week—it just happened that the post she could offer me, head of the short story department, had always been planned on that basis, the vast amount of reading that it entailed being done just as conveniently at home as in the office. I already knew the routine work of the office inside out, having worked there in various more underling capacities, from the time I came down from Oxford to the time I realized I was going to have a baby and fled to bury myself in the country.

Although Mrs. Hitchcock had thus already known me for close on seven years at the time I came back to her (and those seven years included a three-months business trip to New York on one occasion, when I acted as her secretary), I do not remember her ever showing the faintest curiosity about my marriage, my divorce or my child—and that, of course, in my sore and bruised mental state, was precisely what I appreciated. It was not tact—she is too downright to be vary tactful—but genuine refreshing lack of interest, tinged, I suspect, with a sort of bored cynicism. I know nothing about her own marriage, except that it took place a long time ago (she is about forty-five now), and lasted very few years and was childless. I imagine that it was a thorough-going mistake in every way, and that consequently she is never surprised to hear that other people have come croppers too. But after all (as I guess she feels) is that very important? Do private lives really matter as much as people pretend? Isn't all this fuss rather silly? Isn't work more important than futile little emotional muddles?

As I say, I like her. I know exactly where I am with her. Her attitude to life may be a limited one, but there is a pleasant lack of humbug about it.

In appearance she is smart in a severely tailored, 'no nonsense' style. And she runs the office well, strictly, and yet without pettiness.

She is, of course, rather a cruel woman. But even when (a little later in this story) I came directly into contact with this quality in her, I continued to like her. It was no shock to me to find out that she could be cruel. I think I had always known it and accepted it.

* * * * *

Barry, who had been away for a month during his school holidays, came back and resumed his old habit of dropping in in the evenings sometimes. Indeed, now that Rene was living with me, I think he dropped in more frequently than he had done since the day he proposed and I refused him. I expect he felt that it was more suitable for a single man to visit two women together than one alone. (When I laughingly said something of the sort to Rene, she opened her eyes very wide and said, "Well, it is really, isn't it?")

I never told Rene that Barry had wanted to marry me. Rene would have been romantically thrilled, of course, but I have always thought that women, unlike men, talk far too much to other women of their private affairs.

Rene liked Barry very much indeed, and told me so. I think she was quite relieved to find I had at least one friend who didn't frighten her. Mrs. Hitchcock had come down one Sunday and Rene had stared at her like a rabbit at a snake.

Barry, I am sure, also liked Rene at once. He called her to me "your pretty little sister-in-law." Now that her appearance was normal again, I could quite see that Rene was indeed a pretty girl, although to me she had, and would always have, one of those slightly indeterminate 'fluffy' faces. I was not surprised at Barry taking to her, because I had guessed before they met that she would be just the type to appeal to his chivalry and protective instinct. I *was* surprised, however, at the way Rene blossomed out in his presence and prattled to him. The fact that she rarely chatted/to me so easily brought me up sharp against the fact (of which I was already uneasily aware) that I myself was failing with her and failing badly.

It was because I was genuinely pleased about the way Barry and Rene got on so well together, that I was furious with Blakey when she chose, suddenly and unexpectedly, to interfere un-pardonably in our private affairs.

It happened that Barry dropped in one evening after supper when I was just on the point of going out. It had not been certain that he was coming, and therefore I apologized briefly but explained that I must, in fact, leave at once. I urged him, however, to stay and have a chat with Rene, who would, I knew, be glad of his company. (Quite apart from liking Barry, Rene hated being alone, a dislike so foreign to my own nature that I could only accept it utterly uncomprehendingly.)

Just as I was going, I felt that perhaps after all I owed Barry some amends for rushing out of the house the moment he entered it, so I asked him formally to tea the next Sunday.

"Come early," I said, "round about three, if you like, and we can have time to talk to each other properly beforehand. I don't seem to have had a really good talk with you for ages."

I flung in this last sentence purely in amends for my hurried departure on that evening. Blakey, who was passing through the hall, must have overheard it. At the time I thought nothing of it.

Rene told me the next morning that she had had "ever such an interesting talk with Mr. Fortescue about his school."

"Good," I said in vague approval. "By the way, I asked him to tea next Sunday."

Rene looked mildly pleased, and I thought no more about it.

Rene, since she had to wake up early for Philip's first feed, was in the habit of retiring to her room immediately after Philip's two o'clock feed, and going to sleep, with Philip planted out in his pram, under her window. She would usually appear downstairs again about half-past three.

I thought nothing of it, therefore, when, on the following Sunday Rene did not at once put in an appearance. Barry enquired after her and I told him she was resting, but would be down presently.

Barry looked approving, rather as if the idea of women 'resting' appealed to him, as just as it should be. (He has often heard that I am 'busy working' or 'out,' but never, I think, just 'resting.' Even if I was I should have a slight taboo against saying so.)

We talked and I did not notice the time. Presently I heard Blakey and Antonia coming back from their walk. I had given no precise instructions, but I had rather expected that Rene and I and Barry and Antonia would now all have tea together in the dining-room as we usually did.

"Four o'clock! Rene's having a good sleep to-day, it seems," I said.

To my surprise the door presently opened and in came, not Rene, but Blakey, bearing a tea-tray with two cups only on it.

"What's happened to Mrs. Sylvester, Blakey?" I said, swallowing my surprise at this slight departure from custom.

"I've taken a tray up to her room, Madam. She hasn't got up yet, and would like to rest a little longer, if you'll excuse her."

My first feeling was one of surprise that Rene should have plucked up sufficient courage to ask Blakey to bring a tray to her room. Ordinarily she was very loath to give her any direct orders at all. (And Blakey, like the born snob she is, despised her for it.)

"Mummy!" said Antonia brightly through the crack in the door.

"Come along, Antonia," said Blakey, bustling out of the room again. "You and I are going to have tea in the diningroom to-day and, if you like, we'll have it out of your doll's tea-service for a treat."

Well! That disposed firmly of us all. There was nothing to do but pour out the tea for Barry and myself and hope Barry didn't see anything odd in the situation.

I did. I thought it was all very funny; and, although I had been hours and hours alone with Barry in the past and never thought twice about it, this enforced *tête-à-tête* atmosphere made me feel rebellious and cross. I expect I was a little distrait in consequence. Barry, anyway, left soon after tea.

I went straight up to Rene's room to investigate. I was not, of course, in the least offended with her for not coming down. I heartily welcomed this first manifestation of independence of action—if it *was* due to independence of action. *That* was what I was not sure about. There had been a look on Blakey's face as she shut the drawing-room door, a smug satisfied look . . .

Rene was sitting a little aimlessly on her bed.

"Hello," I said casually, "I came to see if you were still asleep."

"Is Philip all right?" said Rene anxiously.

"All right? I don't know. Where is he, anyway? He's not still in his pram in the garden, is he?"

I was more and more mystified. Usually Rene rushed to bring Philip in at the first hint of approaching dusk.

"No, no," said Rene, shocked at the idea, "Blakey told me she'd take the pram into the kitchen. She said he was still asleep, and he'd be quiet in there."

"Seems quite a good plan, but why didn't you come down yourself? I mean—of course, it's *exactly* as you like, Rene, but—"

Rene's strange anxiety over Philip, the fact that she didn't immediately apologize for oversleeping, reinforced my dawning suspicions.

"Look here, Rene," I said directly, "did Blakey *tell* you to have tea upstairs or any nonsense of the sort?"

Rene looked thoroughly uncomfortable.

"Not exactly, Vicky. I mean I do see—honestly and without being offended at all, I *do* see—that you don't *always* want me about the place when you've got visitors."

"Barry isn't 'visitors,'" I said firmly. "As a matter of fact, he was quite disappointed not to see you. Not that that matters—you've a perfect right to please yourself, Rene—but there's one thing I *won't* have and that is Blakey ordering any of us about. Now what *did* she say, Rene?"

"Nothing, really. It was just that . . ."

"Yes. What?" I said inexorably.

"Well . . . I was just settling down after Philip's feed and she brought me a hot-water bottle. I thought it was rather kind of her . . ."

"Part of a deep-laid scheme, evidently," I said unkindly. "Well?"

"Well, she said I looked sleepy, and I agreed I was. So she said, why not have a real good rest and she'd bring me a cup of tea when she got back from her walk with Antonia. I *did* think that sounded rather nice, but I didn't want to be rude—to you, Vicky, I mean—I had forgotten Mr. Fortescue was coming. So I said, 'Won't Mrs. Heron think I'm being terribly lazy?'—half in joke, you know—and she said, 'Mrs. Heron's got company to tea to-day.' She didn't say it exactly nastily, you know, Vicky, but just a little bit as if she meant me to think that—that—"

"—That you weren't particularly wanted," I finished for her.

"Well, just a little bit, you know. Not that I *minded*, Vicky, of course. As a matter of fact, I absolutely understood."

"My dear Rene, I assure you, you needn't have. There was nothing to 'understand.'"

"Oh, of course you'd be far too kind to say so, but I *do* see that you don't *always* want me there when—"

"That's just where you're wrong, Rene. If, on any special occasion, I *did* happen to want a private interview with anyone, I would make no bones about telling you so myself."

Rene, I could see, hardly believed me.

"I hope you don't think I put Blakey up to this—this *disgusting* conduct?" I said fiercely.

"No—oh, no," said Rene in a scared way.

Once again I had frightened her, and must instantly make amends. The only amends I could think of was to assure her fervently that there was nothing I liked better than her company on absolutely every occasion. (And now, to prove it, I should have to forego my cherished luxury of supper in bed, at least for a week or two. Oh dear!)

"But listen, Rene," I finished up, "you must not, you simply *must* not let Blakey bully you. The only way to behave to Blakey is to stand up to her—*then* she'll respect you. In many ways she's got rather a beastly character. For God's sake don't remain immured in your room because *she* tells you to."

"I didn't really," said Rene apologetically, and then immediately gave herself away by adding, "I quite meant to come down when I had had tea, but when Blakey brought my tray she said she'd already wheeled Philip in, so I could go on resting."

I think it was this final touch that really made me angriest of all. The old devil!

"She hasn't bothered to fetch your tray *away*, I see!" I said, and marched out of the room with it.

This time, I was determined, Blakey was not going to get off unreproved.

The fact that, Rene had told me what had happened must, however, if possible, be concealed, for Rene's sake. Blakey must not know Rene and I had talked her over together, or she would take it out of Rene, in various subtle ways. Again, I did not want Rene to know I was tackling Blakey on the subject, or she would be nervous and distressed.

I may here remark that I genuinely dislike (and even despise) intrigue.

I decided to open fire on Blakey that evening when Antonia was safely in bed and Rene busy giving Philip his ten o'clock feed upstairs.

All through supper I silently rehearsed suitable openings, and finally decided on: "Blakey, I couldn't possibly say anything in front of Mr. Fortescue, but *never* do a thing like that again. It was *most* embarrassing, forcing us to have tea alone together like that. If Mrs. Sylvester prefers to have tea in her room on ordinary days that's perfectly all right, but I should have thought you might easily have explained to her that on this occasion she was expected downstairs."

That let Rene out rather nicely, I thought. I rather enjoyed the assumption that Rene would, as a matter of course, order Blakey to bring her a tray if she wanted to!

I primed myself up with a drink just beforehand, and then opened the assault according to plan. Like a good general, I had a scheme for the future development of the battle, but was not going to stick to it too rigidly if other tactics suggested themselves to me.

As a matter of fact, Blakey proved an extraordinary difficult assailant to come to grips with.

"It's hardly my place, Madam, to tell Mrs. Sylvester she ought to come downstairs."

The old hypocrite! And yet, for Rene's sake, I could not unmask her.

"Did you even *remind* her, Blakey, that Mr. Fortescue was coming?" (I enjoyed saying that.)

A mumble.

"What, Blakey?"

She would not say, but I *think* it was something to the effect that Mrs. Sylvester had seen plenty of Mr. Fortescue the other evening when I was out.

I knew what was at the back, of her mind, of course. The maddeningly loyal old woman thought Barry was *my* property and that Rene was preventing a happy little romance from developing between us. I have always known that she would like me to marry again.

"Well, Blakey, I'm surprised at you. I should have thought you'd have had the sense—the *social* sense—not to force me into an embarrassing situation." (There! That ought to touch her up!) "Leaving aside the question of Mrs. Sylvester, why shouldn't Antonia have had tea with us as she generally does? Mr. Fortescue felt quite embarrassed about the whole situation, I could see that."

I do not really blame Blakey for murmuring something to the effect that she had never known before that I felt embarrassed at being alone with Mr. Fortescue.

"Of course not—if it happens in the normal course of events," I said grandly. "But I do object—most *strongly* object—to having anybody *manœuvre* me into a situation of the sort." (Dangerously near the truth that, perhaps, but recklessly, my blood now being up, I swept on.) "And Blakey—you *must* remember this, that Mrs. Sylvester is a member of my family now and that we ought—*all* of us—to make the greatest efforts to—to draw her into the family circle."

Curiously enough, perhaps, I was not conscious of any hypocrisy, as I spoke. Blake's antagonism to Rene *did* arouse a certain family instinct in me. The fact that I could feel no real fondness for Rene myself was gradually making me all the more anxious to do my duty by her.

It was then that Blakey said the one impermissible thing she had said that evening. (All her other rudenesses had been in fair fight and no offence taken, so to speak.)

I am not, to this day, absolutely certain that I heard aright. But I am pretty sure that, as she turned away and slammed a drawer shut, she muttered, "And what sort of a family does *she* come from, I should like to know?"

I think I realized then that, some day or other, I should have to sack Blakey for Rene's sake; and the prospect absolutely appalled me.

Chapter 6

IT WAS A WEEK or two after this that I got a letter from Betty Attenborough.

I had known Betty since I was about eighteen. It was her flat I had so often stayed in during my Oxford vacations, in order to meet Raymond in London. It was her house in Berkshire I had fled to while, waiting for my divorce to come on. She had not—over that business—'taken sides' at all. She had simply been kind to me in an utterly unsentimental way, accepting the fact that I had made my decision and was going to stick to it. She had also continued to meet Raymond, in a friendly social manner, from time to time. (The Attenboroughs and ourselves belonged more or less to the same set in London. We were always being invited to the same parties, and, when I dropped out, Raymond still naturally kept on.) I never needed to ask Betty not to try to mediate between me and Raymond, because I knew she would not. She conducted her own life without tolerating interference from anyone, including her husband, and she extended the same right to her friends. Since Betty had no children of her own and professed no love whatsoever for children, I do not think it struck her as particularly sad that our home should be breaking up at such a moment. I told her about the baby shortly after I arrived to stay with her, and, in the same breath, swore her to secrecy, and assured her that it made no difference whatsoever to my determination, and that I would prefer not even to discuss it. All this she accepted quite calmly.

When eventually I did break the news to Raymond about a couple of months before Antonia's birth—I knew Mother would if I didn't—Raymond not knowing my whereabouts, for I had purposely not told him, wrote back to me c/o Betty, asking me to meet him. I wrote back instantly, telling him that this was quite unnecessary. My mind was entirely made up, and he need feel under no obligation at all to reopen discussion of any sort. Indeed, I would much prefer it if he did not write again. By the same post I wrote to Betty to tell her that I would really prefer Raymond not to know of my whereabouts, and that, if he applied to her, I would be grateful if she would assure him that I was 'perfectly all right,' and he had no need to worry. Fortunately for me, a slight scare about the possibility of Antonia being born prematurely, which occurred just at this time, prevented Mother from trying to persuade me to meet Raymond. (She managed to get out of me that he had suggested it.) The doctor ordered me to stay in bed for a week, and poor Mother had to hold her tongue for fear of agitating me. The scare passed off, but by then there was barely a month to go before Antonia was due and Mother I think decided that she had better give in, since time was so short. Poor Mother! She was torn between her desire to shelter and protect me both for my own sake and the sake of the baby, (Mother is a great believer in pre-natal influence), and her equally strong desire to stop the divorce going through. Fortunately for me the first consideration won,

I can see distinctly to this day the look of disgust on Mother's face when she realized that Betty had known almost all along about the baby. It was a bitter pill for her to swallow.

Mother had always heartily disliked Betty. But what proper mother would not dislike her daughter being, from the age of eighteen onwards, intimate friends with an older woman, who was not only very wealthy but very sophisticated, and, in a smart casual way, utterly disillusioned? Betty was ten years my senior. ("Just the *wrong* age for you!" said Mother darkly once.) At eighteen I did not see her as clearly as I do now—I merely thought her utterly glamorous and entirely admirable. Now that the scales of glamour have fallen from my eyes, I still find a good deal to like in her, although possibly not very much to admire. And yet—I don't know. Cheap as her own standards fundamentally are, she yet lives up to them, and, moreover, spreads a tapestry of grace and wit and 'style' over a poor foundation.

Of course I understand perfectly now what Mother dislikes in her. It is not (as I scornfully thought at eighteen) the outer trappings of sophistication that Mother dislikes—Betty's own men friends, her husband's (Hubert's) girl friends, the way that, living in the same house, they yet give separate parties. An amusing surface possibly this, if, underneath, there was some capacity for deeper feelings. But—and I am pretty sure of this now—in Betty's case, at any rate, there isn't. Not only no feeling, but no capacity for it any more, not towards her husband, not towards anyone. Kindness, yes. Tolerance, yes—the infinite all-embracing tolerance that comes from simply not caring. Feeling, deep genuine feeling of any sort whatsoever towards any person, any cause—no, not a shred. Not only is it not there, but I doubt if it could be there now. I think that, like an unused member, it has atrophied quite away, so that what possibly began as a mere surface gesture ('I must take this well, I mustn't show I mind, I must hold my head up and laugh') has gradually bitten in and sunk down and eaten into Betty's very bones, so that the pretence has become the reality and she has become a person who is surface all through.

That is what I think now, anyway. And sometimes, in the past few years, I have also thought 'There, but for the grace of God and the existence of Antonia, go I.' Betty, I am sure, thinks that I am just such another as herself. Pretence has become her own reality and so, I am sure, she unconsciously dismisses other people's realities as pretence. I have often heard her condemn people's behaviour as 'silly'—by which she means undignified, lacking in style, consistency, gesture. I have never heard her say anything which would suggest that she realized that behaviour comes sometimes from the heart, not from the head.

Well, as I have told before, she and Mother between them helped me through my divorce—an oddly matched pair, who kept well away from each other, but who, nevertheless, each supplied a totally different kind of support. Betty treated me as a sensible young woman who had sensibly and in cold blood made up her mind to break an irksome contract. (I wasn't quite as bad as that, but it was a help to have someone treating me so.) Mother treated me as her child who had got badly hurt and wanted her Mummy. (And I wasn't quite as bad as *that*, but nevertheless a little of it was a comfort.) I 'used' them both shamelessly and neither bore me any grudge—Mother because she is Mother, and Betty because she did not know to what extent I was 'using' her to bolster myself up—not that she would have minded if she had; merely been faintly surprised. The fact that I stayed in her house for five months was nothing much to her. She had money, a large house, a well-trained staff, and rather expected her friends to indicate when they would like to come for a visit.

The letter I now had from her was to invite me to this same house for a week-end. Evidently Betty had not yet allowed the war to get her down. It was precisely the same sort of airy and yet cordially-worded invitation as I might have received any time in the past—". . . a few friends coming . . . think you'll like them . . . send the car to-meet the 3.15 on Friday . . ." I grinned as I read it. Its appeal was positively nostalgic. Did this world of leisured moneyed people really still exist in February, 1941, were there still week-ends to be had in houses with servants, where chauffeurs met trains and one's hostess collected (or, at least, pretended she'd collected) a nosegay of friends, culled for one's own delectation? Evidently there remained still in England some small 'pockets of resistance,' small oases that refused stoutly to be engulfed by the war-time no-nonsense-and-hardwork atmosphere, and evidently Betty's house was one of them. How very shocking; and how utterly delectable to slip back, just for one short week-end, into that other lost (and so rightly lost) world. A 'refresher' course in social futility; a reminder that just here and there in England people still lived in lovely, decorative, extravagant pointlessness. Dope, pure dope—and exactly what I felt I wanted. I made up my mind at once to accept.

I grinned as I read Betty's P.S.: 'Bring your little girl, too, if you like, or haven't anyone to leave her with. I'm sure she'd be no trouble at all.'

No thank you, Betty. Only property children accompany their mothers on visits of the sort, and only property children are 'no trouble at all' on such occasions.

I wrote to accept for myself, and to explain that Antonia would stay behind with Blakey and Rene. Then, the letter posted, I told Rene and Blakey; neither of whom looked at all pleased.

I didn't care, I had made up my mind not to care. This was going to be *my* treat, and my treat alone. It seemed, I thought (a little savagely), about my turn.

* * * * *

Much as I should have liked Betty's chauffeur to meet the 3.15 from London on my account, I yet could not help realizing that I should save several hours by travelling to Betty's house direct from Harminster by Thames Valley bus; and this, accordingly, I did. Betty, on my arrival, loudly applauded my ingenuity.

"How clever of you, darling, to think of it! Now I should just have gone up to London and down again like a little robot." She laughed her attractive laugh. (Betty's manner, her appearance, her laugh, are all extraordinarily attractive.) "You've always had a bit of a practical streak though, haven't you, Vicky? I remember once at a party—when you were about nineteen and looking *too* lovely in white—you kept the whole room absolutely spellbound while you talked about rats in London sewers, and how they were kept down."

"How awful of me, Betty! I promise I won't again."

"But no, darling, that's not the *point*. The *point* is, we were all of us absolutely fascinated. We loved it—*do* do it again. Look, this is your room."

"Fire and flowers. Glorious,"

"This weather ... I mean we all thought England just *couldn't*, didn't we? Siberia—perhaps. But Berkshire—no! And now it seems it *can* happen. Snow! Falling down and piling up the *whole* time, the *whole* time." She gestured with her hands to represent the snowflakes and did not look in the least silly. She is an extraordinarily graceful woman.

"This mirror!" exclaimed Betty, suddenly darting to the dressing-table, "I can't help feeling it's a bit murky. Can you *see* in it, Vicky? No, of course you can't. I must—"

'Ring for another dressing-table,' I finished mentally with a grin, but aloud I said, "Nonsense, darling, I can see perfectly."

"Well, I can't. But then, if I could, perhaps I mightn't like it. I *might* look 'well-preserved' Vicky—do you think? Of course at forty-three it begins to be difficult not to look 'well-preserved'— don't you think?"

"I expect my difficulty will be to look it. You aim so *very* high, Betty."

(Oh, gloriously futile conversation, with what a sense of luxury I snuggled myself back into the old 'Betty' atmosphere.)

"You *do* look older, Vicky darling," said Betty (woman-to-woman-in-frank-affection tone, that used to flatter me so when I was about nineteen). "It suits you though—in a way . . . That line of temple and cheekbone—sharper now, but *very* subtle and taking. . . . Why haven't we seen more of each other recently?"

Affection, compliments, prompted by nothing at all—not insincerity, just nothing. Yet, oddly enough, the magic still worked. Betty 'presented' me to myself as someone desirable and subtle—and immediately my vanity awoke and gave a little luxurious stretch and, like a kitten in front of a cosy fire, purred and fluffed up its fur.

"Yes, it's a long time since we've met," I said, "One way and another. . . ."

"Still with those publishers of yours, Vicky?"

"Yes. Publishers to you always, agents actually to me, but nevertheless, you mean what I mean."

"And how's . . . your little girl?"

"Antonia?" I said (kindly making her a present of the name for future reference). "Very well, thank you."

"Does she go to school yet, Vicky?"

"Not yet. She's not quite five." (It's all right, Betty, you needn't talk about Antonia any more, you've done your duty!)

"Betty, who else is here this week-end?"

"Oh darling, come down and have some tea and I'll tell you. There's just ourselves for tea—isn't that nice? Hubert's away, you know, and the others are arriving later at various times. Not that there's very many—you know, Vicky, nowadays, it's most awfully difficult to fix things up definitely with people, isn't it?"

We went down the stairs, arms affectionately linked.

"I know. They're either in the army or working," I agreed with a grin. "It's a shame!"

Betty laughed. "You needn't be so ironical, Vicky . . . Of course, I know as well as anyone that we've"—her eye fell on a big vase of flowers as we entered the little morning-room, and she finished the sentence abstractedly—"that we've got to win the war. Vicky—I call that vase well arranged, don't you?"

"Very well. Whose handiwork?"

"That's just it, darling. My ex-kitchenmaid. I taught her, of course, but don't you think she's an apt pupil? She's only eighteen. I shall congratulate her. She'll be awfully pleased at that. Darling, sit on the sofa by the fire. Curl up on it, if you like. I'm just going to ring for tea."

"Oh Betty, I am enjoying myself!" I cried, flinging myself luxuriously on to the sofa and piling cushions behind my back. "What's the opposite of 'slumming'? That's what I feel I'm doing now, with all this talk of congratulating kitchenmaids and ringing for tea."

"Don't be absurd, darling, you've missed the point. I said *ex*-kitchenmaid. My dear, she's our *housemaid* now—I just had to promote her, there was no one else to be had. So you see, it *is* a slum now, this house, after all," concluded Betty triumphantly "Here comes our eighteen-year-old to answer the bell. . . . Tea, please, Margaret, and toast, I think, don't you, Vicky?"

"Lovely," I said, and added as the door closed, "But Margaret is not, I take it, your sole domestic prop, Betty?"

"Oh no, there's the cook, of course, and Margaret's mother, who comes in daily to help and a little girl of fourteen in the kitchen—but that's all. It's really awful, isn't it, Vicky? I don't know what's going to happen to all of us. Have you still got your faithful old What's-Her-Name?"

"Blakey? Yes. She's all I've got now."

"Well, of course, darling, there's only yourself and Antonia to be looked after, isn't there? I mean, it's not very many."

"Whereas here," I said, smiling at Betty, "there's not only yourself and Hubert—when he's home—but also" (I counted on my fingers), "the cook, the housemaid, the housemaid's mother, the fourteen-year-old, the chauffeur, and presumably a gardener! A household of eight persons. It makes a difference, doesn't it?"

I did not really think Betty would agree seriously that it did, but I could not resist trying.

For a moment she frowned, and then burst out laughing.

"Ah, but that's not arguing fair, Vicky! What about the size of this house? I can't alter *that*, can I, Vicky? What about all these people I'm having down this very week-end? What about—"

"You win, Betty," I said happily. "I was only being offensive just as a try-on. You can't *think* how I appreciate your house and the way you run it, and your kindness in asking me here. It's heaven!"

"Darling, I'm so glad," said Betty vaguely. "Oh good, here's tea. We'll have it on this little table between us, Vicky, and help ourselves. Thank you, Margaret. Well—as I say, I'm not expecting many people this week-end. There's a rather sweet young Air Force pilot and the Sandersons—you remember the Sandersons, darling?—and Trevor Barrington—have you ever met him? You must have seen him on the stage dozens of times—and Raymond, of course, just down for the day on Sunday."

"Raymond!"

"Yes, didn't I tell you? I thought I had. Oh no, I remember I fixed it up afterwards with him."

"No, I didn't know."

"You don't *mind*, do you, darling? Why, when I saw Raymond in town not so long ago he mentioned that he'd been seeing you. So naturally I took it that you two were on quite friendly terms, meeting in the ordinary course of events and so on like—well, like most people do again after a bit. As a matter of fact, couples usually seem to get on so much *better* after they're divorced, don't you think, Vicky? Vicky, I *am* sorry if you mind! I never dreamt you would!"

She was quite genuine in her surprise, I could see that. Divorced couples re-meeting socially were a commonplace in Betty's life.

"No, I don't mind," I said, wondering, as I spoke, whether this was the truth or not. "It's just that—it's a bit of a surprise. I *have* seen Raymond recently, Betty, but as a matter of fact it was a pure accident. We just ran into each other."

"Oh well—the *first* time it usually is an accident, isn't it? I mean, that makes it easier in a way, and then afterwards everything is perfectly simple. Don't you think?"

"Oh quite," I agreed, since what else, as the well-behaved guest, could I do but 'agree? And then (with a queer little quirk of possessiveness, for I did not want Betty to tell *me* about Raymond), "Betty, you know, of course, about Raymond's T.B.?"

"Yes, poor lamb. A shame, wasn't it? However, he's apparently quite all right again now."

"Yes. Betty, while we *are* on the subject—I mean, you've been seeing Raymond on and off all this time, haven't you?"

"Yes, certainly. On and off, as you say. I'm very fond of Raymond. He's a lamb. So are you, Vicky. Lambs, both of you. What do you want to ask me?"

"Betty, did Sandra chuck Raymond because he got T.B.?"

Ever since I had met Raymond that question had been teasing me. Not that it mattered to me, of course. I only felt that if I *knew*, once and for all, I could stop wondering about it for ever. I could not ask Raymond, and I had not meant to ask Betty, until the opportunity suddenly occurred, and I could not resist it.

I suppose I spoke with a sudden intensity, for Betty stared at me with surprise for a moment and then burst out laughing.

"Oh darling, no! Why, Vicky, you *are* behind the times."

"I expect I am," I said, feeling a little squashed and about nineteen again.

"Sandra chucked Raymond—or he chucked her, I really don't know which—ages ago. I don't remember exactly when, but not so very long after you'd parted. Sandra's had a reconciliation with her husband now. That mythical husband! He turned up from New York or somewhere and, my dear, he's absolutely charming! He and Sandra are positively a devoted couple now."

So! All that agony over Sandra wasted! Pure sheer waste. (Ah! I reminded myself quickly, but was it waste? Wasn't it better to have the agony over Sandra once and for all and get it finished and have it done with, rather than endure and wait for the next time—and the time after—and go through with it again and again, minding less—yes, this was the awful thing, the thing that had panicked me—minding a little less each time, until in the end one hardly minded at all, and one's marriage, which had started so marvellously, had become indistinguishable from the marriages of any other of Betty's friends'?)

"No, I didn't know all that," I said lightly, "I've been out of things so much lately."

"You have, haven't you?" said Betty sympathetically. "This war and one thing and another—it makes life so difficult, doesn't it? I mean to meet one's friends and so on."

"Yes," I agreed with a private grin. Betty patronizing the war as a social nuisance was grand.

"You know, Vicky—stop me if you don't want to talk about it—but—"

"That's a sure gambit, Betty, and always works, as you very well know. Well?"

"Well, if you'd never dashed off to New York with that publisher woman of yours with the extraordinary name—"

"Mrs. Hitchcock, literary agent, you mean. Yes?"

"—At such a *tactless* moment, darling, Raymond would never have got so involved with Sandra. Why on earth did you?"

"Well, Betty, that's a plain question, and I'll give you a plain answer. Or answers. One: it *was* a good opportunity for me—in the office, I mean, and the office, I need hardly tell you, takes no account of domestic tact or tactlessness. Two: funk. I didn't want to be hurt, and I thought if I shut my eyes and ran away everything *might* be over and all right again by the time I got home. Three: pride. I will not, I simply *will* not play the role of the little wifey darning socks at home and waiting to forgive and forget all. There's your answer."

"All the same, it wasn't wise, darling. You'd much better *not* have gone away just then."

"I don't think I care for a marriage that turns into a game of strategy, Betty."

"Oh, Vicky darling! As if one hadn't *got* to—sooner or later—just *plan* a little, here and there.... Why, surely..."

"All right then. I haven't got enough guts to play that game. Put it like that, if you like. I *do* admire your guts, Betty, I do seriously."

"Oh Vicky, what nonsense! It's just a question of—of the right attitude. Of—of not taking things too seriously, that's all."

"Exactly," I said, in a small voice. ('There, but for the grace of God, goes...')

* * * * *

Trevor Barrington I 'saved up' to tell Rene about, like a nice aunt chancing on a toy that would just suit her little niece; Rene, I knew, would be thrilled when I told her that he was exactly as gracious and courtly off the stage as he was on. Distinguished old gentlemen were Trevor's theatrical line, and he was undoubtedly right at the top of his own particular tree. His manner, in private life, was so exactly suitable to the rôles he played on the stage, that one found oneself speculating once again on that old question—do actors act off the stage or are they rather themselves on it? Rene, in any case, would be enchanted to hear about him.

I would not, of course, tell her that probably Betty and Trevor were conducting a liaison together, and that this was possibly the whole reason for the week-end party.

I had, naturally, no direct evidence of this myself, (Betty conducts all her affairs with great decorum), but nevertheless, knowing Betty as well as I did, I was pretty sure I was right. This being the case, I felt it was hard on the young—the *very* young—

R.A.F. boy, to invite him down the same week-end. Not that he would necessarily guess anything; indeed, it would be extremely unlikely that he would. He was too nice. But obviously he thought Betty the most wonderful person he had ever had the privilege of knowing, and, equally obviously, there was a rather nasty eye-opener, of some sort or other, coming to him shortly, in the future. However, it was none of my concern.

The Sandersons were a couple I had known, on and off, for many years. Everybody tended to invite them about as makeweights or useful stop-gaps. They were good, unobtrusive mixers: she, smart without being outstanding; he, good company without being a dominant personality. Really, I think that is absolutely all I know about them—but then I have never, I think, met either of them at all, except at parties—this week-end at Betty's house counting most definitely as a 'party.' The atmosphere was such throughout, not feverishly gay or hectic or anything of the sort, but steadily, unobtrusively 'social' nevertheless. It was rather like being on board ship: at first one was conscious of the beat of the engines that earned one along; later one ceased to hear them unless one deliberately listened, and it was only when one disembarked finally from the house after the week-end was over that one realized that one had been tired and a little wrought-up by this perpetual, almost silent throbbing of the machines.

Not that I did not enjoy the week-end thoroughly. I did. I got exactly what I wanted, what I had come for—a complete change of atmosphere. And, funnily enough, I got something else, something I had been wanting equally badly, but had seen no chance at all of getting—a really good talk with a sympathetic and yet dispassionate listener about Rene and Blakey and Barry, a chance to tell it all to someone as an amusing story and yet as not *nothing* but an amusing story. A confidant, in short, in whom it would not be disloyal to confide.

Raymond was my confidant.

Chapter 7

WE HAD GONE OUT for a walk together on Sunday afternoon. The Sandersons are bridge fiends. I play, but Raymond knows I would usually rather be doing something else. Trevor Barrington and Betty made up the table. For two pins the R.A.F. boy would have accompanied us on our walk, but Raymond—who has a wonderful flair for managing things without giving offence—contrived to circumvent this.

"You didn't want him to come, did you?" said Raymond, as we started out.

Once again, my appearance was far from glamorous. For one thing the snowy state of the ground necessitated gum-boots.

"Good Lord, no! He'd have wanted to edge the conversation round to Betty all the time."

"I'm afraid he would have."

"Poor devil," I said (and knew that, with Raymond, I need not be more explicit).

"Exactly. Do him good in the end though, do you think?"

"Um . . . possibly. On the whole though, *not*, I think. Height of caddishness, isn't it, to discuss our hostess like this while enjoying her hospitality?"

"Except that it's an old-established rule that with you it doesn't count."

"You think that rule still applies?"

"Yes," said Raymond firmly. "Yes—and always."

I sighed, relieved. I think that one of the nicest things about marriage is the exquisite opportunities it gives one for what Raymond and I used to call 'cad parties'—by which we meant those cosy little chats between us about the friends we had just visited or who had just visited us, during which one gaily gave vent to the most malicious observations, happily secure in the knowledge that, as Raymond said, it didn't count. Lovely. I had missed them badly.

"You know, this week-end I can't help feeling I'm taking part in a sort of slightly dated comedy of manners," I said.

"Date about 1935?" Raymond suggested.

"Yes. About then. The *only* thing that really matters is who's having affairs with who—and even that doesn't matter, except superficially. It's just a sort of game."

"Quite. And Betty still keeps on, treating the war, really rather superbly, as 'noises off'!"

"Marvellous, isn't it? I must say I'm finding it the most glorious sort of dope."

"You need dope, do you Vicky, these days?"

"Oh well—who doesn't—these days?"

"Vicky, what's this Rene woman like?"

There was Raymond at his old game, jumping a step or two in the ladder. Quickness as infinitely restful as it had ever been.

"Rene? Oh well..." I began to giggle. "'Cad party,' Raymond?"

"Certainly. Why not?"

"Oh, I don't know. *Really* a bit caddish perhaps. Only there's no one else I *can* to. I can't even to Mother because *I* took Rene off her shoulders, God help me."

"Come on. Be brave. Tell me what she's like."

I laughed and prepared to enjoy myself in the unworthiest way possible.

"Her name's *really* Irene," I said. "But she thinks 'Rene' is prettier."

"Go on," said Raymond, grinning.

"Talking to her is like walking through a bog—squash, squash, squash—never, just *never* do you really crunch on to anything solid. Nevertheless, talking is the breath of life to her."

"You two must get on splendidly," said Raymond, enjoying himself, I think, as much as I was. "Where was the appeal for Philip, do you think?"

"Oh—quite appealing if you *like* that sort of appeal, which I heartily detest. She was lonely. 'Mumsy' was dead, and 'Auntie' died too. She cried on his shoulder. No, to be quite honest, that last is just a guess. Within my utterly caddish framework I will yet try to be truthful, if I can."

"I respect your artistic integrity. What does she make of you?"

"Oh, poor child, she's a bit frightened of me, I'm afraid."

"I never put you in Category H myself, Vicky, Why do you alarm her so?"

"I scold her sometimes. I just *have* to. Oh well, it's a long story..."

"It's a nice long afternoon, Vicky."

It was then that I told him all about the Barry-Blakey-and-Rene episode, and much enjoyed the telling. Raymond had always been the most delightful of audiences, laughter and comprehension mixed in exactly the right proportions—by which, I mean, of course, *my* proportions.

"Vicky," he said. "Forgive me if I ask a rather impertinent question—meaning, of course, as one always does, a possibly pertinent one?"

"Yes?"

"Well. This Barry person. Do you, right underneath, have a sort of feeling that he's your property, even if you don't precisely want him? Are you just possibly cross with Blakey because she acted, on that occasion, as your worser self?"

"No. No, honestly not, Raymond. I don't grudge Barry to Rene in the very slightest. Let him be her friend too by all means—or even her friend *rather* than mine, if that means he'll take Rene off my hands occasionally."

"I see. In that case, you've merely Blakey's machinations to outwit."

"Yes. And the antagonism between Blakey and Rene to contend with ... Oh, it all sounds very trivial, Raymond, but the trouble is, you see, more than trivial issues depend on it. My job, for instance. If things get too unbearable it will have to be Blakey, not Rene, to go. I *can't* sack Rene. But then I *must* have someone utterly reliable to leave Antonia with, on the days when I go to London, and that's not easy to find these days. I don't see Rene looking after both children and doing the cooking and house as well. It wouldn't be fair to ask her—apart from the fact that I wouldn't trust her.... Oh Lord, Raymond, for God's sake stop me! I'm simply not going to bore you with my domestic problems."

"Date definitely 1941, not 1935. Only I'm not bored, Vicky. Believe it or not, I'm passionately interested. . . . Vicky, it's a small point, but why didn't you tell Rene who I was that night I saw her? Or did you tell her afterwards?"

"No, I never told her, Raymond. I don't know quite why not. Possibly just because she's not the sort of person to take that sort of thing in her stride. I mean, she'd have goggled. And anyway, what the hell business is it of hers *who* my friends are?"

"Do you know, Vicky, I begin to see why poor Rene is frightened of you?"

"Oh, so do I, Raymond! And you needn't go to tell me that I'm not very nice about Rene, that I've drawn an unfair picture of her. Of *course* I have. If you don't *like* a person, obviously you're not going to see their nicest side, are you?"

"Vicky, my sweet, don't go so violently on the defensive! I'm not criticizing you. I'm enjoying you, and I'm still on your side. I only just wavered towards Rene for one moment when you said that about it being no business of hers *who* your friends were. The emphasis on the 'who' was almost savage."

"Yes, well. As a matter of fact, I had a reason for being a trifle savage and secretive about your identity. I would permit Rene to know my other friends more readily—witness Barry. The truth is that once Rene and I had a bit of a quarrel about you."

Even as I spoke I knew that Raymond's interest, together with my desire to clear myself of appearing unnecessarily unkind to Rene, were together luring me on to speak of things I had really better not refer to.

"About me? An odd choice of subject when there must have been so many better."

"Yes, it was, wasn't it? It wasn't much really—I wouldn't *dream* of discussing you properly with Rene, Raymond," I said haughtily.

"Thank you," said Raymond, but I saw his lips twitch and guessed that his unspoken comment was again, 'Poor Rene!'

"—It was merely that Rene seemed to have the idea that you'd more or less knocked me about, and were *nothing* but a good riddance to me and Antonia, and naturally I resented that, Raymond, and told her so."

"Was it worth quarrelling about, after all these years? Ah well, Vicky, I'm very touched that you should think so, anyway. It was a very loyal gesture on your part, to defend me to Rene."

Perversely enough, this rather nicely-turned little speech of Raymond's annoyed me. I think it was the word 'gesture' which touched me up. Real honest anger is no gesture, nor had I been moved by any abstract conceptions of 'loyalty,' nor had I even stopped to think whether the subject was 'worth' quarrelling about. I had acted on impulse and from the heart, and of course afterwards regretted it. I did not want to be congratulated on a good gesture.

Rather to my own surprise, I burst out and heard myself saying, "Oh *Raymond*! This admiration of 'gestures' has been our undoing! Your undoing *and* my undoing, we're alike in that. We ought to pull ourselves up before it's too late."

Raymond looked interested.

"I'm not quite sure that I see what you mean, Vicky."

"No? It's difficult to explain precisely . . ."

It was, for I wanted to avoid all concrete examples from the past, to express myself in general terms, and yet, now that I had so recklessly embarked on the subject, to make my point, and make it strongly.

"I only mean that we're too damn *civilized*, both of us, Raymond. We've both of us almost grown out of all the primitive instincts, we don't understand them any more. We don't understand about people loving passionately or hating passionately or worshipping passionately. We've grown out of jealousy, we've grown out of revenge, we've grown out of saying prayers. Instead of behaving naturally, instead of grabbing and praying and crying, we stand a little aloof, smiling faintly and behaving beautifully in an arrogant sort of way. We're too proud to fight, Raymond, that's our trouble. And possibly we think it's just a little bit vulgar to feel passionately over anything. We're awfully good at behaving *well*, but I'm not at all sure that that isn't our worst vice. It might often be much better, if we behaved really badly—and *naturally*—for a change."

"Could you give me an example?"

"No, because I'm rather carefully not being personal. I'm sure you can think of heaps for yourself. I can." (Supposing I had rated you like a fish-wife and thrown the fire-irons at your head when I first became jealous of Sandra, instead of giving you to understand you had my blessing and disappearing with a halo of bogus broadmindedness to New York? Supposing you, Raymond, had *insisted* that I should have a baby when *you* wanted to start one—a year after our marriage—instead of agreeing so chivalrously that it would be a pity for me to give up the office just as I was getting on so well there.) "I only mean," I finished, "that if we hadn't been so damn civilized, you and I, we might have made a better job of things. I'm not talking about our marriage particularly, you know," I added hastily, and, I'm afraid, a little unconvincingly. "I'm just talking generally."

"Quite," said Raymond reassuringly. "And you're being very interesting, Vicky. Only I think you depict us as further gone than we really are. One can have feelings—real primitive tough ones—without necessarily showing them, can't one?"

"Yes. Only if the poor things *never* get a run off the chain, they pine away and die."

"It's better than never putting them on the chain and letting them bark and jump about all over the house all the time. That's hell!"

"Oh, quite. Only you and I would never be in danger of that. Our danger is that, if we don't *ever* let them out, one day we'll find we simply haven't got them any more."

"I wonder. Vicky, even after all these years, did you find yourself totally unmoved at the prospect of seeing me again this week-end? I know I didn't."

"I thought we could carry it off perfectly well."

"Oh yes. That's self-control though. Not—unfeelingness. Different, isn't it?" He paused and then added softly, and half as if he was apologizing for saying such a thing, "I know I nearly said I couldn't come after all when I heard you were to be here."

"Why, Raymond?"

I knew it was a mistake to ask. I knew the conversation was edging on to dangerous ground. I knew things dead and buried had better be left dead and buried. And yet, for the life of me, I couldn't help wanting to know.

"I didn't want to get hurt, I suppose."

(*Hurt? Raymond* hurt after all these years? Had it been as bad as that for him at the time then? Of course I had never imagined he had got off scot-free from unhappiness, but, selfishly wrapped up in my own agony, I had not at the time *felt* his pain to any extent. And now I, perhaps, was the less vulnerable of the two of us. How strange.)

"I don't think," I said slowly, while all this flashed through my mind, "that it's any good trying to conduct one's life on the principle of not getting hurt. You lose too much that way. Besides—you *don't* find my company hurtful, do you, Raymond?"

"I find it delightful as a matter of fact, Vicky. I should like to go on seeing you from time to time, if I may. Let's see—I know your office telephone number, I think."

I was relieved to find an undercurrent of mockery in his voice again. We had, I felt, edged round a dangerous corner together.

"Yes, I'd love to meet you again sometimes, Raymond," I said heartily, and meant it. Then, suddenly, I laughed;

"What's the joke?" said Raymond, smiling at me.

"Nothing."

"Nonsense. Tell me what you're giggling about like that at once."

"Well—only that I had a sudden vision of ourselves ten years ago overhearing this conversation of to-day—time suddenly going wrong you understand me, in a Priestley-Dunne sort of way—and us being utterly horrified. And then I imagined a companion picture—us overhearing this conversation five years ago and how blissfully soothing and reassuring it would have sounded."

"Yes, I suppose it *was* just ten years ago we got married," said Raymond.

We were walking up the drive back to the house. I wanted our outing together to end on a light note.

"I put my hand upon my heart" (I quoted mockingly),
"And swore that we should never part,
I wonder what I would have said
If I had put it on my head."

I had come across that recently in some anthology or other, and it had amused me. I thought it would entertain Raymond now and would round off our conversation on the correct note.

I had forgotten to allow for Raymond's quickness and for his infuriating capacity for getting in the last word.

"Yes," said Raymond smoothly. "Or, to alter the rhyme a little to suit the situation of five years back, instead of ten—

"You put your hand upon your head,
And vowed you'd stick to what you'd said,
It might have been the better part,
If you had put it on your heart!"

He grinned at me triumphantly.

"Just to turn the tables on you, darling, and to punish you for being airy about me."

"Raymond! Oh well . . . it was very clever of you to make that up on the spur of the moment like that. One couldn't expect it to *apply* in the circumstances."

"No?" said Raymond teasingly; and we entered the house together.

* * * * *

Betty, clad in a glamorous garment (of the genus 'wrapper' rather than plain 'dressing-gown') came and sat on the-end of my bed on Sunday night, and seemed prepared for what I did not particularly want—a girlish chat.

"Darling, I've hardly seen *anything* of you this week-end, after all," she said in prettily-simulated regret.

"I know. The time seems to have gone in a flash. I *have* enjoyed myself, Betty."

"I'm so glad, darling. . . . It's the office you're going to to-morrow at crack of dawn, is it?"

"Yes. Three days a week, I generally go."

"Don't you find it rather a strain, darling, still keeping on working like that?" She gazed at me sympathetically.

"I should find it much more of a strain *not* having an office to go to, Betty. Apart from the work interesting me, it gives me two atmospheres to move about in—home and office. It's refreshing, you know."

"Darling, I think you're marvellous! Such energy! You always had, hadn't you? . . . All the same—it must *be* tiring in the end, whatever you say." She picked up a tassel from her sash and twiddled it round her fingers, "Somehow I always thought you'd marry again, Vicky," she finished.

"Oh? No, I don't think that's likely," I said nonchalantly.

I was, as a matter of fact, tired and wanted to go to sleep. But I could hardly, in the circumstances, tell her to mind her own business.

"Not attracted by the idea, darling?" hazarded Betty.

"Not particularly by the idea. I'm not averse to it or anything, but I don't want it particularly," I said truthfully. "And I'm certainly not attracted by any particular person."

"And yet you're so attractive to men, Vicky," said Betty, who says this sort of thing without the slightest hesitation. "Surely there must have been *somebody* in these last few years who has tempted you. Hasn't there?"

She flashed me a sideways look under her lashes.

"No, nobody at all, Betty. I won't say I haven't had a few dishonourable proposals, so to speak, and one entirely honourable one—but I couldn't take much interest in any of them."

"What a pity, darling," said Betty sympathetically.

I did not want her sympathy. Indeed, it annoyed me.

"In fact, if you really want to know, Betty," I added, "I have lived in complete chastity ever since my divorce, and there seems every prospect of my continuing to do so."

I thought it was about time somebody gave Betty a healthy shock of the sort. Shock it undoubtedly was. She looked quite horrified.

"But *darling*! It must be so *bad* for you."

"Rubbish!" I said briskly.

"Oh no, it's not rubbish," said Betty seriously. "Vicky darling, if you start talking like that I'm going to feel worried about you—I really am!"

"My dear Betty, surely you don't expect me to take a lover as a sort of tonic or pill or something?"

"Now Vicky! You're just talking like that to put me off," retorted Betty, not without a certain acuteness. "You know perfectly well that I only mean that it would be *natural* for you to want—well, not to be lonely—any longer."

"I'm not lonely," I said, deliberately misunderstanding her, and enjoying doing so. "I've got Antonia and Blakey and my sister-in-law to keep me company."

"You're being very naughty and perverse to-night, Vicky," said Betty, laughing. In spite of the laugh I could see that she was a little annoyed with me. Perhaps, for the first time, she realized that I was now at last utterly free of her, emotionally speaking, and of her long-wielded sway over me. "You really know perfectly well what I mean, don't you?"

"Well yes, I do, Betty," I admitted, slightly penitent. For after all, according to her own lights, she had always been and would always be extraordinarily kind to me. "But I really don't see that there's anything to be done about it. And I'm certainly not, generally speaking, at all unhappy."

"No?" said Betty, doubtingly. "All the same, darling . . . You know Hubert and I and several others of us, we quite thought you'd eventually settle down with Charles."

"Charles? I haven't seen him for years. He's in New York, I imagine."

"That's where he really lives, is it?"

"Yes. He was only over in London on business, you know, that time we all saw so much of him."

I slightly emphasized the 'all,' but Betty was not to be put off.

"He went back to New York, didn't he, just about the time *you* went there?"

"He did indeed. *And* I saw quite a lot of him over there. I was very fond of Charles," I said calmly.

"And he of you," said Betty meaningly. "But all the same—oh well, we all guessed wrong about him and you, did we?"

I was not really cross with Betty for her insinuations—not even though there was just enough truth in them to get home. Charles *had* been in love with me and I *had* enjoyed the fact that he was. That was all, and Raymond had never appeared to mind. No, I was not cross, but I *did* want to close the conversation. There had been, I felt strongly, enough raking up of the past already that day.

"If you guessed that—that Charles was to me what Sandra was to Raymond, you *did* guess wrong, Betty," I said firmly. "And if you guessed that there was anything 'collusive' about our divorce, you guessed wrong too."

"I didn't guess either of those things *exactly*, Vicky. I only thought that perhaps Raymond and you came to some sort of understanding about everything. And that was why, shortly after you got back from New York, Raymond and you stopped living together and you started divorcing him. But, of course, if you say Charles didn't come into the picture at all, I'll believe you."

"The only 'Understanding' that Raymond and I came to after I got back from New York," I said wearily, wondering how on earth I had allowed the conversation to go so far, "was the understanding that I couldn't *stand* the situation of Sandra and him any longer. Very hysterical of me, no doubt. And, as a matter of fact, I wanted to be the one to clear out of the house, and Raymond only went to stop *me*, so, morally speaking, *I* left him. That's all. But Charles, as you see, didn't come into the picture at all. As a matter of fact, I've never set eyes on him since I said good-bye in New York."

"Poor old Vicky!"

"No, I'm not setting myself up to be the virtuous wronged wife," I said quickly. "The reasons for a divorce are *never* utterly simple, and the question of which partner happened to commit adultery may be really rather irrelevant—outside the courts."

I believed this to be true, as I said it. I did not mean exactly that adultery 'didn't count,' but I *did* mean that the circumstances which had led up to the adultery counted more. I knew that Betty, even if she missed this implication, would agree.

"Oh, of *course*, darling," said Betty instantly. "Of *course* you're right. And I'm so glad you can talk about it all so sensibly. It does show that if you *do* ever want to marry again—and I'm sure you will one day, you know, Vicky—you won't have any sort of silly 'thing' about marriage."

"No, I haven't got a 'thing' about marriage," I said, yawning.

"Darling, you're half-asleep! You must tuck up at once. I mustn't stay another moment. Good night, darling. You must come here again soon."

"Thank you, Betty, I'd love to if I can manage it. Good night."

But, after Betty had gone, I found that, tired as I was, I couldn't sleep. Betty's insinuations about Charles, sincerely as I had denied them, had started a fresh train of thought in my mind. Supposing I hadn't started a baby at such an extraordinary inapposite moment . . . supposing the width of the Atlantic had not separated Charles and me after my break with Raymond . . . supposing that, on one particular occasion in New York (Charles and I alone together in his flat, Charles in love with me, I secretly unhappy because of a letter from Raymond with references to Sandra in it), supposing that a party of Charles' friends *hadn't* happened to call in on him, interrupting us at a very tense moment. . . . Supposing that circumstances (not ourselves, just circumstances) had been just a little different for Charles and me—should I possibly be married to him now? And, if so, should I be happier than I now actually was or less happy?

This 'if' frame of mind! Once you get into it, there's no escape from it—particularly at twelve o'clock at night when you're still tossing about awake in bed. If's and if's, further back and further back. If's about Charles, now if's about Raymond. If Raymond had urged me to give up my job when I got married. . . . If I'd had a baby quite quickly, then I'd probably have had another, why not? (Ah, but neither of the horrid little things would have been *Antonia*, bless her! Or would one of them? Wilder and wilder speculations and sleep further off than ever!) If my father hadn't died when he did, the very week after my return from New York, would I have run to Mother earlier on in the story and possibly come back to forgive Raymond rather than to issue ultimatums—with agony inside and a top dressing of nonchalant 'It's-been-good-fun-while-it-lasted' sophistication? (Ah, but 'forgiveness' was one of the things Raymond and I laughed at; had, we assumed, grown out of.)

If's about Charles, if's about Raymond, if's about me. And, finally (although I tried to beat my way out, to escape from this nightmare of coiling, spiralling suppositions), an 'if' about Raymond and Charles and me all enlooped in one vast tentacle. If I hadn't flaunted Charles so gaily, so arrogantly in Raymond's face, would Raymond have taken up, to quite such an extent, with Sandra?

But here, at this point, with an enormous mental effort, I broke free and landed back (almost, it seemed, with a thump) into the solid realities of the present. Useless, utterly useless to go on threshing about in the past in this feverish way. It was the present that mattered. Here I was, aged thirty-three, divorced, a mother, holding down a job and running a household that included Rene. These were facts. And the best thing I could do was to go to sleep on them.

Perhaps, in the circumstances, I might permit myself a couple of aspirin.

I did (three). And, eventually, went to sleep.

Chapter 8

FOR SOME WEEKS after my visit to Betty, life was, or appeared to be, extremely dreary and tasteless. The weather continued extraordinarily cold, causing me to do frightful things that I had never done before in my life, like wearing an old sweater over my pyjamas in bed and even then getting up in the middle of the night to boil up the water in my hot-water bottle again. Antonia, who did not seem to have read the bit in the book about healthy children glorying in frost and snow, disliked the cold as much as I did, and was often peevish. Blakey got chilblains. The kitchen seemed always full of Philip's nappies in various stages of staying rather wet. Rene said this weather really wasn't *fair* on a little baby, and I said that Philip was the only one it *was* fair on, and that if only somebody would tuck *me* up in a nice snug cot or pram all the time, I would ask nothing better of life. The pipes froze. Mother wrote that she had a streaming cold and couldn't travel to Oxford to meet me after all. It thawed. It froze again, and I fell down and cut my knee. Philip rolled off the sofa while in my charge, and although fortunately uninjured screamed loud enough to bring Rene running. Blakey reported that Antonia had refused to say her prayers and that consequently she, Blakey, had, as a punishment, taken away her much-loved Mickey Mouse gas-mask for a week. (And, at the time, I had not enough spirit to see anything funny even in this.) The butterfly-nut off the mincing machine mysteriously disappeared. Blakey, on no grounds whatsoever except the excellent ones of personal dislike, suspected Rene, and Rene suspected me and I suspected Antonia.

Life, in short, seemed full of minor irritations and singularly bereft of major or minor pleasures. I had lunched with Raymond once in town, but, ridiculously enough, had spent most of my time trying to get used to the look of him in uniform. He had got his War Office; job and seemed very pleased at finding himself working just under an old friend of his. I was pleased, too, for his sake, but, as Raymond talked more and more about this friend of his, I began to wonder, a little crossly, whether it was for this I had taken trouble over my appearance and asked Mrs. Hitchcock for a longer lunch-hour than I usually took. Afterwards I was cross with myself, rather than with Raymond. For what on earth had I expected of this lunch? Nothing at all, naturally, so why be piqued when it passed off quite ordinarily?

Perhaps it was merely that a vista now stretched ahead of me with nothing perceptible to look forward to at all. If I was as I had firmly resolved, henceforward going to live solidly in the present, eschewing all 'might-have-beens' and 'if's' and like woolinesses of the mind, well then the present might, I felt reward me by displaying some slight interest in my existence—just a little variety or entertainment, no matter what.

The only variety that came my way was Rene's illness, which happened just at the beginning of March. It was not the sort of entertainment I had hoped for,

Rene got a mild form of 'flu. It was not serious, but did necessitate taking to her bed one Sunday evening and staying there. Rene was still feeding the four-months-old Philip, and I assumed that she would carry on while in bed, at least partially. She was not very ill and she had been, I knew, very keen not to wean Philip before it was really time—an attitude in which I heartily supported her. I was, therefore, more than a little indignant when I came home from the office on the Monday evening to find that the doctor had called and brusquely told her to "put that child on to bottles," as he went. Rene was almost in tears about it.

"I haven't tried a bottle yet," she said, "because, honestly, I don't know how, Vicky. I fed him myself at six o'clock, as I always have, and he seems to have settled off to sleep perfectly happily. Oh, of course I must do what the doctor says, but it *does* seem a shame!"

"Oh, good gracious Rene, if you don't want to give up feeding him—and I think you're absolutely right to want to keep on—I certainly shouldn't do what the doctor says," I said.

Rene gazed at me, round-eyed. "Oh Vicky! Won't he be cross with me, then?"

"I shouldn't tell him. He isn't coming again, is he? Didn't you argue about it with him at all at the time?"

"No, because he just said so and then went, before I had time to say anything."

"Oh, he probably thought you'd be only too pleased at an excuse to drop it."

"You don't think he meant it for *Philip's* sake?" said Rene, reverently.

"Oh no. I shouldn't think so. I expect he was thinking entirely of you. Doctor Saunders doesn't care a rap about babies, you know. If he was thinking of Philip, he'd have left you with more instructions about what to give him and so-on, wouldn't he? You know heaps of very good doctors hardly know a thing about infant feeding, and care less."

Rene looked shocked.

"I never have him for Antonia, you know. I have a woman doctor—rather a friend of mine, Doctor Mary Lambert—who knows all about that sort of thing. Would you like me to ring her up and ask what *she* thinks?"

"Oh, I *would*, Vicky. Would it be all right, do you think?"

"Oh yes," I said recklessly. "We can reckon we're consulting her for Philip, not for you."

I went straight to the telephone, and was lucky enough to catch Dr. Mary herself. I was a little horrified when she immediately took it that I was expecting her to pay a professional call on Philip, but, as soon as she mentioned how very busy she was, I saw my way out and assured her that a little advice over the telephone was all I needed. I did not say anything about Dr. Saunders. I merely told her the facts of the case, that Rene was not really ill and that she was very anxious to go on feeding Philip.

She said, as I had thought she would, that if Rene's attack was really only a mild one, she could certainly continue to feed Philip, and that it was improbable that the milk would upset him. Rene should proceed with caution, noting results carefully, but by no means doing anything drastic and sudden. *That*, she said definitely, would be a great pity. She added some instructions about how to prepare a supplementary feed for Philip, if temporarily necessary, and said that she would call in on us towards the end of the week to see how we were getting on.

Well, I couldn't stop her coming, if she wanted to. Probably Rene would be up and about again by then.

Fortunately I had not to go to the office the next day, and really I quite enjoyed myself nursing Rene and Philip together. I find it a bore to be vaguely 'nice' to people, but no bore at all to do something definite and practical for them. For the first time I really felt quite fond of Rene, and proud and fond too of Philip. I had always thought him a nice healthy little baby, but now I was amused to find myself discovering him quite particularly sweet. I had him in my room at night, as it seemed healthier while Rene was ill, and quite enjoyed his company.

I enjoyed being competent too. (It is so easy to be competent over other people's children—one is never seriously worried about them). I took Blakey's scales from the kitchen and test weighed every feed for Rene. I was quite pleased when a few supplements (mixed most carefully by myself) proved necessary. Rene was inclined to be distressed—she had had no trouble at all hitherto—but, in my best professional calm cheery manner I assured her that it was nothing but a temporary expedient.

That was Tuesday. On Wednesday I was due to go to the office again. Rene was better, but clearly needed another day or two in bed. It was quite obvious that she dreaded the prospect of being left to Blakey's ministrations on the morrow.

I had taken such a lot of selfish pleasure in being the One on whom everyone was depending, that I had not bothered very much about co-opting Blakey into my little act. On Tuesday night I realized that this was a mistake. Blakey, I saw, was distinctly disgruntled. Probably, had I appealed to her earlier on to rise well to a crisis, she would—like the true servant she is—have risen beautifully. As it was, I had just ignored her all day, and she was retaliating by registering complete indifference to Rene and Philip. Things boded ill for the morrow.

When Rene suddenly said, "Oh Vicky! You *have* been sweet to me to-day. What *shall* I do without you all to-morrow?" and turned appealing eyes on me, I suddenly made up my mind to do a thing I had never done before in my office career. I went straight downstairs and telephoned to Mrs. Hitchcock to say that I was terribly sorry, but a domestic crisis prevented me from coming to the office the next day.

Mrs. Hitchcock, I could tell, was not pleased, but, in my exalted ministering-angel mood, I hardly cared. Blakey was not pleased either when I told her. The perverse old creature had been robbed, at a stroke, of a grievance and a chance to show her mettle, and, although I saw this, I did not care either. I made Rene some Ovaltine, superintended Philip's last feed, tucked them both up, and went to bed in a glow of smug self-appreciation. I had, I thought cosily, now two more whole days to be wonderful in.

I had. And I was. The nice thing was that both Rene and Philip progressed splendidly under my rule. By Thursday evening it was evident that Rene could perfectly well get up, for a little the next day. Philip showed no signs whatever of being upset. What a splendid reliable person I really was! If only everybody always did exactly what I told them to, how smoothly things would always run!

It was in such a mood I returned to the office on Friday. Brisk, refreshed, ready to make up for lost time. As it turned out, I needed all my energy.

Mrs. Hitchcock, after an extremely perfunctory, not to say disapproving enquiry after 'my invalid,' handed me a letter with the remark, "Well, you see what's happened *now*. Something will have to be done about that woman."

The letter was from the woman editor of one of the most reputable women's monthly magazines. I glanced through it quickly.

The editor wrote to say that she was returning a story by Dorothy Harper entitled *Mermaids in Bloomsbury*, recently submitted to her by us. This story had already been refused by her a week or two ago when sent direct from Miss Harper. Would we take care to see that this did not occur again, as it wasted everybody's time?

Now, as I had explained to Barry, we could not prevent Dorothy Harper sending stories to editors on her own, much as we disliked it. We could, however, and must prevent her from handing on to us stories which had been previously rejected without telling us the names of the magazines which had already seen them. This was right against etiquette, and extremely bad for our reputation—as Miss Dorothy Harper very well knew.

"Of course she didn't say anything to you about anyone having already seen it when she sent it in?" asked Mrs. Hitchcock.

"Not a word. She gave me to understand it was smoking-hot from her pen."

"I wonder if she sent it anywhere *else* first," said Mrs. Hitchcock darkly. "I wouldn't put it past her."

"Nor would I," I agreed. "I suppose she hoped nobody would bother to write and tell us, so she wouldn't get found out."

"Yes. Or she may have even hoped it would get accepted the second try-on with the same magazine. It's amazing what people will hope for." Mrs. Hitchcock looked grim. "This *must* be stopped. I wish it wasn't so necessary not to offend her. I've great hopes of her new novel, you know. She's writing it with an eye to serialization first, and I believe I've got Miss Page interested."

Miss Page was the editor of one of the best-paying monthly magazines, and the new novel, to which Mrs. Hitchcock referred, was not yet actually in our hands, although we had seen some of it—and very promising it was too. It certainly seemed a very bad moment to offend Dorothy Harper.

"Well," said Mrs. Hitchcock firmly, "you'll have to have that talk with her after all. Write and ask her out to lunch."

"Won't *you*?" I said weakly.

"No, no. You undertook to do it before, if you remember," retorted Mrs. Hitchcock with a steely glint in her eye which showed she remembered only too well the circumstances in which I had promised before. "Besides, you're the head of the short story department and this *Mermaids in Bloomsbury* business is *your* affair. You'd much better do it. Be tactful, you know, but make it clear she just *mustn't* do that sort of thing."

"All right," I said wearily.

"And of course don't send out that story again until you've seen her and found out where it *has* been to. Perhaps you'd better not send out *any* more of hers until you've got the truth out of her. I don't trust that woman." Mrs. Hitchcock stalked out of the room with a disgusted expression.

I sat down to my typewriter forthwith and rattled out a note to Dorothy Harper. Friendly it was (according to our office code which favours friendliness and the personal relationship between agent and author) and yet deferential. I had a notion that Miss Harper was herself all for the deference side. She always treated *me* as if I was the office-girl she was giving a bit of a treat to.

I did not fancy the job. Too much hung on it for my taste—not only the necessity for not offending Dorothy Harper but also the necessity for showing Mrs. Hitchcock I could be more tactful than she had once been. I showed the letter to Mrs. Hitchcock before it went, and she approved.

I should have liked her to say something encouraging about "I'm sure you'll manage the woman beautifully," but naturally, being Mrs. Hitchcock, she didn't. All she remarked was, "That's O.K. Bring her back to the office if you like after you've given her lunch and said your piece and I'll be genial to her for a few minutes."

This was, of course, no comfort at all—rather the opposite. I sent the letter down to the girl who deals with the post and tried to forget all about it. I had left Dorothy Harper to fix the date, and probably it wouldn't be for a week or two.

I worked very hard all the rest of that day and returned home dead tired and planning an immediate bath and bed.

Blakey met me in the hall.

"Ever such a to-do we had this morning with the doctors," she said instantly.

The very last thing I wanted to hear about was 'to-do's' of any sort whatsoever. I suddenly remembered how, airily, I had told Betty that I found it 'refreshing' to live in two atmospheres, home and office. On this particular evening I saw no prospect of being refreshed at all.

"*Doctors?*" I said mazedly. "*What* doctors? How's Mrs. Sylvester?"

"Oh, *she* seems all right," said Blakey, "but I'm afraid she's got you into trouble with Doctor Saunders—*and* with Doctor Lambert too."

I think at that moment I really hated Blakey. Not only was she evidently taking a ghoulish pleasure in retailing bad news, but she was referring to Rene in the tone of voice which I most disliked—and which I certainly ought to pull her up for, were I not so tired.

"You'd better tell me what happened, Blakey," I said coldly.

"It was just before lunch this morning, and Mrs. Sylvester was just finishing getting up—like you told me she would—when Doctor Saunders arrived."

"I didn't know he was coming again," I interrupted.

"No. There was no need, I'm sure. Perhaps Mrs. Sylvester made herself out worse than what she really was when he came before," said Blakey.

I almost slapped her.

"Blakey, will you please leave all remarks about Mrs. Sylvester put of it, and simply tell me what happened?"

"Well, Doctor Saunders was up there in the bedroom seeing Mrs. Sylvester when who should drive up but Doctor Lambert. *I* didn't know why she'd come, I'm sure. Nobody had told *me* anything about it."

"Go on," I said grimly.

"Doctor Lambert seemed to be expecting to see Mrs. Sylvester and the baby. I showed her into the drawing-room and asked her to wait. I thought it best not to say anything about Doctor Saunders being up there. Of course *I* knew nothing about it all, but it seemed a funny thing if Mrs. Sylvester wanted to see two doctors at once."

"Of course she didn't," I said impatiently. "Now Blakey, don't pretend you know nothing about how it happened. I know for a fact you heard me ringing up Doctor Lambert the other evening. I dare say I oughtn't to have, done it, but it was *my* doing, not Mrs. Sylvester's. Couldn't you have been clever about it somehow? Kept Doctor Lambert in the drawing-room until Doctor Saunders had gone or something?"

"I was just trying to think how to act for the best," said Blakey self-righteously, "when Mrs. Sylvester spoilt it all."

Incorrigible old fiend!

"How?" I said wearily.

"She came downstairs with Doctor Saunders, just at that moment. Wearing a dressing-gown she was, over her clothes. I suppose she meant to show Doctor Saunders to the front door. There was no call for her to do that, I'm sure," added Blakey spitefully, "*I* was ready to hand him his coat and hat in the hall."

"Well?"

"Mrs. Sylvester, *she* said before I could stop her, 'I expect you left your coat in here' and opened the drawing-room door and there was Doctor Saunders and Doctor Lambert staring at each other."

"Did Mrs. Sylvester realize who Doctor Lambert was? She's never seen her."

"Yes, because Doctor Saunders said, 'Oh! Good *morning*, Doctor Lambert!' at once in a surprised sort of voice, and then Mrs. Sylvester looked ever so put-out and said. 'Oh dear!' If she hadn't showed so plainly that something was wrong I might have managed to pass it off even then," said Blakey, so thoroughly enjoying herself by this time that I felt I simply could not bear to hear a word more.

"All right, Blakey. You needn't tell me any more. It was all very unfortunate, and I shall have to explain how it came about to them both, if I get a chance. It was entirely my fault, not Mrs. Sylvester's at all."

I made as if to go up the stairs.

"Oh, Mrs. Sylvester told them *that*," said Blakey with unction. "I heard her say—I couldn't help hearing her say, she spoke so loud—I heard her say 'Mrs. Heron said it would be all right to ask you *too*, Doctor Lambert.'"

I would not swear that I did not give Blakey a distinct push as I passed by her on my way upstairs.

"Vicky!" called an entreating voice from Rene's room.

"Hello," I said, opening the door and going in.

The moment I had got home Blakey had enjoyed herself at my expense. Now Rene wanted to unburden her mind on to me. It wasn't fair, I thought childishly. Men breadwinners have slippers laid out warming for them and a loving welcome from little wifey.

"Oh Vicky, I *am* so sorry about this trouble I've got you into about the doctors. Blakey was telling you, wasn't she? I *am* upset about it, I really am. I couldn't help crying after they'd gone."

"Never mind, Rene."

"I feel it was all my fault, I really do."

"No, it wasn't, Rene. It was my doing in the first place."

"You see, I'll tell you exactly how it happened. Just before lunch—"

"Yes, yes, I *know*, Rene, Don't bother to tell me all over again."

"I thought and thought afterwards about all the different things I might have said to them to make it look better, and I am so awfully sorry that I did actually say *you'd* said it would be all right. I could have bitten out my tongue after I'd said it."

"That's all right, Rene. It was I who rang up Doctor Lambert, after all. Anyway, I don't imagine they turned on you and demanded an explanation, did they?"

"Oh no—nobody said anything really except me, who tried to sort of explain."

"M'm. Well, it, was unlucky, Rene, but it just can't be helped, so don't let's talk any more about it. How are you this evening? You don't look too bad."

"Oh, I'm better, thanks. If it hadn't been for this upset I'd be practically well."

"Good. I'll tell Blakey to send you up your supper. I'm going to have mine in bed too, as a matter of fact. Where's Philip? In my room?"

"Yes, in his basket on your bed. I'm so sorry, Vicky... I didn't realize you'd be wanting your room just yet."

Poor Rene! I had said good-bye to her that morning like a competent nurse going temporarily off duty. I had come back a tired breadwinner, with first claim on any comfort there was going.

"Bring him back in here, Vicky. He's sound asleep, I think. I don't think the light will wake him."

"No, I tell you what. I'll pop him in Antonia's room till ten o'clock. Then you can have him again after that, if you like. You're so much better now, I'm sure he can go back to sleeping with you."

"Oh yes, I'm sure he can, Vicky. Don't bother to get out of bed to bring him to me at ten this evening. *I'll* get up."

Poor Rene! If I wasn't going to play at nurse any longer, she couldn't continue to be the grateful but utterly dependent and submissive patient. Here she was going all apologetic and 'don't-let-me-be-a-nuisance' again.

"No, no," I said quickly. "Don't get up again to-night. To-morrow you shall be considered quite well." I meant this as a promise. I only hope it did not sound too much like a threat. "To-night I'll bring him to you at ten—or probably, I shouldn't wonder, soon after half-past nine."

Rene looked shocked at such a scandalous suggested departure from routine; but did not, poor child, like to protest.

I went and had a bath, during which I found time to muse on the strange ill-luck which had, from the very start, dogged my relationship with Rene. Sometimes we *began* to get on well together, but always, before we had time to develop any real friendship, Fate seemed to take a malicious pleasure in tripping us up and sending us stumbling headlong again. Fate had thrown that wedding photograph at Rene's feet and embarrassed her during our first real talk together. Fate had contrived the Blakey-overhearing-us *contretemps* which had put an end to my efforts to 'take Rene into my confidence.' Fate had allowed us to play prettily at Nurse and Patient for a little, and then arranged that the interlude should close not gracefully but with an unfortunate muddle over the doctors, which left a bad taste in everybody's mouth.

Recalling all these incidents to myself, as I lay in the hot water and soaked the fatigue out of my limbs, I was, for the first time, quite struck by the sheer bad luck of it all. It did seem, on the face of it, that Rene and I had been victims of a far greater number of unfortunate coincidences than one would really have expected. Then, thinking a little deeper, I was not so sure.

I have never believed in 'good reasons' for quarrels, I only believe in quarrels. The reasons are, I am perfectly certain, usually irrelevant, and the people who quarrel are the people who really like quarrelling and so will find 'good reasons' without much difficulty. Well, Rene and I very seldom openly quarrelled, but I could not help finding the same line of argument applicable to us. So few points of contact existed between us, so many points of potential disagreement, that really 'unfortunate coincidences' were not bad luck at all on the part of Fate, but sheer probability. I could not believe in 'reasons' for not getting on with someone, any more than I could believe in 'reasons' for quarrels. I could only believe in incompatibility. It was a conclusion that I would really rather not have come to.

* * * * *

These early months of 1941 seemed to be a trying time for almost everyone. If I have not referred much to the war in this book, it was not for want of thinking and worrying about it—merely for want of any comment that has not already occurred and been given expression by thousands of others. The war was always in my thoughts—not necessarily in the foreground, which space I kept reserved for private pre-occupations and troubles, but as a dark background. It was almost a disappointment to me as it must have been to many people, to find that I still minded about little things just as much as ever. One might have thought that, by comparison, one's trivial worries would dwindle to vanishing-point. On the contrary. Whether it was that one's nervous resistance was permanently slightly below par, or whether it was that one's personal radius of activities necessarily shrank and consequently every little episode loomed disproportionately large in one's mind; whatever it was, little things seemed to matter enormously. However much one thought about the Czechs and Poles and told oneself one was really astoundingly lucky, I, and everyone else I had the chance of observing, seemed to feel the same.

Barry, more idealistic by nature than I, probably took the war itself harder. But even he found plenty of time to bother about his private worries. Just about this time he was very, upset about an unfortunate occurrence in his school. One of the housemaids found that she was expecting a baby, and accused one of his undermasters of being the father of the child. The man denied it, and the man's wife appealed to Barry to believe her husband and to show no mercy to the erring girl. It was a horrid sordid muddle for Barry to untangle. It brought into direct conflict his Puritan streak and his desire to believe the best of everybody. I suspected that he was not much of a hand at guessing which of the parties was lying, and no hand at all at taking a robust, practical, commonsense point of view of the matter. He told me he felt very unhappy about the whole thing and personally 'smirched' by it all.

"Oh Barry! What nonsense," I said briskly.

"Yes. I do. I should have hoped—I have *tried*—to make the atmosphere of my school such that such things just *could* not occur. I must have failed somewhere, Vicky."

It is rather amazing that Barry can say such things without sounding the most howling prig. He can.

"You're not tough enough, Barry," I said. "You have too high an opinion of people. You're too hurt when they behave badly. You're not the sort of person to deal with a muddle like this."

"I know," said Barry sadly. "That's why I wanted to ask *your* advice, Vicky."

I was touched.

"Barry darling, how can I be able to be any help to you? I've never *seen* the housemaid *or* the master *or* the master's wife. How could I have an idea who's telling the truth?"

"Sometimes . . . I thought a woman's point of view might be a help," confessed Barry.

"You ought to have a wife, Barry," I said directly. "A nice, practical, good-tempered wife. A really thoroughly out-and-out *nice* wife. That's what I'd prescribe for you."

"You know whom I wanted for my wife, Vicky."

"Yes. And you were wrong. Oh Barry, you *were* wrong, believe me. It really would be such a tremendously good thing if you'd forget all about ever having wanted to marry me and—and consider yourself free to find someone else."

"Vicky! Please! Are you telling me to go out and look for a suitable wife as one might engage a housekeeper or something?"

"No, no, you needn't put it like that. You know quite well what I mean." (I paused, struck by a strange echo of my conversation with Betty over a possible husband or lover for myself. My own rôle was now reversed with a vengeance!) "I only mean acquire the state of mind in which you *might* find someone. You simply mustn't be a bachelor all your life, Barry. It's too—wasteful."

"There's absolutely no hope of your ever changing your mind, Vicky?"

"Absolutely no hope at all, Barry dear," I said steadfastly.

He changed the subject; and afterwards, I felt a pig. He had come to me for comfort and help in trouble and what had l given him? Advice that might be good but was certainly hurtful.

I reflected sadly that these days I seemed to have lost my old talent for 'handling' people well.

Chapter 9

IT WAS APRIL, and less cold at last. Springtime. Even though Benghazi had just been evacuated by the British, the Germans had invaded Greece and Yugoslavia and the Budget announced our Income Tax of 10s. in the pound, I felt a little more cheerful. The end of the war seemed as far off as ever, or possibly a little farther, but at least we had struggled somehow through a winter of rationing, raids, black-out and bitter cold. Dunkirk was nearly a year ago. Even if we were not yet winning, we had not yet lost. In those dark days it was all we could hope for, and now at least we had the summer in front of us. It is well known that nothing is ever quite so bad in summer as it is in winter.

Blakey's cat had kittens, Philip was learning to sit up. Barry and Rene sometimes went walks together on Sunday afternoon and left me in luxurious, selfish peace. I took Antonia to meet Mother in Oxford and the child enjoyed herself ecstatically. (Trains and meals in awful tea-shops suitable to children are Antonia's idea of heaven.) Dorothy Harper went away on a holiday and couldn't possibly accept my kind invitation to lunch for a month. I amused myself inspecting all the schools in Harminster and making my choice for Antonia, who would shortly have to be flung into the mill of English education. Raymond rang me up at the office one afternoon to say he had suddenly acquired a couple of stalls for a play that evening, and would I come?

I would. The invitation came at just the right moment. I was beginning to feel I had the energy once more to go out and enjoy myself.

Raymond is good at creating a party atmosphere. In the old days we had always as a matter of course gone in for all the accessories—evening dress, dining out first, taxies home, and so on. On this occasion, Raymond was in uniform, and I in my office clothes, and there was no question of dinner first as the performance started so early. Nevertheless, *from* the first moment it felt like a party. Very gay we were, very witty with each other, very amusing in our comments on the play, very much at ease with each other and with the world, very assured and very heart-whole.

I could never have believed that an evening which started under such splendid auspices could have ended so—peculiarly. I do not think it would have done so had we not, by the merest chance, encountered Sandra and her husband.

Funnily enough, when one remembers my old vindictive day-dreams, we *did* meet in the bar during the second interval. Everything else was, of course, quite different. There should have been nothing in the least upsetting in the encounter for me. I was furious with myself for feeling upset.

I could never have guessed, if anyone had told me I would never have believed that, at the sight of Sandra, I would have been assailed by a rush of the most agonizing emotion. For years I had been able to think of her calmly, to speak of her normally. Why then, at the sight of her face, should all my inside suddenly feel as if it had been turned to water? It couldn't be true, it *must* be bogus emotion, I assured myself desperately, even as I moved forward to the inescapable encounter. (She had seen Raymond and hailed him with just the gay insouciance I had once imagined myself showing.) How *could* I mind a little incident like this when, at the time, I had felt so very little of the conventional wife's fury towards the Other Woman?

Delayed shock. That was the only explanation I could fling confusedly to myself. Delayed shock, all the worse for not having been felt properly at the time. I was suffering now because I had not once *allowed* myself to think about her as I should really have liked to think.

Raymond's touch on my elbow steadied me. At the time I thought it was accidental. All this turmoil was happening inside me—I was retaining perfect control of my behaviour, I thought.

"You are absolutely cured again then, Raymond?" Sandra was saying. "I *was* so distressed when Betty told me about your . . . your . . ."

"T.B.," said Raymond. "Say it. No taboo. Yes, thank you, Sandra, I'm perfectly all right again now."

"May I get you another drink?" Sandra's husband politely asked me. (I do not know if he knew who I was. There had been—mercifully—no introductions by surnames, and, even as I accepted his offer, I wondered for a moment whether he knew of Sandra and Raymond's past. Sandra's name had not been mentioned in the evidence in the divorce courts. Raymond had gone through the dreary farce of taking another woman away for a week-end and sending me the hotel bill. At the time I despised Sandra heartily for this.)

"Are you living in London again now, Vicky?" said Sandra to me.

Her manner, her appearance were, as far as I could judge, just the same as when I had last seen her. Smart, polished, a general effect of glitter. I had never known her at all well. As soon as I had begun to be unhappy about her and Raymond, I had gone to some secret pains to avoid meeting her.

"No—I just come up from Harminster when necessary," I answered.

She wasn't interested, of course. Why should she be?

"Why don't you two come on to Betty Attenborough's afterwards?" said Sandra's husband. "We're going on to a party there. These people know Betty, don't they, Sandra?"

"Know Betty? Of *course* they do, darling! Why, Vicky's one of Betty's oldest friends, aren't you, Vicky? Yes, *do* come, both of you."

She spoke with only the right amount of conventional enthusiasm, but I saw her eyes flicker towards Raymond, and tried to interpret the glance. Mischievous? Questioning? I did not know.

The great thing was, I felt, that there should be no awkward pause at this point. Wild horses were not going to drag me to Betty's party myself, but the very last role I was going to play in front of Sandra was that of killjoy or backer-out. Let Raymond speak.

He did. Instantly.

"Thank you very much, Sandra. We will drop in for a few minutes if we can."

I liked the 'we.' I liked the assumption that he and I were united for the evening with other possible plans for entertaining ourselves.

It now only remained to explain to Raymond afterwards, quite quietly and without the slightest suggestion of making a scene about it, that I would not actually accompany him to Betty's flat. He, of course, must go.

The bell for the last act rang, and a commissionaire in the corridor called out, "Hurry up, please." We all moved out and became separated again into two couples. Just as she drifted off, Sandra called over her shoulder to us, "If I get there first, I'll tell Betty you're coming—or we might share a taxi?"

Raymond smiled and nodded. The curtain was going up and we hurried back to our seats.

During the whole of that last act I felt quite sick with apprehension. If only I could have mentioned casually to Raymond at once that I was not coming on to Betty's with him! There had not been time, and now I was working myself up into a state of nerves about it. If only I could pretend that I had to catch a train home at once. Unfortunately, Raymond knew that the trains ran until midnight.

Not for worlds would I give Raymond my real reason for not wanting to go to Betty's—that the sight of Sandra and him together made me feel literally and physically sick. It was a reason

I myself heartily despised. I was a coward and would have to take the coward's way out—a headache or some such excuse of the sort.

There, that was the end of the play. The first two acts I had thoroughly enjoyed, the last hardly taken in at all. *God Save the King*. Stand to attention and *don't* fumble. Now! Say quickly to Raymond . . .

"This way! Quick, Vicky!" said Raymond, taking me by the elbow.

The main exit was at the back of the auditorium, but, before I knew where I was Raymond had shepherded me through a side fire-exit. We were on the pavement, in a side-street.

"Now, round this corner and with luck we'll pick up a taxi before the crowd," said Raymond, still completely in charge.

"Raymond, look—I think I ought to be getting back to Harminster. I don't think . . ."

"Taxi?" said Raymond, waving.

The taxi drew up. Raymond handed me in. Hypnotically, I acquiesced.

"Raymond, don't give him the address of Betty's flat because I—"

"Don't worry, I'm not going to!" said Raymond. (Oh! the heavenly decision in his voice. I was so relieved that I did not notice to where he did actually direct the driver.)

Raymond climbed in. The door slammed. The taxi drove off.

"A neat get-away, you must admit, Vicky," said Raymond, turning to me with a grin.

"Oh Raymond! I thought you wanted to go there," I said idiotically.

"*Me?* Good God, no. I only accepted to prevent discussion. *You* didn't, did you?"

"*Me?* Good God, no," I repeated absurdly, and then we both laughed.

"Where *are* we going actually, Raymond? To the station for me?"

"Station? Certainly not, not yet. You needn't, need you?"

"Oh no, I needn't."

"Good. Complete agreement again. As a matter of fact, quick action of some sort being necessary, I gave the driver the address of my flat. Do you mind?"

"Mind? No, of course I don't mind—oh Raymond, I do nothing but repeat things after you and then agree!"

"A very good course to pursue, Vicky. As a matter of fact, I had thought before that we'd go out and have supper somewhere. Having made our get-away, we can now re-direct the driver, if you like, Vicky. He won't mind. He knows all customers are mad, anyway."

"Oh, let's go to your flat, Raymond. I'd like to see it. Where is it?"

"In the Temple—the bit that hasn't been bombed. But you must want something to eat, don't you, Vicky?"

"Can't we find something to eat there?"

"There's some bacon and tins of things, I think. Wouldn't you rather go out though?"

"No," I said decidedly. "I'd *much* rather picnic in peace at your flat."

"All right then," said Raymond, without further demur. I was a little surprised at him showing even the amount of hesitation he had.

Raymond's flat was up a lot of stone stairs, up which our feet clattered coldly. The names of the occupants were written over the doors. It was curiously reminiscent of an Oxford college.

"I've just taken it furnished for three months at a time," explained Raymond, opening the door and showing me into a room that might well have been a college room—nicely proportioned, a 'good' room (not a box in a centrally-heated, steel-framed block of flats), but somehow an austere, a slightly impersonal room. I did not feel that I had very much right to be there.

"I suppose women are *allowed* in here, Raymond?" I said absurdly.

"Good gracious yes! What are you talking about?"

"I only felt the atmosphere was rather—monastic."

"Is it?" Raymond glanced round vaguely. "Well, if you want the Nun's Retreat it's just down the passage on the left."

"Thank you."

I went and spent some time doing up my face again—a glance in the mirror assured me that it needed it. On the way, I passed the half-open door of what, I thought, must be Raymond's bedroom. I glanced in. It also looked bare and impersonal, and rather dreary in the half-light from the passage. It gave me an odd sensation to think of Raymond sleeping alone in this room every night. It was not a painful sensation; it was just—funny. I could find no other word for it.

When I came back to the sitting-room, the place looked more welcoming. The gas-fire was roaring cosily, Raymond had pulled up chairs and was in the act of getting out glasses.

"Gin-and-lime, Vicky? You look better now."

"Better?" I said surprised. "Was I so very untidy, or what?"

"Not so very untidy," said Raymond, carefully measuring out some gin. "Just white."

"*White? Was I? Did* I really? I didn't realize I'd . . ." My voice trailed away. I might have realized Raymond would see through my pretence of nonchalant chat to Sandra. Damn his perception! Especially as I still felt that I didn't really believe in my own reactions.

"Raymond—I didn't *really* mind meeting Sandra, you, know," I said feebly.

"Didn't you? I did," said Raymond briefly.

Well. Already my inside had 'turned to water' that evening, in the conventional way, and now blessed if my heart didn't seem literally 'to sink.' I began to think there was more in these old novelist's phrases than I had imagined.

"Not for myself, of course," added Raymond casually. "Only for your sake. We were having a lovely time—and she spoilt it. Vicky, you didn't *really* think I was going to try to take you on to that bloody party, did you?"

"Yes, I did. I was even prepared to agree with you that one *ought* to go. Why not, I mean, and all that."

"Correct gesture in fact?"

I nodded.

"The woman who told me that 'admiration of gestures had been our undoing' being presumably in eclipse?" suggested Raymond.

"Oh, yes. I'm only a prig on Sunday afternoons. This is Wednesday evening. *Quite* different."

"Oh, of course, I see. *Quite* different," retorted Raymond gravely.

"Raymond—just to restore my slightly damaged self-confidence. You don't think anybody *else* noticed I'd gone white—or whatever my revoltingly dramatic reaction was—do you?"

"No, I'm sure they didn't. Your *sang-froid* was admirable, Vicky."

"And yours, too," I said politely,

"Mine? Oh, mine wasn't *sang-froid*. It was pure cold-bloodedness. A literal translation which means something utterly different. In the words of the grand old cliché, 'What's over is over.' There now, that's *quite* enough of that, thank you. Have another drink. How's Rene?"

"This is where I'm competent in the kitchen with bacon, isn't it?" I said, accepting his lead, as I usually accepted it. (So his feeling for Sandra *was* quite 'over,' was it?)

"I'll come and watch and tell you *that's* not the way to open tins," said Raymond.

We knocked up a scratch meal together—bacon, fried bread, a tin of beans, coffee—the sort of meal that seems bed-sitting-roomish and dreary if a woman makes if for herself, but rather cosy and intimate if concocted in congenial mixed company. Over supper I entertained Raymond with what he called "The next instalment of your Rene story." I found no difficulty at all in making the history of the two doctors sound quite amusing.

"Thank you, Vicky. That was most enjoyable. I can hardly wait for the next episode in 'The Life and Adventures of Rene Sylvester.'"

"It ought to be written from Rene's point of view as well—and the two histories bound up together. A very valuable document for social workers, it would be. All the same, I'm sure you oughtn't to encourage me to be such a cad about Rene. You're not a feminine man, Raymond, but you have a most dangerous feminine capacity for being a good listener."

"I wouldn't call you a masculine woman, Vicky, but you have a most dangerous masculine capacity for shouldering dependents. Is Rene yours for life, do you suppose?"

"God knows! I can't *sack* her, can I? Yes, I expect she *is* mine for life—and when we're two old hags mumbling toothless by the fireside we'll still have our little disagreements from time to time. Philip and Antonia will be able to join in and take sides presently. It will be fun for them. Oh well! Raymond, it's *your* turn to bat now. Tell me—do you ever think of writing another novel?"

Raymond said not, he thought. The conversation passed to books, which we had always enjoyed discussing, and thence to the office and thence to Raymond's job in the War Office. Time passed quickly, and it was Raymond who finally said, "Vicky, I simply hate to end this, but what about your train?"

I glanced guiltily at the clock.

"Oh Lord! Yes, I ought to go. What a fag!"

Suddenly, as I rose, I felt very tired; and the prospect of all that long journey back to Harminster, with twenty minutes cold walk in the black-out at the end of it because the buses would have stopped running, absolutely appalled me.

"*What* an effort," I said drearily. "Can I get a taxi to Paddington, do you suppose, Raymond?"

"I'll come down with you and we'll see if we can pick one up in the Strand. They're not as frequent as they used to be at this time of night, but we'll probably get one all right."

"Oh, I hope we can. It seems about a hundred years since I left home this morning."

Raymond shot me a quick glance. "I'm sorry if it hasn't been worth it, Vicky. I rather bounced you into it I know."

I suddenly woke up to the fact that I was behaving rudely and ungratefully.

"Oh *Raymond*! I didn't mean that. I've had a *lovely* evening. It's only the prospect of this awful trek home . . ."

"Frightful, I agree. You ought to have a club or something, Vicky, where you could stay the night occasionally."

"M'm. Only I don't go two days running to the office usually, you know. Although, as a matter of fact, I *could* do with putting in an extra half-day to-morrow . . . Raymond!" (A brilliant idea struck me.) "Raymond, *I* know. Let me spend the night on your sofa here."

Raymond and I had often in the old days put up belated party-goers on sofas or camp-beds. I swear that, as I spoke, my suggestion seemed exactly on a par with situations of the sort. Raymond's instant negative response was all the more of a shock to me.

"No, I'm afraid you can't do that, Vicky," he said, firmly.

I suppose it was a very long time since anyone had told me categorically that I could not do something I wanted to. Immediately I felt injured and defiant.

"Why ever not, Raymond? It's a perfectly sound idea. You needn't even *see* me to-morrow morning if you don't want to. I'll get up early and go out to breakfast."

"Don't be absurd, Vicky. It wouldn't do at all, and you know it."

I don't think Raymond had ever spoken to me in that tone before. I did not dislike it as much as I should have thought I would have done. Nevertheless, I was not going to give in weakly.

"Have you gone *conventional* in your old age or something, Raymond? Have you got a charwoman who comes in early or something?"

"No. It's not that. She doesn't arrive till ten. All the same, you're not going to, Vicky."

"Why ever not? You might at least tell me."

"All artless and innocent, aren't you, Vicky?" said Raymond impatiently.

That stung. Like a fool I could not let it pass and go with a good grace.

"Yes," I said crossly, feeling just like an overtired child on the brink of tears because thwarted, "Yes, if you want to *know*, Raymond, my suggestion—and I *still* think it a very good one—

was made quite artlessly. If you think there's an ounce of—of flirtatiousness or coquetry or whatever you like to call it left in my attitude to you now, you're just plain wrong. We're past all that—thank God!"

Furious with myself because I was almost in tears, I seized my coat and plunged my arms into it. My back was turned to Raymond, and so I could not see his face when he answered dryly, "We're past all that, you say? I congratulate you, Vicky."

"Well, *aren't* we?" I said, challenging him angrily.

"Certainly, if you say so. All the same—"

"All the same—what?"

"All the same if being 'past all that' is going to upset us and cause scenes of this sort, perhaps we'd better not see too much of each other," finished Raymond.

I did not like that. I did not like it at all. I attempted airiness.

"Nonsense, Raymond. Anyway, it wasn't *me* who let the party down. I'm not 'upset.' I'm just cross, because you're conventional and stupid."

"Exactly, Vicky. You're *not* conventional, and so you just *can't* be stupid, can you? Don't forget your gloves. We must run for it."

We did. Fortunately Raymond found me a taxi quickly. During the journey to Paddington I was so occupied in wondering whether I should catch my train that I had no time to worry over this strange end to our evening together.

I did just catch it; and then, of course, found I had nothing to read and nothing to do but meditate on what had just occurred. I did not feel I had come out of it all very well.

First I had been silly over Sandra, and Raymond—damn him—had noticed it. Next, I had grumbled very rudely about having to go home. Thirdly, I had nearly cried over nothing at all and practically—horror of horrors!—made a scene.

No, it was not a very brilliant exhibition from someone who was, in her own words, 'past all that.'

The funny thing was that I was really honestly speaking the truth when I had said that I was 'past all that.' I was—even if the sight of Sandra *had* hurt badly for a moment. Fundamentally,

I felt perfectly settled. I had, in my life, two big things. Antonia and my work. I honestly did not feel the need for much else. Raymond I enjoyed seeing enormously—but in between times I forgot all about him.

I did hope Raymond understood this. If I had not been so cross and tired I would have tried to get the idea across to him in a calmer way—although wasn't really this idea implicit in our whole relationship? I had, of course, believed it so—and therefore how very unnecessary it had been to shout rudely at him those remarks about my casual attitude to him nowadays.

Raymond himself had been anything but 'casual' to me when he had noticed the effect Sandra had had on me. He had been extraordinarily thoughtful on my account and saved the situation with the minimum of fuss. He had been thinking of *me*. But I had hardly been thinking of him when I made my get-away scene from the flat.

No, I hadn't been thinking of him, not for one instant, selfish pig that I was. That was a funny last shot of his, just as we were leaving: "*You're* not conventional Vicky, and so you just *can't* be stupid, can you?"

Stupid? Me *stupid*? I nearly laughed out loud in the railway carriage at the incredulity with which I received the suggestion.

Stupid, what about? Or did the very fact of asking myself what about convict me instantly of the fault?

Oh dear, I *was* tired. Far too tired to go on thinking muzzily about who had been stupid to whom about what. Clatter-clatter-clang-clatter went the wheels. There was a button missing on the purplish-brown upholstery opposite me. Clatter-clatter-clang-clatter. To-morrow I must interview the butcher and ask him why he never seemed to keep any liver for me. Clatter-clatter-clang-clatter. Sandra had had a lovely fur-coat—was it mink? . . . Antonia wanted some new socks. How horrible these little black, cone-shaped lampshades over the carriage lights were. When peace comes (if ever) shall we have pink with frills? Clatter-clatter-clang-clatter. Life was made up of a million utterly incoherent details. (Damn that missing button. I might go to sleep if it didn't worry me so.) A million incoherent details and the wonder was that anyone ever succeeded in making any sort of a sensible pattern out of it.

Chapter 10

I REALLY CANNOT go into detail about the next big row Blakey and I had over Rene. Even at the time the triviality of the whole thing infuriated me. Even at the time I saw the three of us as a group of undignified, idiotic petty women. Even at the time, while realizing all this, I knew that this storm in a tea-cup was going to have disastrous results.

It did. The worst happened, and I sacked Blakey. I don't know which of us was the more appalled at this disastrous culmination. Blakey, who had, I think, believed I would never really do such a thing. Rene, who said, Oh dear, I *didn't* think it was all her fault, did I? Or myself, who had to face the, prospect of coping with the office and Antonia without my infuriating but utterly reliable domestic retainer.

It happened about a month after my party with Raymond, and was of course led up to by episodes, each one very trivial in itself, each one heightening the tension between the three of us a little more. There was the Episode of Blakey falling over Philip's pram in the dark scullery and barking her knee—followed by the Episode of Rene presenting Blakey with a new pair of stockings in compensation and Blakey refusing them. There was the Episode of Rene turning out her own room to help Blakey one particularly busy morning, and Blakey turning it all out again grimly and thoroughly that very afternoon. There was the Episode of Blakey "not holding" with veal broth and nonsense of that sort for babies, and letting Rene's bones boil dry on the stove and ruin a saucepan. There was (as a private sideshow for myself particularly) the Episode of Barry overhearing me give Rene an impatient little lecture on how to handle Blakey ("For heaven's sake *bully* the woman back, Rene! It's the only thing she understands!") and hinting afterwards, oh! so gently and tactfully and idealistically that Rene was far too sweet a person to find that sort of advice comprehensible. There was—finally—the Episode of the Fireguard, of which I will merely retail briefly the bare facts.

Rene left the sitting-room unoccupied one day when I was at the office, without putting the fireguard up. A spark flew out and burnt a rather nasty hole in the hearthrug. This hearthrug was not part of my landlord's furnishings, but belonged to me. Blakey discovered the damage and took the line that Rene had endangered the lives of everyone in the house by her criminal carelessness, besides destroying irreparably one of my most valued possessions. (I never found out exactly what she said to Rene, but it was enough to reduce her to tears and to keep her sobbing, on and off, until I came home an hour later.) Secretly infuriated by Rene's tears, and inwardly resentful of consolation and sympathy being required of me the minute I set foot inside the door, I went out to the kitchen to take the line it was all a ridiculous fuss about nothing and the hearthrug, which wasn't a particularly nice one anyway, could easily be repaired. But Blakey, while I was in the course of establishing this as an Official Pronouncement, said so many intolerable things—("Of course, if you don't *mind* what happens to your things, it seems a pity I take so much trouble to keep everything nice," and "There's been twice the work since Mrs. Sylvester came here, and does she mean to live with you *all* her life, I should like to know?" were two fair samples)—that it very shortly became apparent to me that there could be only one end to this sort of discussion. A really splendid burst of anger swept me off my feet and made the actual pronouncement positively enjoyable.

Both anger and enjoyment had, of course, completely ebbed away from me by the next morning. I woke up early and put in a good hour's worrying before breakfast-—an exhausting procedure that I can recommend to absolutely nobody. In the end, I got up half an hour earlier than usual, fished Antonia out of her bed and brought her into mine "for a treat." The child, who was of course as bright and chatty as only children *can* be at seven o'clock in the morning, was enchanted. Naturally she had no conception of why I had suddenly had the excellent idea of requiring her company, and her artless pleasure and surprise consoled me considerably. Extraordinary how children can be simultaneously an awful problem and a tremendous consolation. Who on earth was to look after Antonia and keep house *now* on the days when I went to the office? Rene, I felt sure, was just not capable of doing everything. Even if she offered—and why should she, after all?—I would not let her—if only for Antonia's sake. I felt very stranded and forlorn. However, I told myself that I must remember that to Antonia—and to Rene too—I was a rock, a refuge and a fortress in any storm. And anyway, Blakey would not, I thought, leave me until I had found a substitute.

On this cold crumb of comfort, I finally got up to breakfast.

The period that followed was, naturally, an uncomfortable one for everyone. I had vowed to myself that no word of reproach to Rene should ever cross my lips. Rene had evidently vowed that not more than half an hour should ever pass without the topic being apologetically and uneasily brought up by her. Blakey seemed to have made up her mind to show us what a treasure we were losing. We were all of us on our best behaviour; and really I almost preferred us when we were biting and scratching like fighting cats.

I put an advertisement in the local paper and received three replies—one from an elderly Nanny who expected "the nurseries" waited on. Well, we hadn't any nurseries, so that disposed of her. The next was from a girl of sixteen whose previous employer reported her to be "good-tempered and willing, but a little unreliable with soldiers." I did not enquire too closely what that cautious phrase meant. The third was from a Welsh girl who said if I would forward her her fare from Aberystwyth she would come immediately for an interview. I didn't.

It did not make things easier that conscription of women was being foretold in all the papers about this time. Already 'registration' had begun.

Once again I looked forward to my days at the office as a temporary escape from domestic worries. The fact that, as usual, Mrs. Hitchcock was totally uninterested in my private problems and that I never spoke at all about my home to her, was, once again, a considerable relief. Barry, to whom Rene of course prattled of our difficulties, attempted to talk sympathetically to me about the situation and got his head bitten off for his pains.

I do not know quite why I have such a strong personal taboo against being sympathized with, but I certainly have. I suspect that while it was always dormant in me, it flourished and grew noticeably just after my divorce. Perhaps there are only two courses open to a woman who is left to run her life single-handed against a certain amount of odds; She may either become a bit of a 'poor little thing' (with a top-dressing of slightly bogus bravery and gallantry) or else she may go to the other extreme and become rather too self-sufficient and bossy. Finding the first course utterly detestable, I naturally inclined to the second attitude. I expect the psychologists would call it 'over-compensation.' The fact that I know a certain amount of their jargon and am quite good at standing a little apart from myself and thinking out my behaviour does not, I need hardly say, make it any easier for me to feel differently—a disappointing conclusion that always seems slurred over in the helpful little psychology books.

I half-envied and half-despised Rene's utter lack of any inhibitions against lapping up sympathy. It was either jealousy or scorn that made me be so horrid to Barry when he attempted to condole with me.

"Rene's told me all about the fix you're in over Blakey going," he said one evening when we were all three having coffee in the sitting-room.

Rene gave a deprecating little cough. I knew, without looking at her, that she was now shooting a slightly nervous glance in my direction.

"Blakey going?" I said, a little deliberately vaguer. "Oh yes. Yes. It is a nuisance, but we'll soon find someone else."

When I was married to Raymond it was part of my code never to mention domestic worries of any sort to him. I thought that, since he had agreed so amicably that I was going to keep on my job, that was the least I could do in the circumstances—and I kept most resolutely to my vow. I suppose it was partly habit that made me speak so airily to Barry now. A moment's thought might have shown me that Barry and Rene would probably prefer not to feel slightly squashed.

"Oh Vicky, I'm so glad! I was afraid you were worrying. You looked *so* tired the other night!" exclaimed Rene impulsively.

Silly ass, I thought ungratefully, can't you see I'm pretending and why?

"I do hope you do find someone really suitable, Vicky," said Barry in his slow gentle voice, "It must be so important to have the right person to look after a child."

As if I needed telling that! As if I didn't lie awake worrying about whether Antonia would be upset by the change! As if I didn't have absurd nightmare visions that I laughed away regularly in the daytime about a new Person who slapped Antonia for no reason or let her run out into the road in front of cars.

I said absolutely nothing. If they thought I was an utterly casual mother who didn't care in the least who looked after her child, let them. I was, it may be observed, in an extraordinarily prickly mood.

"Of course, you don't necessarily need a trained babies' nurse, do you, Vicky?" Barry continued, not, I think, at all perceptive of the 'atmosphere' I was surely radiating by this time, "because *Rene's* always there for Philip." He treated Rene to an approving smile. She basked. I swear, she perceptibly basked.

"Yes, Philip's got his Mummy," said Rene smugly.

"Yes, that's very nice for Philip," I said dryly. "Antonia has to put up with second-best."

They did not, I could see, know quite what way to take this. To be honest, I did not know quite where or at what I was hitting out myself. I would almost have liked to have said that Philip was lucky because he hadn't got a Mummy who had to support the expenses of a home. Not that there would have been much meaning in this gibe—because Rene, of course, paid her expenses with me. My only real grievance was one I could never express—that Blakey and I had always got along well until Rene's arrival. And even then I was prepared to admit that it was Blakey, not Rene, who had made mischief.

"Well, one thing, Vicky," said Barry comfortingly, "it must be a consolation to you to feel that Rene's here to superintend things on the days when you're at the office."

"Oh yes," agreed Rene helpfully. "And, of course, Vicky, if you do get a young untrained girl I'll be only too willing to help all I can. Blakey never would *let* me, you know."

"I know she wouldn't. She was maddening," I snapped. "But all the same I *do* want someone a bit better than a young untrained girl. I *must* have peace of mind while I'm at the office."

There was a rather nasty silence. I had time to reflect that, by implication, I had been extremely rude to Rene.

Barry certainly saw it too. He shot a quick shocked glance at me, coughed, and said, "Of course, naturally you want the best for Antonia, Vicky. Everyone sees that. I was only suggesting that at least you're better off than you would be if Blakey was going and Rene wasn't with you."

I didn't say it. I swear I didn't say it, although the retort 'Blakey never *would* have been going in that case' nearly fell, of its own weight, off my lips. What I *did* say was ungracious enough. I exclaimed, "Oh, for God's sake let's drop the subject. It's a very boring one, and why we're discussing it I can't imagine."

Barry got up. "In any case, it's late. I must be off," he said.

"Oh *do* wait another twenty minutes!" exclaimed Rene. "Then it will be time to get Philip up for his last feed and you can see him properly."

I really do not think Rene had noticed that I was, to put it mildly, in the beast of a temper, that evening. She was blessedly thick-skinned. In any case, the thought of showing off Philip to anyone was enough to drive all other considerations out of her head.

Barry, I could see, thought this very charming and proper of her. I could also see that he was puzzled and upset about me.

Well, if nobody was going to send me out of the room until I could behave myself (which was, I absolutely saw, just the treatment I needed) I had better send myself.

"Yes, do stay, Barry," I said quickly. "As a matter of fact, if you'll excuse me, I'll go and get in a quick bath now before other people want theirs. It's a bit of a queue in the evenings, you see, because Blakey takes one too then . . . So, if you won't think me very rude, I'll leave you and Rene to entertain each other till Philip's fetched."

"Of course, Vicky," said Barry politely, "I think you're very wise to get in an early night when you can. You look tired."

"Oh, I'm not going to sleep," I said, perverse to the last. "I've got about six short stories to read in bed. However—good night."

"Good night," they chorused politely.

I went thankfully out of the room. I felt like a nasty schoolmistress leaving her class to a much-needed break. I felt like a sulky child who had refused to join in the other children's jolly games. I felt simultaneously very old and very babyish. I felt nobody liked me, and I didn't blame them particularly. I didn't like myself.

* * * * *

The following week I got on the track of a suitable-sounding woman. She was a widow, aged forty, who had been a Nanny before she was married and seemed willing to undertake cooking as well as the partial care of Antonia. I wrote off to her, and felt better. Even though the Germans had entered Athens and on another front captured Sollum, even though there had just been another heavy air-raid on London, I felt better. Of such stuff are we women made.

I met Raymond again—just for lunch—and it all passed off most flippantly and excellently. I told him, of course, about Rene and Blakey and he took just the line I liked and wanted—passionate interest strongly tempered with humour. I suppose it was sympathy of a sort I got from him—but certainly not of the tabooed variety.

I also told him (since Raymond is perfectly familiar with my childish streak) of the game I was playing on my dressing-table with a counter, Antonia's chalks and a large sheet of squared paper. It was a version of snakes-and-ladders—the difference being that Life laid out the board as one went along. On a normal day when nothing particularly nice or nasty happened, one simply moved one's counter along one square. On a day when something nice had occurred, one gleefully drew a ladder (appropriately graded as to length according to the extent of the 'niceness') and shot up to the top. Bad days necessitated drawing snakes, similarly graded, and descending down them. I amused myself by making them as brightly coloured and horrifically wriggly as possible, and even by giving them faces with some caricatured resemblance to either Blakey or Rene or Mrs. Hitchcock, as the case might be. I am not at all good at drawing, so I trust that this private amusement passed unnoticed. Both Blakey and Rene in any case thought I was slightly mad when they saw it; Antonia, on the other hand, although not entirely comprehending the rules of the game, obviously welcomed it as a really sensible idea, and, of her own accord, pressed me to borrow her most treasured chalk—a particularly virulent scarlet—for the snakes' tongues.

"How do you know whether you've won or not?" asked Raymond.

He was the first person to take a really intelligent interest in the game. My heart warmed to him.

"Well, I definitely lost in April, but then I only played for half a month. I'm starting the May board now. I think you've won if you get 'home' by the end of the month. Very exciting, the last week of the month, as you can imagine."

"The temptation to cheat must be terrific towards the end," suggested Raymond.

"Oh Raymond, you shock me! My integrity is such I just *couldn't*."

"Well, let me know if it's a near thing and I'll try to produce a ladder for you at the crucial moment. Or am I being smug in supposing I could qualify as a ladder sometimes?"

"Oh, of *course* a nice outing with you is a ladder, Raymond. The only thing is I'm not sure that a deliberately-produced ladder wouldn't be cheating. What do you think?"

"Yes. I see. One needs notice of that question, perhaps."

"There's going to be the hell of either a snake or ladder towards the middle of this month," I said. "My lunch with Dorothy Harper. It's on Wednesday week. Settled at last."

"Dorothy Harper?" Raymond looked enquiring.

"Yes—didn't I tell you all about that? Oh no, of course I didn't. It was Barry I once bored with the whole story."

"Tell me now."

"No, it doesn't matter. It's a long story, and it isn't really very interesting and anyway, I've no business to talk about our authors outside the office."

"You seem to have told Barry," said Raymond.

I saw, to my surprise, that he looked a trifle hurt.

"I know. I had no business to really, although actually Dorothy Harper isn't her name."

"In that case, can't I hear about it too?"

"No—I don't think so, please, Raymond. Not so much for reasons of professional secrecy as because—well, as because it's a long story and will take up all our time together, and anyway I'd rather forget about it and enjoy myself while I'm out of the office and with you."

"'Good-time-Raymond'—eh?" said Raymond a little sardonically.

"Any objection?" I said, surprised.

"Of course not. No objection in the world. Tell me, have you read that new book by . . ."

And so on. It was a nice lunch together. That evening I went up a three-runged ladder, and the next day I had a letter from the widow person to say she could come to Harminster for an interview on the Tuesday week. I was very anxious for her to see the house and Antonia and what she would be taking on really properly, so I wrote back immediately clinching this and asking her to come to lunch and tea that day. It was the day before my lunch with Dorothy Harper. With any luck, I should now be able to interview that annoying woman with an easier mind. Again, I felt better.

Just to keep me in order, Antonia caught a cold. This, at the beginning of May, seemed a little unnecessary. However, since the weather *was* so much better, I thought it could not possibly amount to much. I did, however, decide that a bottle of Parrish's food would do the child no harm. There was no doubt that she was growing very fast these days and beginning to look rather all legs and eyes. As a connoisseur of legs, I appreciated her growth. As a mother, I felt a trifle wary.

Rene was, I think, quite disappointed when I pooh-poohed her suggestion that Philip should have some Parrish's food too. I am sure she was secretly looking forward immensely to the time when she could 'dose' him.

Chapter 11

ALTHOUGH IT IS PART of my code always to refer to Antonia with a confident airiness, I am always surprised when people (not unnaturally) assume that I never worry about my child. I disapprove of worrying, being perfectly aware of the fact that the best type of mother for a child to have is one who takes the whole business instinctively in her stride—affection, correction, demands, obligations and all. I am also perfectly aware of the fact that I am not that type of person, and that I have often to make do with intelligence as a substitute for instinct. I try very hard not to appear to take my child too seriously, and I think on the whole I put up a pretty good show. But I do not—alas?—deceive myself.

Had Antonia been a 'difficult' or 'delicate' child I might have had an even harder time of it. But she had always been, thank God, both healthy and normal. Of course I privately thought her very intelligent for her age, but that, I knew, was both healthy and normal of me.

Apart from a bad cold or two, Antonia had never been ill at all until this time—ten days or so after my lunch-party with Raymond, I could hardly believe my ears when I was wakened in the middle of this Friday night by sobs from her bedroom. The cold she had had was practically gone, and in any case I had not had a disturbed night from Antonia since she was a tiny baby. Smugly I had attributed it to *my* virtue, not to hers. "Good care and management," I had thought, "is absolutely all that is required."

With surprise, rather than alarm or compassion predominant in my mind, I hurried to investigate. The fact that I had to draw the black-out curtains before I put on the light, and, in fumbling with them, knocked over a vase on the window-sill, rather spoilt the effect of utter calm and reassurance that I would have wished to produce.

Antonia, no longer crying but with the tears still wet on her cheeks, enquired with interest, how many pieces it had broken into.

I felt a little cross. Was there anything the matter with her or not? She was sitting up, I now saw, and looking a little flushed perhaps.

"What's the matter, Antonia?" I tried to speak calmly, kindly and yet with a certain healthy briskness. "What on earth was that funny noise about?"

Antonia, contriving suddenly to look pathetic, seemed uncertain of the answer to this question. Finally she remarked that she was too hot.

I decided to accept this explanation and close the incident as quickly as possible. I took a blanket off her bed, turned her pillow over for her, blew her nose, assured her cheerfully that now she would be lovely and comfortable again and be able to go straight off to sleep, kissed her and said good night.

"Mummy!" said Antonia, just as I was leading the room.

"What, darling?"

"You haven't pulled the curtains back again."

As a matter of fact I had deliberately forgotten to do this. I very much hoped Antonia would not disturb me again, but, lacking all precedent, for this sort of performance, I thought it prudent to prepare silently for the worst. However, since the last thing I wished to-do was to put any ideas of the sort into her head, I now obediently pulled back the curtains again and then said good night once more.

Antonia gave a satisfied little sigh and seemed to smuggle down quite happily. It was more than I did, when I got back to my own room. I suppose mothers who have, in their time, weathered a certain number of disturbed nights, learn to fall asleep again instantly after a little midnight excursion of the sort. I couldn't, although I think Antonia did. I lay awake for a solid hour, and there was no sound from her room. She did not call out again until I was once more heavily asleep. This second time was about three o'clock in the morning.

Our conversation this time was a little more staccato.

"Darling, what *is* the matter? You *can't* go on waking us all up like this." (Was I being too sharp with her?) "Have you got a pain anywhere, darling?" (Was this last too sympathetic?)

"Yes," said Antonia.

"Where?" Rapidly I tried to recall what she would have eaten that day. I had myself been at the office. Blakey had reported nothing untoward, but I now wished heartily that I had had more opportunity of observing Antonia myself the previous day. Perhaps this divided control was a mistake after all.

Antonia did not seem to be sure where the pain, to which she had so instantly assented, was. Again I wondered if she was merely playing an entertaining game with me.

"Does your tummy feel uncomfortable?" I suggested.

"Yes," said Antonia readily.

I had my doubts. However, I fetched a hot-water bottle, filled it at the hot tap and adjured her to go to sleep again cuddling it to her. Even as I did this, I thought it was probably a poor idea. The hot-water bottle would get cold or she would lie uncomfortably across it and get wakened up again. Still, I had at least had the illusion of doing *something*.

There were, however, no more disturbances that night. Obviously, had I been the calm competent, non-fussy mother I so passionately pretended to be, I need have lost no more than about twenty minutes sleep in all. I did, however, lose between three and four hours, and when Blakey brought me tea at half-past seven I felt as if I had hardly slept at all. I also felt that, at the very moment when she knocked on the door, I was just slipping out of uneasy dozing into really deep and refreshing slumber. With an effort I roused myself to ask Blakey if she had heard the disturbance in the night, and whether there had seemed anything in the least wrong with Antonia the previous day.

The great thing about Blakey is that she permits me to be Antonia's mother. (Trained Nannies 'in entire charge' cannot, I think, help feeling that the mother is merely an irrelevant nuisance.) Blakey is generous enough to think my remarks about Antonia rather more than the foolish prattlings of an untrained amateur, and consequently I talk to her frankly without silently joining battle in an attempt to keep my end up. I confided to her now my doubts about whether or to what extent Antonia had been 'playing up,' and Blakey did not insinuate once that it was a pity *she* hadn't dealt with the situation—*she* would have known.

Indeed she was at her nicest, with all her real qualities of humanity and warmth of heart uppermost. I felt once again she was 'one of the family,' and it was a very comforting sensation after all that had happened between us. Of course it made the thought of so shortly parting with her much worse, but, for the moment, I would not allow myself to think about that.

Blakey, on my instructions, peeped round Antonia's door to see if she was still asleep, and came back to report that she was. "And, if you don't mind me suggesting it, Miss Vicky, the best thing you can do is to go to sleep again yourself, and I'll bring you your breakfast on a tray later. Anyone can see you haven't had a good night yourself by the looks of you."

"No, I think I'll get up to breakfast as usual, and rest this afternoon, perhaps," I said.

Tired as I was, my tumbled bed repelled me. I had been too long wakeful in it already that night.

Antonia was still asleep when I went down to breakfast. Although I was by now fairly well persuaded that there was nothing much the matter with her, I decided as a matter of convenience to take her up breakfast in bed when I had finished my own, and let her get up immediately afterwards.

When I brought up her breakfast-tray she was awake and greeted me with a cheerful, "Hello, Mummy, is it half-past seven? Can I come and dress in your room?"

Probably, I thought, she had entirely forgotten she had woken me twice in the night. Well—so would I, and dismiss all thoughts of her being ill out of my mind at once. Obviously she was perfectly all right.

"No, it's much later than half-past seven! You were still asleep when I went down to breakfast, darling, so I've brought you yours up on a tray and you can have it in bed before getting up to-day."

"For a treat?" said Antonia brightly.

"Er—yes."

"Oh, how *lovely*!" said Antonia gleefully. "Shall I wear my dressing-gown and sit up with the pillow behind me like you do sometimes?"

I wanted to hug her and smack her simultaneously—hug her for being so thrilled about her 'treat,' smack her for fooling me that she was going to be ill.

"Here's your cornflakes, Antonia. Now for heaven's sake be careful and don't spill anything."

"What else am I having besides cornflakes? I know—BACON! I can smell it. Oo, good, bacon."

I had not the heart to tell her that I had meant her to breakfast invalidishly off cereal alone, and I now saw no necessity for suggesting to her that she was ill and had better do so. Bacon, it was true, *had* been cooked for Rene and me, and I was pretty certain there was still some left. I told her to eat up her cornflakes while I went and fetched it. I did so, cut it up, removed her empty cornflake bowl, handed her the bacon-plate and spoon, and proceeded to tidy up the room while she ate. In a way I rather enjoyed dancing attendance on the child like this, although in another way I resented the slight feeling that I had been made a fool of.

"Mummy—" said Antonia suddenly, in the middle of some trifling conversation.

"Yes, darling?"

"Need I finish my bacon?"

I looked at her, surprised. Bacon is one of Antonia's favourite foods and she had seemed particularly delighted at the novelty of eating it in bed. Was there something really the matter with her after all? Oh, how heartily sick I was of this seesawing to and fro! Couldn't I make up my mind once and for all?

"Darling, is your tummy still feeling funny or *what* is it? Now do tell me just what it is."

"It's not my tummy, Mummy. It's my ear. This ear. It's feeling funny and hurting again—like it did last night."

"But *darling*!" Full of amazement and compassion I knelt by the bed to put my arms encouragingly round her. "Why *ever* didn't you tell Mummy so last night? You never said a word about your ear."

"I didn't . . . I wasn't sure . . . I thought p'raps it *was* my tummy when you said so," was Antonia's rather uncertain answer.

I did not press her further. Children's behaviour is often inscrutable at the best of times, and I suddenly saw that Antonia was suffering from exactly the same difficulty in this business as I was—inexperience. If I, from lack of practice in illness, found it hard to make up my mind whether there *was* anything the matter with her or not, so precisely did Antonia. She knew no more than I did about how to behave on such occasions, was just as uncertain as I had been about whether she was being naughty or hot last night. We were a puzzled pair who had yet to work out between us the correct pattern of behaviour between sick child and ministering mother.

I peered anxiously down the small pink ear offered for inspection, and was alarmed to see a slight discharge, already apparently dried up. Horrid thoughts of bursting abscesses floated into my mind. I knew absolutely nothing about ears, and would have chosen a tummy upset for preference any time. Having been a bilious child myself in my youth, I knew all about *those*—including the fact that one nowadays calls it 'acidosis' and explains to one's friends that it is not greedy but clever children who are prone to such attacks.

I murmured non-committally but reassuringly at the ear, kissed the nape of Antonia's neck because it suddenly looked rather appealing and pathetic, and remarked brightly that I thought we'd get Dr. Lambert to come and have a look, and tell us how to stop the ear being so silly and naughty. Antonia should stay in bed until she came.

"Oh, but I thought you said I could get up as soon as I'd finished my breakfast, Mummy? I want to go and play in the sand-pit."

Really it was extraordinarily difficult to know how ill a child was feeling!

"But it will be much more fun to play when Dr. Lambert has stopped your ear hurting," I said reasonably.

"It's stopped hurting now," said Antonia instantly.

"Never mind. It had better have a little rest," I said firmly.

For some unknown reason the idea of her ear 'resting' appealed to Antonia as extraordinarily funny. She giggled all the time I was tidying her bed and taking her temperature. She was, I discovered after a good deal of peering, a fraction above normal. Anxious as I was about her, I felt almost relieved that my line of conduct was now clearly marked out—bed and the doctor. I was also heartily glad to think that I had not to go to the office again till Monday. By Monday, surely, she would be recovered? I had always Beard that children's powers of recuperation were marvellous.

All the way downstairs to the telephone I reassured myself, and then, while I was looking up the number I laughed at myself for finding so much reassurance necessary. Things *really* weren't serious enough to have to tell oneself they weren't so bad after all.

I could have wished that there did not exist this unfortunate coldness between Dr. Lambert and myself. As I took off the receiver I damned Rene once more for her share in that disastrous business—just as heartily and just as unfairly as ever.

* * * * *

There followed a time I prefer not to recall in detail. Antonia—although very far from being recovered by Monday—was not by any means dangerously ill. Some of the time she hardly seemed ill at all, but her ear obstinately refused entirely to clear up, her temperature continued to go up at nights, and she was, of course, confined to bed. It was, I learnt, what one nowadays calls an 'otitis media'—the modern version of the old-fashioned earache, and Dr. Lambert called every day, not, she assured me cheerily, because there was anything she could do, but because ears were "funny things" and must be watched because there was always the possibility of mastoid which was, she need hardly tell me, a "nasty thing." Dr. Lambert paid me the compliment of treating me as a sensible mother who would not panic. I did not—outwardly. But inwardly the word 'mastoid' gave me the jitters, and really I would much rather she had taken me a little less into her confidence. I had always supposed that mothers naturally worried over their children when they were ill, but I had never realized that I should find it practically impossible ever for a moment to think about anything else. I told myself feebly that if it had been anything but 'ears,' I should have been more sensible. I told myself that it was my good luck with Antonia hitherto, my sheer lack of practice, that caused me to worry so much. I told myself that I was suffering a good deal more than Antonia. All these things were, I think, true. But none of them helped much.

Sunday night was the worst. Antonia had hardly eaten anything all day, and her temperature rose to 104 degrees. I felt perfectly certain that she was in for mastoid, particularly when I discovered, to my horror, that she was quite deaf in the affected ear.

I decided, then and there, that wild horses would not drag me to the office the next day. It was not that I did not trust Blakey to do all for her that I could do, which was very little. It was just that I felt that I simply could not face being separated from her for close on twelve hours, and missing Dr. Lambert's promised visit at that. Blakey, to her credit, understood this perfectly, and took no sort of umbrage. She was, during all this time, the staunchest and loyalist of supporters. On Sunday night, at my request, she went and telephoned Mrs. Hitchcock at her house, to say I would not be at the office the next day.

I did not funk telephoning Mrs. Hitchcock myself. I was really past all that. It was merely that I was busy making Antonia's bed for the night and wanted to act instantly on my decision. Blakey came back after a few minutes to say Mrs. Hitchcock wanted to know if I could come on Tuesday instead.

"Tell her I'll let her know later," I said impatiently. "Oh no—wait a minute. No, Tuesday I definitely can't. Say I'll certainly be in on Wednesday."

On Wednesday I certainly must be. It was the day of my lunch with Dorothy Harper. Tuesday was the day the widow was coming to see me and Antonia. It was hardly a propitious moment to have chosen, I thought distractedly, but I did not dare put her off now. I might lose her altogether if I did, and to feel I ought to start advertising and casting about again at this precise moment would be the last straw, I thought.

Blakey retired with this curt message, and I finished reading a footling story about rabbits to Antonia, as I had promised. Even with a temperature of 104 degrees she appeared to take her usual interest in literature.

She was, poor darling, touchingly 'good' all this time. A sick child is, of course, a spiritless child, and dealing with her was pathetically easy. Later I was to find that a convalescent child is a peevish child, a very different matter altogether.

"That Mrs. Hitchcock seems to think she's somebody, doesn't she?" remarked Blakey when I came downstairs.

"Oh well, she *is*, after all," I said vaguely, and then, suddenly seeing the point of Blakey's comment, "Why? Was she annoyed about me not coming in on Monday?"

"She seemed to think she had a right to know just *why* you couldn't," said Blakey with a touch of indignation.

"Oh well, Blakey, she has. She's my employer, after all."

Blakey sniffed. I am in her eyes above all things 'a lady.' It is slightly *infra dig.* for me to be at the same time someone else's employee.

"I hope you told her the reason, Blakey?"

"Oh yes, I told her. Now don't you worry about that office of yours, Miss Vicky. If that Mrs. Hitchcock can't carry on for a day or two without you, what's she there for?"

I smiled at this slightly twisted logic. Nevertheless there was something very comforting about Blakey. I liked the look of her white apron, of her not very prepossessing but utterly familiar face, of her gnarled working-woman's hands. Above all, I liked the feeling that she was staunchly 'on my side,' willing to identify her life with mine in a way that domestic servants (very rightly, no doubt) never do nowadays. I would miss her terribly. I did not doubt but that she would miss me either.

"Blakey, you remember, this woman's coming on Tuesday? I'm sorry Antonia's in bed, but you'll help me all you can to show her everything, won't you?"

"Oh yes, Miss Vicky. I only hope she's a decent body."

A decent body! From what I could judge of her letters, Mrs. Dabchick (for such was her peculiar name) was not setting up to be anything quite so satisfactorily humble as *that*.

* * * * *

Sunday night was, as I have said, the worst. On Monday morning Antonia's ear was discharging again, and after that it mercifully began to clear up. On Monday night her temperature was normal, and on Tuesday morning she was hungry for her breakfast. Dr. Lambert, who called early on Tuesday, seemed to think convalescence would now be rapid and straightforward.

I was, of course, enormously relieved, and more than a little cross with myself for having endured such unnecessary agonies. I also was suddenly aware of feeling extremely tired.

Antonia, on the other hand, suddenly got bored with bed and bored with being good. Peevishness was now obviously going to be her line until she was allowed to get up again. Once again I felt slightly at a loss to know at what point one resumed normal disciplinary action.

The situation was complicated by the fact that, although I had prepared her for "someone coming to see her" on the Tuesday, I had not explained who this person was, or might be. She did not yet know Blakey was going. I had thought it preferable not to tell her until the date was settled. I passionately wanted Antonia to be at her best before Mrs. Dabchick, but could see no way of stage-managing the interview to ensure this. It would have been so much simpler had Antonia been about, coming and going, in the normal way.

Mrs. Dabchick arrived while Antonia was having her mid-morning rest. Her appearance I can only describe as, like her letters, a trifle on the gushing side. Scarves were wreathed round her neck, a swagger coat floated in folds behind her, trimmings bobbed on her hat. A spate of conversation poured from her lips, interspersed with high-pitched laughter. She certainly bore no resemblance to the grim-faced Gorgon I was anxious to avoid at all costs for Antonia, but even less resemblance possibly to Blakey's 'decent body.'

I was prepared to be very 'friendly' to her and explain frankly my circumstances. For a long time I did not have a chance. She was exquisitely friendly to me instead, and told *me* all about herself.

She was, I was given to understand, a lady, a lady financially badly placed, but oh! so brave and sensible about it all. All her friends said to her, my dear, they said, you *can't* go out and work in somebody else's house, but what did she answer? She just answered that of *course* she could, why ever not? For years she had done everything—yes, *everything*—in her own house so, why not in someone else's, she would like to know?

She paused expectantly, as if awaiting a flood of protestation from me, but really I hardly thought it was my place to join the ranks of her friends, indignant on her behalf. I merely nodded and asked if she had not then worked as a Nanny before her marriage, as I had been given to understand?

Mrs. Dabchick laughed a little shamefacedly and said coyly that she would let me into a little secret. This post had sounded so much the sort of thing she was looking for—being a sort of second Mummy to a little girl whose own Mummy couldn't be much at home—that perhaps she had *pretended* a little bit in order to get at least an interview. She hadn't *actually* been a real Nanny ever—when her father was alive he wouldn't have *heard* of such a thing—but she had always been crazy about children and had often and often looked after her little nephews and nieces when they were tiny. It was the greatest grief to her that, when she was married, she never had any little ones of her own. Now *please* I mustn't be cross with her for this tiny deception, which she had meant to explain frankly to me the moment she saw me. It was just that she had liked the sound of my letters to her so much that she felt that this—yes this! (flinging an arm expansively out)—was *just* the place for her.

I did not, by any means, share her conviction. However, I said cautiously that Antonia was nearly five and hardly needed a trained Nanny now in any case.

"And that darling baby I caught a glimpse of as I came in, peeping at me out of his pram? That's your sister-in-law's little boy, you mentioned in your letter, is it?"

"Yes, that's Philip."

"*What* a pet!"

"Yes. Er—you do understand, Mrs. Dabchick, don't you, that you wouldn't be in charge of him? Mrs. Sylvester looks after him."

"Oh, of *course* I understand! You put it all so plainly—*and* so nicely!—in your letter. *He's* got his Mummy all the time, so of course I shouldn't dream of interfering. You won't think I'm blowing my own trumpet, will you, Mrs. Heron, if I say I've always been considered rather a tactful person? I absolutely understand that it's *your* little girl who's my business."

"And the cooking," I said, a little baldly. This picture of a more or less motherless and forlorn Antonia annoyed me. "I'm only at the office three days a week, Mrs. Dabchick, although of course I work at home the other days. I like to take over Antonia quite a bit when I'm home. Blakey and I always worked it out between us quite well—although I must admit Blakey was marvellous in doing all the cooking and housework. I wouldn't expect—anybody else—to do quite so much." (As a matter of fact, I had. But a sudden vision of Mrs. Dabchick scrubbing the floor, scarves, hat and all, upset me with its obvious incongruity.) "I'm quite prepared to get a charwoman. There is, after all, more to do now Mrs. Sylvester's living with me—although I know Mrs. Sylvester wants to help now too . . ." I stopped. I seemed to be making the whole situation out more of a muddle than it really was. "I'm afraid we're a rather peculiarly constituted household," I finished up with an apologetic smile.

"But that's what's so delightful!" exclaimed Mrs, Dabchick gaily. "That's *just* what attracted me when I read your letter! Like you, I hate formality and conventionality. Let's all share the work together in a friendly way, that's what I say!"

With such smiles and enthusiasm did the woman speak, that I was almost hypnotized into agreement. I had, quite sternly, to dismiss from my mind this pretty picture of us all picking up pails and mops and dancing and singing about the room—to remind myself brutally that, on the contrary, I *did* like a certain modicum of formality and conventionality, and that, even more brutally, I was proposing to pay Mrs. Dabchick to *do* the work, not to share it.

"Would you like to see Antonia now?" I said, thinking it better on the whole to change the subject for the present. "I'm awfully sorry she has to be in bed to-day, as I explained just now."

"Poor little mite! Is she a wee bit delicate perhaps?"

"Not a scrap. She's never been ill before in her life," I retorted, a little squashingly perhaps, but the woman couldn't have it all her own way. "Come up with me, won't you?" Antonia had had a really good night, and had not now, I felt sure, gone to sleep. It was time to rouse her for lunch and I thought it a good moment to introduce them. Antonia was always pleased to be told she could stop resting.

As we went up the stairs together I heard a slight scuffle from behind Antonia's door. When I went in she was in bed, but I could not help noticing that a teddy-bear, which I remembered lying unclothed on the floor when I left her, was now wearing trousers and sitting on the windowsill.

This was, of course, definitely Naughty, by any nursery code, and at any other time I should have been severe about it. It was only Mrs. Dabchick's presence that made me decide quickly to be unobservant and not notice.

"Well, darling!" exclaimed Mrs. Dabchick. "Do you know, I believe you and I are going to be great friends!"

"Why?" said Antonia, not unreasonably, I thought.

I had warned Mrs. Dabchick that Antonia did not know that Blakey was going. It was a silly opening in the circumstances. I waited with some amusement to see what the woman would find to say next.

As a matter of fact, she did not behave nearly as foolishly as I had expected. She turned the conversation instantly to Antonia's toys, many of which were piled rather untidily about the room, and Antonia responded rather well. Half-pleased, half-annoyed (for downstairs I had practically made up my mind that she was hopeless and that I didn't care anyway how the two got on together), I faded into the background. When Mrs. Dabchick picked up Teddy and admired his trousers, Antonia sent a slanting mischievous glance in my direction, which I pretended not to see. The ringing of the luncheon-gong disturbed quite a merry little chat, between them.

"*What* a darling!" said Mrs. Dabchick, as we went downstairs.

I could not help my heart warming to her slightly.

"She liked you," I said generously. (I always feel I am conferring a medal on someone when I say this.)

"She liked my scarves and my hat, didn't she?" said Mrs. Dabchick happily. "Children always like pretty gay things, don't they?"

I agreed. The fact that I personally found Mrs. Dabchick's clothes both foolish and unsuitable probably merely convicted me of snobbishness.

We went in to lunch. The spate of conversation continued—with this difference: that Rene was now present, and made a much more sympathetic and nicer listener than myself. Indeed, Rene and Mrs. Dabchick got on so well together that, over the pudding, they practically had a nice cry together about Mrs. Dabchick's unborn children. She had hoped and *hoped*, she told us—and *once* it really had seemed as if her dreams were going to come true after all . . . but alas! no.

"Oh, I am so sorry," cried Rene impulsively, her eyes big with sympathy. "*What* hard luck on you when you love children so!"

Mrs. Dabchick registered gallant resignation.

"Ah well! These things just happen to some unlucky people. Please don't think I grudge anybody else their children, even the tiniest bit. If I can be of some help to someone else who *has* been luckier than myself, that's all I ask now."

I really thought Rene was going to forget herself and impulsively promise Mrs. Dabchick a home here immediately. Hastily I suggested we should have coffee in the sitting-room. We moved and resettled ourselves. The flow of conversation poured on. I sat a little apart, feeling aloof and beastly.

I could not help deeply distrusting this damned up vicarious motherhood. I felt Mrs. Dabchick would be only too ready to let it sweep over Antonia like a torrent, and I had an uneasy feeling that Antonia might possibly respond rather too well and get mentally softened and cosseted just when it was important for her to become more independent. Also, quite apart from this question, I wanted someone who really was a capable cook. I would have preferred a little less about the unborn children, and a little more interest in what the kitchen and scullery were like.

As against this, it was not, I knew, going to be at all easy to find the utterly reliable sort of person I wanted. A very young girl was out of the question. An elderly trained Nanny would not be likely to want such a post. Mrs. Dabchick was, for all her foolishness, a vicar's daughter. In some ways, at least, she would never let me down. That counted for *something* in these difficult days.

I hate indecision. It worries me in other people, but infuriates me in myself. In the end I excused myself for an hour before tea, on the plea of work, and put the whole question firmly out of my mind.

I was, indeed, horribly behind with my office stuff.

* * * * *

"Well?" said Rene enthusiastically as the door finally closed on the last chatterings and flutterings.

"I don't know, Rene. I simply don't know. You liked her, didn't you?"

"Oh yes, I thought she was *awfully* nice. So friendly and sweet."

"Friendly, certainly. Do you think she could really manage the cooking, Rene?"

"Oh, surely between her and me we could, Vicky. That was what I really liked so much about her. She'd be such a nice person to work with, don't you think?"

"Personally I should want her to quieten down quite a bit first. All that talking would drive me crazy. However, that's possibly more your look-out than mine, as you'd see more of her."

"I think she's been lonely and just hasn't had anyone to talk to for a long time. I felt so sorry for her. She told me all about her husband's death after you'd gone, you know."

"I'm sure she did. That's just it."

"What do you mean, Vicky?"

"Well . . . Rene, don't think me utterly cold-blooded and awful if I say it's just that sort of thing that puts me off. *I'm* sorry for her too. I think all that about longing to come here so much and how she was going to be on tenterhooks until she heard from me was quite sincere."

"I thought it was awfully nice and genuine too."

"Yes—only *unsuitable*, Rene! That's what I mean. Her whole manner was unsuitable. Now don't misunderstand me—I don't mean in the least that I wanted her to fold her hands and call me Madam. I only mean that when one's applying for a job one *shouldn't* talk about one's dead husband and one's unborn children. It's off the point. It's an unfair appeal for sympathy. I shouldn't dream of going on like that myself if I wanted a job."

"Not for an office job, of course, Vicky, I see that. But domestic work is rather different, surely?"

"Yes, it is more personal. But even so—!"

"I think she wants a home more than a job," suggested Rene sentimentally.

"Oh—you're a pair, you and her!" I said, laughing, but nevertheless a little annoyed that Rene could not apparently see what I was driving at. "I shall have to express myself more brutally, I see. Look here. It's for *me* to say what I'm offering her, not her—

and, in point of fact, I'm offering wages for a job, *not* a home for someone I'm sorry for."

"It is your house, Vicky. I quite see that, and that you must do as you like," said Rene in a small voice.

Well, it was better that Rene should say it was my house than that I should. Nevertheless, I had driven her to it, and now felt slightly ashamed.

"Oh well," I said hastily, "the question of whom we get does affect you too, of course—in some ways more than me. I certainly want to hear your views, Rene. You'd really like this woman, would you? I can't see her sitting in the kitchen somehow. I think we'd have to have meals with her and that sort of thing."

"But that's just what I should *like*, Vicky!" said Rene, cheering, up again instantly. "That's to say, if you wouldn't mind."

"Oh well, I'm out such a lot or working in my room . . ."

"Yes, that's just it. I mean—" (Rene looked confused for a minute but plunged bravely on), "I mean sometimes—although it's absolutely nobody's fault—I *do* get a little bit lonely. Mrs. Dabchick would be company for me the days you're out."

Poor Rene! I had a sudden vision of her moping about the house in solitude, Blakey sour and inscrutable in the kitchen, nothing to look forward to but my own arrival back in the evening and my prompt retirement to my own room. It wasn't much of a life for her, and if Mrs. Dabchick could brighten it, would not that be really to my own advantage?

"Well, I'm glad to know what you feel about it, Rene," I said sincerely. "I'm not going to commit myself one way or the other for a day or two, but I promise you I'll seriously consider at least trying her."

"There's no harm in *trying*, is there?" said Rene happily.

Perhaps there wasn't. Nevertheless, as I went up the stairs to my own room I had a nasty recrudescence of the feeling that it was, after *all*, my house, and would I ever feel it was with Rene and Mrs. Dabchick prattling cheerily to each other all over the place?

Chapter 12

THE FACT THAT Dr. Lambert had, at least on her first visit to Antonia, showed by her manner to me that she considered that there *was*, a certain coolness between us on account of the 'two doctors' episode, had contributed slightly but perceptibly to my general wretchedness at the time. When I saw her on Tuesday morning she had suggested that I should ring her up on Tuesday night to let her know if I wanted her to pay Antonia a visit on Wednesday or not. She thought it would probably be unnecessary, but she would be quite willing to come if I wanted her.

By Tuesday evening it was plain to me that the bit in my little book about the wonderful recuperative powers of a child was coming true all right, and I went down to the telephone to tell Dr. Lambert she certainly need not bother. I hoped, as I took off the receiver, that we might possibly have a cheery little chat together which would finally restore us to our previous very friendly relations.

I reported progress, and even tentatively suggested that Antonia might possibly be allowed to get up for an hour or two on Wednesday afternoon. Her temperature had been normal since Monday evening.

"No, no," said Dr. Lambert, still, I was sorry to note, a trifle brusque, "I'll come again on Thursday and let you know what I think then."

"Of course, just as you say," I answered meekly. "It's just that she seems to be *so* bored with bed and—"

"It won't do her any harm to be bored for a bit," retorted Dr. Lambert. "That was a sharp attack, you know, and you'll have to go on being careful for a bit."

Absurdly enough, I felt like bursting into tears. To treat *me* as if I was a casual fool! *Me!* Had *she* gone through the agonies, or had *I*?

"Oh, I know," I said hastily, "I've been wondering whether there was anything I could get her that would help to pull her up again a bit now? Children have cod-liver oil and oranges anyway, these days, don't they? I can't quite think what I mean, but perhaps you could?"

What a fool I sounded, I thought! The trouble was, I was so desperately tired!

"A holiday—not immediately, but in a week or two's time—wouldn't do her any harm," suggested Dr. Lambert. "Harminster's rather a relaxing spot, you know. A change does everyone good from time to time."

"Do you mean take Antonia to the sea?" I said, a little blankly, thoughts of barbed wire, blown-up piers and landmines rapidly ousting my primary immediate mental pictures of sand-castles and pierrot shows and shrimp-teas on the beach.

"Not necessarily the seaside. That's not too easy these days, is it? Good country air—somewhere bracing, preferably—would do just as well. Just a little change from this Thames Valley mugginess you know."

"Would the region of Ashdown Forest in Sussex be suitable? It's lovely country and quite high up, I believe."

"Yes, I should think that would be excellent. Do you know of somewhere you could go there?"

"Yes. Some friends of mine keep a hotel there, and there's a bungalow in the ground they let out as part of the hotel, with sendee. If I could get it that's so much more suitable for a child than just being in a hotel full of grown-ups. Not that Antonia isn't quite sensible now and all that, but . . ." I stopped. I suddenly had the strongest impression that Dr. Lambert was not profoundly interested in all this—and indeed, why should she be? "Well, anyway, I mustn't keep you," I finished quickly. "Could you just tell me when you think it would be best to take Antonia away?"

"Oh, in about a fortnight to three weeks, if all goes well, as it certainly should now."

"I see. The beginning of June, in fact. I'll see what I can do about it. I'll have to arrange with the office to let me have my summer holiday early this year. Thank you so much. Good-bye, Doctor Lambert."

"Good-bye."

No. Things were certainly not quite as they had been between us. A trifle frigid, still. Obscurely, I felt that it was all the more important that I should do what she suggested about Antonia. I had, after all, no other plans about a summer holiday. In a way I rather welcomed this decision being forced on me.

It would do Antonia good. It would give me a rest from Rene. It would refresh us all and give us a breathing-space. Really, it was an excellent idea.

On impulse I took up the telephone receiver again, dialled O, and asked for the number of the hotel in question.

It is really wonderful how circumstances sometimes respond to a fit of decision. There was no delay on the line. I was able to speak to my friend personally. She and her husband both thought it was an excellent idea that I and Antonia should pay them a visit. Yes, by very good luck, the bungalow was free from the 5th of June to the 15th—a booking had just fallen through. The hotel was very full, there were so many officers' wives in the district, so it was extremely fortunate I had rung up just at this moment. Otherwise I might not have got a room, even in the main building. Yes, certainly, the bungalow was ideal for children. They had had so many families staying there that they had made a paddling-pool and a sand-pit in the bungalow's garden, and perhaps Antonia would invite any other children who happened to be staying in the hotel to come and play with her in it?

I think it was this final touch that enchanted me more than any other. I saw myself charmingly welcoming the children, and then retiring to read in luxurious peace while they all played happily together in the garden. They would, without exception, all be very nice children of just the right age. Antonia would love their company, their parents would be very grateful to me, and nobody would be able to help noticing that Antonia was prettier and had nicer legs than most of them. I dwelt on this idyllic picture so long that, by the time I went up to bed, I was firmly convinced that it would be unthinkable to go to any other place at any other time. If I imagined anywhere else at all I imagined instantly over-furnished rooms, red plush, antimacassars and (to get away from such horrors) long walks in the pouring rain with a fretful Antonia dragging at my heels. Could there really be any choice?

I had told my friends—Margaret and Harry Smith by name—that I would let them know for certain the following evening. They promised to hold the bungalow for me until then.

* * * * *

The worst of hating indecision is that one tends to rush things. Had I really considered the matter instead of letting my imagination take fire in this dangerous way, I would have seen that Wednesday morning was hardly the most propitious time to tackle Mrs. Hitchcock for an instant decision about my summer holiday. I would have realized that I had not been to the office since Friday, and that to Mrs. Hitchcock sick children were a nuisance and absolutely nothing else. I would have realized that all remarks about the doctor recommending a holiday in the country had much better be omitted, and the request formulated purely as a matter of ordinary fixing-up of staff holidays. I would have realized that Blakey had done me no good by telling Mrs. Hitchcock over the telephone that I could not come in on Tuesday because it was essential I should interview a new Nanny that day. I would have realized that I had always hitherto taken the greatest pains *not* to behave to Mrs. Hitchcock in a 'harassed housewife' kind of way, and that it was really a measure of my success that her attitude was clearly now that I was 'letting her down' and she had never expected it of *me*.

I saw my mistake quite quickly, and tried to defend myself. Of course I made things rather worse.

"I suppose it will be all right for you to take your holiday then instead of later," said Mrs. Hitchcock grudgingly, as I finished my unwisely frank and full explanations. "I hadn't really got round to arranging holidays yet, but still—all right. As long as that's the end of it."

I would have done much better at this point to thank Mrs. Hitchcock and retire. Instead, like a fool, I took her up. I suppose I was in a rather nervy state.

"The end of *what*?" I said, on the defensive at once.

"The end of all these requests."

I stood silent a moment. What a *beastly* woman she could be!

"I don't think there have been *many* requests," I said stiffly. "I've had *one* day off and one only because of Antonia."

"*And* one when your sister-in-law was ill," retorted Mrs. Hitchcock. "*And* you wouldn't come in on Tuesday instead of Monday because you had to interview a Nanny or some such thing."

Obviously, to Mrs. Hitchcock, interviewing Nannies, was an almost flippant pastime. I saw that it would be the greatest mistake to suggest to her that it was a serious matter. Quickly I changed my ground.

"I'm sorry about both those things. They were very unfortunate. I didn't realize you so particularly wanted me on Tuesday or I might have . . . I never *do* come on Tuesdays, after all, do I?"

"No. But I had no opportunity of explaining to you personally—since you didn't come to the 'phone yourself—*why* I wanted you."

"Why did you?"

"Dorothy Harper rang me up on Sunday evening and wanted to know if you could change your lunch together to Tuesday instead of to-day. If you hadn't rung me I was going to ring you about it."

"Oh. I'm sorry. *Is* she coming to-day or has it been cancelled?"

"No. She said she could manage to-day after all."

"Oh."

I did not honestly feel that there was any great grievance involved here. Dorothy Harper was the type of woman who *always* rang up at the last minute to try to rearrange things, as Mrs. Hitchcock very well knew. Mrs. Hitchcock had often been quite firm with her in the past and held her forcibly to her word.

"Well, as I say, I'm sorry," I said. "But as she *can* come to-day after all, perhaps there's no great harm done."

It was a silly thing to say. Too airy. I could see it irritated Mrs. Hitchcock afresh.

"As it happens there *is* no great harm done," she admitted. "But all the same, I should like your assurance, Vicky, that this sort of thing isn't going to keep on happening."

It was at this point that I realized that Mrs. Hitchcock really was rather a cruel woman. Tiresome as it was for her that I had been absent once or twice, it was very hard on me, in the circumstances, to take up this attitude. Antonia's illness had shaken me considerably, and I was, naturally, still a little worried about her. I did not expect or want Mrs. Hitchcock to sympathize with me over this. I merely thought she might have refrained from badgering me about the future. It was cruel, yes, it *was* cruel.

"Mrs. Hitchcock!" I burst out. "*Honestly*, I think you're being rather unfair. I'm extremely sorry I've been absent twice, but which of us in the office isn't ill occasionally without all this fuss? Miss Spenser had 'flu for a week and I did most of her work, and nobody thought of being nasty to Miss Spenser when she came back."

"If you're ill yourself, that can't be helped. It's this staying away on other people's account that I dislike, Vicky. Where is it ever to end?"

"If you're asking me for a promise that I'll *never* stay away again on Antonia's account, Mrs. Hitchcock, I just can't give it," I burst out recklessly. "All I can say is it's happened extraordinarily little so far—*never* before this time I think—and I don't see why it should happen any more in the future. I'm sorry now that I told you the truth. It would have been much better to have said I was ill myself. As for this question of my summer holiday, *don't* give it to me in June if it makes you so angry that it's on Antonia's account."

"Don't be ridiculous, Vicky," said Mrs. Hitchcock sharply. "I've told you you *can* take your holiday then. That's settled. As a matter of fact you look as if you could do with a holiday yourself. *You'll* be the one to be ill next."

Perhaps this was meant kindly. It was not, however, reassuring. Mrs. Hitchcock was almost hypnotizing me into thinking myself a crock surrounded by crocks. Of all the injustice!

"In all the years I've worked here," I said angrily, "I think I've been away less than anybody else in the office. Just think—haven't I?"

She would not even admit this, perfectly true as it was.

"For goodness sake drop the subject, Vicky, and let's get on with the work now you *are* here again!"

Beast!

I went angrily back to my room. I had got my way about my holiday, but at *what* a cost! The lovely vision of the children and the sand-pit was all spoilt for me, and, moreover, I had now to cope with Dorothy Harper with my self-confidence well drained away in advance.

* * * * *

Mrs. Hitchcock had even shaken me about my appearance. I peered into the murky, spotted little office mirror, and decided I undoubtedly looked a battered hag.

I was not late at our rendezvous, a quite expensive and fashionable restaurant, but Dorothy Harper was. I had a bit of trouble with a waiter insisting that our reserved table should remain reserved; I think I should have lost it had not an old friend of mine, John Martindale, drifted up and greeted me at the crucial moment.

John Martindale is now a very well-known actor and well established in the hearts of the great British public. I have known him ever since we were children together—his father was a friend of my father and we lived in the same London square once—and, although never knowing him really intimately, I have never altogether lost sight of him, and we naturally call each other by our Christian names. The waiter's manner to me altered very perceptibly after John drifted up. He recognized him, of course—his profile is extremely well known—and, when he heard him calling me 'Vicky,' was immediately all deference and servility again, and not a word more was said about tables only being kept reserved if customers claimed them promptly. I loathed the waiter for this change of front, but was nevertheless grateful to John for his unconscious championship.

John went off to join his own party at the other end of the restaurant, and Dorothy Harper finally arrived, vaguely apologetic in a way that was obviously intended to be very charming and gracious. Of course, I let her think that I was completely won over by this exhibition.

"You business women frighten me sometimes!" declared Dorothy Harper, playfully. "You are so *very* business like, aren't you? Now don't be offended, dear—I didn't mean you particularly and, as a matter of fact, I *love* your hat, where *did* you get it—I meant Mrs. Hitchcock, for instance. I quite shook in my shoes when she told me I'd *got* to lunch to-day and no other day!" She laughed merrily, and then patted my arm confidentially. "Tell me! Doesn't she frighten *you* sometimes?"

I laughed warily. Even for the sake of getting on well with Dorothy Harper, I was not going to demean myself by discussing my employer with her—all the more because the previous events of that morning *had* made me feel rather like the office-girl with a grievance.

"Business-women wouldn't be much good unless they *were* business-like, would they?" I said, playing for safety.

"Yes, that's very true," agreed Dorothy with as much intensity as if I had just given vent to a profound and novel thought. "Of course, in the case of the artist . . . I don't know that they should even *try* to be business-like. It might—stultify something in them, don't you think?"

I laughed silently. What a good opening for what I had to say to her! Not that I would follow it up immediately—that would be clumsy. It was as well, however, to know that Dorothy was in her 'artist' mood to-day. It was a very easy one to play up to. I flattered myself that I could do it on my head—*and* without letting her have the faintest suspicion that I knew it was utterly bogus in every way. Dorothy Harper was no victim, willing or unwilling, of the 'artistic temperament.' Swelled head was all she suffered from, nothing more artistic than that—swelled head and a snobbish desire to appear aristocratically superior to all those middle-class virtues—sticking-power, business instinct, and so on—which actually she indubitably possessed.

I followed up Dorothy's lead and we talked about 'artists' and 'creators' with splendid sentimentalism and woolliness. The war, we agreed, was perhaps harder on such people than on anyone else. I did wonder a little bit whether Dorothy considered herself an artist by virtue of her competent magazine stories, but I was not so gauche as to ask, and presently she let drop a rather deprecating reference to her 'pot-boilers' and followed it up by a confidence. She was, she said, writing a play into which she was putting "all of herself—not just a little bit."

"How interesting," I said. "I'm so glad. I hope you'll let us see it when it's finished. We *have* got a play department, you know." (It was past two o'clock. We must get down to brass tacks *some* time.)

"Oh, it's not nearly finished yet," said Dorothy, instantly becoming vaguer.

"No? . . . By the way, while we *are* on the subject of your work, we had a little bit of bother about one of your short stories—*Mermaids in Bloomsbury* was the name."

"Oh? Let me see . . . Oh yes, *I* remember the one."

I felt quite sure that she remembered it very well.

I proceeded cautiously. "It's not a very great matter, Miss Harper, but it's just that naturally it's our job to be careful that that sort of muddle doesn't occur. I'll tell you what happened." I told her briefly about the letter from the editor. I made fairly light of it, and ended up, "So you see, I've been rather held up with your short stories since in consequence. I haven't liked to send any out just in case one or two of the others have been seen by someone already." I paused, wondering for a moment whether to make any point about how unfair it was on us to behave like that, and then decided not. She knew now that we might quite possibly find out if she tried the trick on again, and that was the main thing.

"Oh, my dear!" cried Dorothy gaily. "Have I committed a terrible crime? I'm so sorry—all your funny little rules quite perplex me. *What* was that frightful argument about 'split commissions' I heard a bit of one day in your office?"

It was a good red-herring, but I wasn't to be drawn.

"It's our job to handle your work so that you shan't be bothered with all that sort of thing," I said persuasively. "Only I'm sure you see we can't do it unless—well, unless we *know* what's happening."

"I'm so sorry, dear. Did I get you into trouble with Mrs. Hitchcock? What a shame! Don't bother any more about that silly little story. Just tear it up."

"Oh no! Please! That would be a great pity. It's a very good story. We can very probably sell it—if you'll just let me know . . ."

"Really, my dear, it's not worth bothering about! Just one of my little pot-boilers that I toss off and then forget all about! I'm afraid I take even less interest in their fate than I used to do since I started on my play."

Damn the woman. It was like arguing with a butterfly! I would not have minded so much if she had really been as foolish as she made out.

"Ah, but *we* take an interest in their fate," I countered. "A very great interest. Could you tell me if *Mermaids in Bloomsbury* has been already seen by anyone else? And the other stories we have on hand too, of course. I have a list here as a matter of fact—"

"Isn't that John Martindale at that table over there?"

"Yes," I said briefly.

"Are you *sure*?" (The butterfly seemed suddenly to have developed a power of concentration.)

"Yes, quite sure. I know him, as a matter of fact. I was talking to him before you arrived."

"Do you *really*?" I saw her give me a quick all-over sort of look. I knew exactly what it meant—'How on earth does this girl out of an office come to know John Martindale? Perhaps there's more in her than I thought.'

"Yes. Not very intimately now. We used to meet in the Park as children," I said, kindly relieving her unspoken curiosity.

"I wonder if you'd introduce me?"

She tried to say it lightly, but the effect was rather that of a command. I felt considerably taken aback. If there's one thing I hate it's presuming on a chance acquaintanceship with someone well-known.

"You see, I'm on a committee that's getting up a dance and cabaret in aid of the bombed-out Londoners," explained Dorothy. "Those poor East-Enders, you know. And it would be such a feather in our caps if we could get John Martindale to come. Funnily enough, we were just wondering how to approach him—the personal approach is *so* much better, don't you think? Oddly enough, none of us happens to know him—not even old Lady Mansbridge who knows *everyone*. Now you understand why this sudden request! It's not for *myself*, of course."

Except that it will be a feather in *your* cap if you're the one to get him, I thought. Aloud I said, to gain time: "But he's not a cabaret artist."

"Of *course* not!" She gave a patronizingly indulgent little laugh. "When I say a 'cabaret,' I don't mean quite the usual thing. I mean something rather better ... more *suitable* for what the ball's in aid of. We'd like John Martindale to do a speech from Shakespeare, perhaps, or something of the sort."

"Oh, of course—how stupid of me! I was getting muddled and thinking for a minute that the bombed-out East-Enders would be coming to the ball themselves and might prefer George Robey," I said naughtily.

Dorothy Harper flung me another quick look. I could see that, once again, she didn't know quite where she was with me.

"It could all be managed quite naturally if we happened to go out of the door together," said Dorothy persuasively. "Look—he's calling for his bill. We'd better get ours. Waiter!"

Well, really, I thought. The woman's my guest and for sheer bad manners ... ! What am I to do now?

"Wouldn't it be better if I gave you a note of introduction and you wrote to him?" I said. "After all, he's with a party ... It's a little—"

"Oh, nonsense, my dear! It's the easiest thing in the world. Just do it casually, you know ..."

At this point the waiter tried to hand our bill to Dorothy, and I think it was only the interruption that stopped her from telling me in a kindly, 'hints-to-girls' way *how* to introduce someone to someone else.

I really felt furious. The most maddening thing of all was that I had by no means yet said all I wanted to say to her. I should have liked to have given her, there and then, a strongly-expressed lecture upon how and how *not* to behave both professionally and socially. She badly needed it.

"Quick! They're getting up!" hissed Dorothy. "Just leave the money on the table, and you go out first and I'll follow."

I should have liked to have sat tight and called, "Hi! Miss?" to punish her. Instead I found myself bluffed into rising with her.

She had not managed badly, I will say that for her. We *did* meet in the doorway. John had four or five people with him, all talking. He smiled at me (we had already had our little chat and exchanged such minor news about ourselves as we always did), and stood aside to let me pass out. I did, together with the other women of John's party. Dorothy Harper, I supposed, was behind me.

She was. Close on my heels, as I found when we were all on the pavement. The other women closed in round John, jabbering again. Dorothy nudged my elbow.

I think it was this final unnecessary nudge that really put my back up. The last thing I wanted was to introduce her to John anyway, but at least if I *was* going to do it, I was going to do it in my own way.

A taxi, on the lookout for a customer, prowled by John waved to it and sprang in.

"*Must* fly!" he called cheerily. "Terribly late. Good-bye everyone."

He was gone.

The others melted away. I was left face to face with Dorothy! I had not, after all, made the slightest move to introduce her.

"I'm sorry," I said (but I do not think I sounded very sorry), "but, as you see, it wasn't a good moment. He was in a hurry."

"You, could easily have stopped for a minute in the doorway," retorted Dorothy, now anything but vague in manner.

"There were so many people about."

"I shouldn't have kept him a moment. Just a smile and word or two. You didn't imagine I was going to ask him there and then about the cabaret, did you? It was only just to—to make a contact that I could follow up afterwards."

I did not see the slightest reason why I should go on apologizing. I had had quite enough of being alternately patronized and bullied by her.

"Shall we go back and have some coffee now?" I said coldly. "We were discussing your work, weren't we, when we *got* interrupted?"

I thought that the phrase "got interrupted" was putting it generously. I hoped that, by coffee and perhaps a promise of a letter to John, I could retrieve the situation. I was an optimist.

"I don't believe you really know him at all!" cried Dorothy; venomously.

I looked at her, frankly surprised. I had always thought her a frightful poseur, and a social climber. I had not realized quite how easily the veneer would crack, nor that her voice could have that fish-wife note. It was now my turn to feel snobbish and aristocratic. I looked at her and thought, and enjoyed thinking, that she looked like a thoroughly ill-bred woman in a thoroughly nasty temper.

Perhaps she saw something of this in my face. In any case the checked herself slightly, glanced at her watch, exclaimed, "I'd *no* idea it was so late, no, I can't possibly stay a *moment* longer, I must fly," hailed a taxi, leaped into it and was gone in a flash.

I was left on the pavement, ruefully contemplating the vanishing taxi. I had been away from the office a good two hours, had spent a considerable sum of the firm's money on lunch, and had, in the end, accomplished absolutely nothing. Indeed, to say that matters stood exactly as they had done before was putting it perhaps a trifle optimistically.

* * * * *

"You didn't even manage to get out of her whether *Mermaids in Bloomsbury* and all her other stories *had* been seen by anyone else or not?" said Mrs. Hitchcock.

She had listened to my account with some sympathy. Mrs. Hitchcock, although a hard and unimaginative woman, was by no means, on her own ground, a stupid or brutal employer. In our opinions of Dorothy Harper we were at one, and she made no sort of pretence that she found her easy, herself, to deal with.

I shook my head disgustedly.

"No, I didn't. I *would* have got that out of her—I wasn't doing too badly at that time—if it hadn't been for this blasted John Martindale interruption."

Mrs. Hitchcock was silent, apparently wrapped in thought. For no real reason I felt nervous.

"Do you think that I ought to have introduced her to him at any cost?" I said, hopeful, perhaps, of a little reassurance.

"No. No, I really don't see why you should have. The office really can't be expected to help her with her blasted charity balls. The only thing is I don't quite see why you had to part so abruptly immediately after."

"Well—I've explained how she sort of bounced me out of the restaurant—"

"Yes, yes. I understand all that." (Mrs. Hitchcock sounded impatient. She is far too concise a person herself ever to want to hear anything twice over.) "But couldn't you have got her back to the subject of her work afterwards—asked her to walk back to the office with you or something? I did ask you to bring her back after, didn't I?"

"Did you?" I'm afraid I looked a little blank. "This morning?"

"No, no. When we first wrote the letter inviting her."

I remembered then. Mrs. Hitchcock *had*. Damn.

"Yes, I'm afraid I had forgotten that," I said. "But honestly, even if I had remembered it I don't think she'd have come. She suddenly discovered she was in a tearing hurry. I *did* suggest going back to have coffee."

"And what did she say?" said Mrs. Hitchcock.

"Actually she said, 'I don't believe you really know him at all.'"

"And what did you answer?"

"I didn't say anything, as a matter of fact. I think I just looked at her."

"Angrily?"

"No, not really angrily. Not at all angrily, really. Just rather taken aback, sort of surprised—interested almost. I suddenly sort of saw her for what she was."

It was a perfectly truthful answer. It was, perhaps, an unfortunate one.

"And it was after this look of yours that she discovered she was in a tearing hurry?" pursued Mrs. Hitchcock remorselessly! "I see."

I did not like the tone of that cold 'I see.'

"Anyway, I didn't lose my temper with her—not apparently, not for an instant," I said defensively.

I really was not alluding to the time when Mrs. Hitchcock had begun the whole business by more or less losing *her* temper with Dorothy Harper. But I am afraid Mrs. Hitchcock thought I was. She gave me a quick look and said, "Losing your temper with clients isn't the *only* thing that matters—some of them it does good to."

"Good Lord! You don't mean I ought to have flared out at her, do you?" I said, bewildered.

"No, no, of course I don't. I only meant—oh, surely you can see for yourself what I mean, Vicky."

"No, I can't. I honestly can't."

"Well then—with a touchy snob like Dorothy Harper, better anything than going all superior."

"Superior?"

"Yes. Superior. You told me yourself you looked at her and saw her for what she was. I imagined you *knew* that already, Anyway, you didn't take her out to lunch for that purpose."

"I think you're taking up my words and using them against me," I said, a little stiffly. "I only told you what I *thought*. I didn't say anything at all."

"Quite. You just looked at her," retorted Mrs. Hitchcock meaningly. "She won't forgive you very easily for putting her so thoroughly in the wrong."

There was a nasty silence. Indignant as I was at the accusation of 'going superior,' I could not help feeling that Mrs. Hitchcock had unerringly jumped on my one false move. Dorothy Harper was a slightly taller woman than myself, and yet, as I cast my mind back to visualize us standing together on the pavement after John's taxi had driven off, I saw myself mentally as towering momentarily over her. That was certainly a clue to my state of mind at the moment—and, if it had shown in my face or even by implication in the fact that I looked at her without speaking, it was no state of mind for Dorothy Harper to appreciate as from *me*. Just for a second or two I had 'forgotten myself'—by which I mean I had forgotten to keep the office foremost in my thoughts. Mrs. Hitchcock, in whose mind the office always came first, had scented this out instantly. The fact that she shared my opinion of Dorothy Harper's behaviour was irrelevant.

Our luncheon was doubly a failure. Dorothy had built up a fine façade of gracious airy patronage and then given herself away badly. I had first played up to her well and then by a single contemptuous look, allowed her to suspect that I was merely acting a part. No, certainly she would not forgive me readily.

I sighed.

"I'm sorry," I said drearily. "I've wasted time and money and done no good at all."

"Yes," agreed Mrs. Hitchcock coolly.

So reduced was I by this time that I was almost grateful to her for leaving it at that estimate.

I turned to go. As I reached the door, Mrs. Hitchcock spoke.

"You might let me have all the short stories of hers you've got on hand, will you, Vicky? I'd better look through them, and think what to do next."

"Yes." I swallowed. "I gather you don't want me to take any further action myself about her?"

"No, certainly not. Don't do anything at all."

She did not actually say: 'I can't trust you any more'; but that was what I felt her meaning was.

"I'll get them right away," I said in a small voice. That, at least, would get me out of the room.

It did, since Mrs. Hitchcock merely nodded.

I went and collected the short stories, every one of which struck me now as bearing a particularly nauseating title, and carried them drearily down to Mrs. Hitchcock's office.

I could not help being strongly reminded of a painful episode in my childhood, when an aunt had given me an embroidery set, from the contents of which I had with much preliminary glee and subsequent feverish exasperation tried to make a very small table-mat. Not only had the mat been an utter failure, even in my own prejudiced eyes, but kind but firm adults had removed the rather mangled remains of the set. I should have it again, they said, when I was older and cleverer and wouldn't spoil it all.

My sensations as I delivered up the box to authority on that occasion were extraordinarily similar to the feelings I now endured on handing the Dorothy Harper stories over to Mrs. Hitchcock—hurt pride, an outraged sense of possession, angry disappointment and, underneath, a faint substratum of relief.

Oddly enough, it was no help to reflect that I could now merely laugh over the embroidery episode and that undoubtedly in years, or even months to come, I would certainly be able to raise a smile over Dorothy Harper. At the moment I felt far too tired and battered even to raise the energy to *believe* in future laughter.

Chapter 13

"How's Antonia?" I enquired instantly of Blakey, as I entered my house that evening.

"Quite all right. No temperature again to-night, and is getting back her appetite nicely. She's a bit cross, on and off, but I suppose that's only to be expected. She's bored with bed, now she's so much better."

"Good," I said, relieved. In the train on the way home, I had had a recrudescence of worrying about Antonia, and would not have been altogether surprised to hear she was worse again. Now I could at least feel exhausted in peace.

I strolled into the sitting-room, thoughts of bath and supper in bed uppermost in my mind. Rene was in there and greeted me cheerily.

She was sitting knitting, looking young, untired, pretty. Not perhaps a bad person to come back to after a hard day's work, I thought, with a sudden softening of the heart towards her—due perhaps to the fact that I was thoroughly 'down' myself that evening. Rene was, at least, no shrew or bully. The atmosphere of the home which she would have made for Philip might have been a bit sickly for my taste but would never have been hard or comfortless. She would not have been a stimulating companion, but her very softness might have been a pleasant refuge.

In a burst of humility I suddenly conceded that Rene was probably far better fitted to be a wife and mother than myself.

Just so (only with more affection—warm kisses, and so on) would she have greeted Philip on his return home from the office. Just so would she have instantly prattled to him about little Philip and what the man at the grocer's had said to her. Just as I was doing now, would Philip have stood and smiled down at her, the burden of the day's work easing a little off his shoulders.

It was not a design-for-living that I or Raymond had ever tried for, or even wanted, but it was a very solid, old-established matrimonial pattern, to which perhaps the majority of men and women instinctively conformed. Possibly they were the lucky ones.

I did not go off instantly to my bath, as I had intended. I lingered, half-listening to Rene's prattle, half-musing about the various lines men and women chose, or felt unconsciously impelled, to work out their marriages along. Presently I became aware that Rene was waiting for the answer to a question.

"What? Oh yes—yes it *is* all right about my holiday," I said, suddenly realizing that I had heard her query with my ears, if not with my mind.

"Oh good! I'm *so* glad!" Rene looked genuinely, unselfishly pleased.

"Yes, I must ring up the hotel this evening and confirm it."

I was not, of course, going to confide to Rene that Mrs. Hitchcock's attitude had spoilt most of my pleasure in the whole plan.

"Vicky—"

"Yes?"

"Have you come to any decision about Mrs. Dabchick yet?"

I don't know if I scowled outwardly, but mentally I scowled. Yes, I thought, with a change of mood, yes, just so might Philip have scowled had Rene forced unwelcome matters upon him too shortly after his return home. Not, I admitted instantly, that the analogy was quite fair. Rene would not have needed to appeal to Philip for decisions about Mrs. Dabchick and her like—they would have been purely her concern. For a fleeting instant I grasped once again the difficulty of Rene's position in my household, and answered gently.

"No, I'm afraid I haven't, Rene. I just haven't had time to think about it to-day. I will to-morrow, I promise you."

And now, I thought, for my bath, quick!

Rene was quicker. Probably the gentleness of my tone had encouraged her.

"It's just that *I've* been thinking, Vicky, and—"

"Yes? I know *you* want her, Rene. I'll remember that."

"Yes, I know *you* know I do, and I wouldn't dream of trying to over-persuade you, Vicky, I wasn't meaning that at all. I wanted to say something else."

"Well?" (Get on, can't you. Don't fuss about 'overpersuading' me. You couldn't, anyway, whether you, wanted to or not.)

"It's just that—if you *do* decide to try her and if you *are* going for your holiday on June the fifth, wouldn't it be a good plan for her to come here just then and we could be all settled in by the time you come back? I know you hate changes. You said they worried you. So perhaps the change could happen while you're away?"

I stood thoughtful a moment. I had a strong impression that things were going a little too fast for me.

"I don't *know* if that's a good suggestion, of course," said Rene carefully, "because I don't know exactly when Blakey's going."

"Nor do I. That's to be arranged between us. She'll stay until I get someone, I know, But I don't want any overlapping."

"If you did engage Mrs. Dabchick, did you mean her to come at once—before your holiday?"

"I really don't know, Rene. I haven't thought it all out yet. I don't want to throw Blakey out at too short notice, so perhaps not."

"The only thing is, it's leaving it rather a long time to ask Mrs. Dabchick not to come until after you come home again, isn't it?"

She wasn't exactly badgering me. Nevertheless, I felt a movement of irritation—the more so in that there *was* some sense in what she was saying.

"Well Rene, honestly, I think I've got to decide *whether* I want Mrs. Dabchick before I decide *when*," I said.

"Oh, of course, Vicky. This is all—all—"

"Hypothetical," I suggested impatiently.

"Is that the word? Yes, I suppose it is. It was only that I was just wondering about your holiday and how it would fit in and everything."

"Probably it won't fit in at all well—these things never do. There's one thing I'm not going to do and that is tell Blakey to go to-morrow, so to speak. Especially not as she's been so nice over Antonia recently."

"But it's three weeks to your holiday, isn't it, Vicky?" said Rene.

I had never realized before quite how persistent Rene could be. Evidently she had spent the whole day thinking things out. It *was* partly her business, of course—and, even if I would have preferred personally to discuss it another time, how was she to know this? I had said nothing about having had a hard day at the office, and, and, anyway, why should I always dictate my own times?

I looked at her and suddenly realized what might well be at the back of her mind.

"I expect you're not particularly keen on being left here *tête-à-tête* with Blakey while I'm away?" I suggested.

Rene shifted and looked uncomfortable. "I—I shouldn't *like* it much," she admitted. "Oh, I know it's silly of me, Vicky, but I can't help feeling awfully uncomfortable with her somehow."

"I know. I don't blame you. She can be perfectly awful, that I freely admit."

"Of course if it was necessary, I'd just have to put up with it and that's that," said Rene bravely. "But if I *could*—if it *could* be arranged that it was Mrs. Dabchick instead with me—and really the dates do seem to fit rather well, don't they, Vicky?—well, that would be just *lovely*."

It was extraordinary how, at the mere mention of Mrs. Dabchick, Rene's whole face shone.

"You mean, what you'd really like would be Mrs. Dabchick to come just as, or immediately after, I'd gone away? Frankly, Rene, now I come to think of it, I just don't *want* her here before. I don't want to have to *cope* until I've had my holiday and feel I've got the energy."

"Oh yes, Vicky, I *do* see that. I wasn't thinking only of myself and not wanting to be alone here with Blakey. I was thinking of you too. Wouldn't it save you a lot of the sort of bother you hate if, when you came back from your holiday, you found Mrs. Dabchick already settled in and knowing her way about?"

Just for a moment this prospect, as put by Rene, certainly sounded enticing. Without considering it further, I said:

"Yes, it's not a bad idea."

The effect of this casual statement on Rene was electric. She jumped up, clapped her hands—I had thought people only did such things in books—and exclaimed enthusiastically, "Oh! I'm so glad you agree with me."

A wave of horrid misgiving suddenly engulfed me. I had a sudden vision of coming back home to find Mrs. Dabchick only too well ensconced in my house. I would come in and she and Rene would be having tea together, their heads close together prattling as hard as they could go. They would jump up and welcome me charmingly, and at first I would feel like an honoured guest in my own house. Later, as their prattle died down, it would become apparent that I was indeed the outsider, the stranger, the discordant element. Mrs. Dabchick would slink off to the kitchen, and I would be left remembering that she was a vicar's daughter in reduced circumstances and feeling generally awful about her.

It was an exaggerated and nightmare-ish vision, no doubt. Nevertheless, there was more than an element of good sound foresight in it.

"Don't go too fast, Rene," I said. "I *really* haven't decided to engage her yet."

"No, no. But if you *do* . . ."

"I can't promise even that, Rene. When I said it was a good idea just now to have her come while I was away, I wasn't really thinking."

Rene stared at me blankly, like a disappointed child.

"I only thought it would save you such a lot of bother," she hazarded timidly.

"Well, so it doubtless would. Only the point is—I don't really *want* that sort of bother lifted off my shoulders."

"You mean you'd rather I didn't sort of help you? Oh Vicky, I *would* so like to. All along I've felt I didn't *do* enough in the house."

Oh dear, I thought.

"I'd be very grateful for your *help*, Rene," I said, slightly emphasizing the last word. "But—well, help's one thing, and very welcome too, but—but *training* someone into my ways is rather a different thing, isn't it? I expect you and Mrs. Dabchick would settle in splendidly and then I should come back and upset everything, and it would all be a muddle."

I thought this was putting it as delicately as possible. I thought, nevertheless, that Rene would grasp and appreciate the point that I had, after all, a right to 'upset everything' if things were not *my* way.

She did not. The word 'training' seemed to be the one chiefly to catch her attention.

"I don't think Mrs. Dabchick is the sort of person one 'trains' exactly, is she, Vicky? I wouldn't have suggested it if she had been."

It was, I think, about the most annoying thing Rene could say in the circumstances.

"Exactly," I snapped. "That's just my objection to her. That's just my objection to the whole situation. It's all a splendid idea and we're all going to get on like a house on fire and share all the work so nicely together, and it's all lovely—*except* that it isn't what I personally happen to want. And it is, after all, my house."

I knew, as soon as this last fatal sentence had left my lips, that I had in my own eyes at least at last committed the worst social crime against Rene I could possibly commit. Even if I had had a particularly awful day at the office, even if Rene had, in some measure, driven me to it, I felt that it was a shocking thing to say. The fact that all over England owners of houses were saying or implying precisely the same thing to the evacuees, refugees or paying-guests they had probably at first welcomed, did not comfort me in the slightest. I had gone into this business with my eyes open, only about nine months had passed, and at the end of this short time I was ending discussions with the one remark that should never in any circumstances have been made.

The fact that Rene did not seem particularly insulted, only made me feel more of a cur than ever. Had she flared up, had she reminded me, as she might very well have done, that she had never behaved as if the house was not mine, I might have felt better.

As it was, the discussion tailed off inconclusively; and a sense of penitence, which I could not express for fear of making matters worse, caused me to punish myself by having supper downstairs with Rene after all.

* * * * *

I have, as a minor luxury I greatly prize, a telephone extension by my bedside. I was almost asleep that night when Raymond rang up.

He had never rung me before at home—always at the office. It was an odd sensation to lie in bed, talking to him, so strangely like old times and yet so very different.

"I just wondered whether you knew yet whether you were winning or not," explained Raymond.

"Winning?" I said, stupidly.

"Yes. Your game. Snakes and ladders."

"Oh, *that*! I'm very sorry to tell you, Raymond, things are so bad I haven't the heart to play it any more."

I expected him to laugh and tease me. I had spoken half-humorously, although God knows it was the truth. Instead, he enquired very sympathetically what the trouble was.

I pulled myself together. Luxurious in a way as it would have been to drip tears of self-pity down the telephone receiver,

I was not yet quite so far reduced as to wail at Raymond. Not once, in our whole life together, had I ever wailed at him. Not even when things were at their worst.

"Oh, just a terrific conglomeration of snakes—office snakes and domestic snakes and private snakes," I said. "Positive boa-constrictors, some of them."

"Poor Vicky! Just one of those patches, is it?"

"It is indeed!"

"Shall I send you a poker-work calendar with 'It's not life that matters, but the courage you bring to it' inscribed on it in Gothic letters?"

In spite of myself, I giggled. Raymond and I, both agreeing that poker-work mottoes and illustrated rhyme-sheets were about as horrible as they could possibly be, had once 'collected' them (mentally only and by report to each other) as atrocities. Many were the moments I had spent in front of arty-crafty shops, my lips moving, silently memorizing some new perpetration for Raymond's benefit.

"It would be a rather subtle insult to one's paying guests if one suddenly caused the house to break out into a rash of texts and mottoes preaching forbearance and courage, wouldn't it?" I said.

"Yes. On the day they entered the house you could ostentatiously remove 'Don't worry—it may never happen' from the hall, put up 'If' in the sitting-room, and in their bedroom hang out 'Oh wad some power the giftie gie us, To see ourselves as others see us'," suggested Raymond.

"Yes. I think the crowning subtlety would be that one would put up more and more mottoes, more and more to the point, hoping passionately that they would take the hint and go, and it would only be years afterwards that one would learn casually from a friend that the *one* thing that had helped them to put up with everything else was the fact that they liked the house so much—so cosy, so furnished, so home-like, with not a bare space on the walls!"

"Are things too desperate for a two-runged ladder to be any good, Vicky? Saturday isn't one of Your Days, I know, but what about lunching with me one Saturday soon and topping it up with a matinée or a visit to Kew or something of the sort?"

"Lovely, Raymond," I said gratefully. "Things are not so desperate yet that I'm forced to reserve my free Saturday afternoons to have a good cry in, for want of finding any other possible boo-hoo time."

"But there is plenty to boo-hoo about?"

"Well, roughly speaking, the position is 'Don't worry. It *has* happened and is just as nasty, or possibly even a little nastier, than you thought it would be.' However..."

"May I hear the details when we meet?"

"My dear Raymond. Of course I shall talk of absolutely nothing else! What do you take me for?"

"Splendid! You shall cry on my shoulder. It will be a new experience for both of us."

"I'm looking forward to it enormously, Raymond."

"I'll let you know the date of the gala performance as soon as I can. It won't be quite immediately, I'm afraid. I must just make sure which day I'm absolutely free. I'd hate anything to interrupt us."

"So would I. I should be deeply insulted. Who wouldn't be? Good night, Raymond."

"Good night, Vicky."

A click from the receiver. A click from my bedside light as I turned it off again. The day, the extraordinarily long, the extraordinarily harassing day, was finally over. I was alone in the dark, with only my worries as companions.

I was not, however, as, miserable as I had been before Raymond's call.

* * * * *

I think if Rene and I had never had our 'this-is-my-house' discussion over Mrs. Dabchick I would not have engaged the woman at all. It was chiefly the fact that I was left with a bad conscience about Rene after this argument that led me to decide to give her a trial. I still, however, stuck to my decision about not having her arrive while I was away, partly out of genuine prevision of calamity, partly out of obstinacy and partly out of a feeling that it would be sheer waste to have made myself so unpleasant and then not stick to my point.

Rene, being of a truly humble and forgiving nature, appeared delighted when I told her, a day or two later, that I had written to Mrs. Dabchick to offer her the post, and even more delighted when Mrs. Dabchick wrote a four-page letter by return, accepting with joy and saying that it really suited her splendidly not to come until the middle of June. It would give her time, she said, to stay in the neighbourhood she was in a little longer, and "help to settle" her new tenants into her "wee bungalow."

She had, I had already gathered, a bungalow of her own in a London suburb, which she had already arranged to let—partly for the money, partly to escape the loneliness of living perpetually by herself.

I pitied her new tenants profoundly. I could just imagine her popping in and out all day asking them if they felt cosy yet.

Matters had arranged themselves so quickly that there was still more than a fortnight to run before I went for my holiday. It occurred to me that if Blakey was to go anyway as soon as I came back, she might as well go, if she preferred to, when I went away. I sounded her, and she expressed a definite preference for doing so. I do not think she liked the prospect of being left alone with Rene, any more than Rene did. She had, I am sure, a bad conscience about Rene underneath.

It honestly never occurred to me that I ought to have asked Rene first before sounding Blakey on this point. Rene had told me that she was afraid she would feel uncomfortable alone with Blakey, and I therefore jumped to the conclusion that she would prefer to be quite alone. Rene had, I knew, been longing for some time to stop being waited on and do things for herself. She was, I also knew, domestically inclined and liked cooking, and had once told me that she had planned never to have a maid when she was in a home of her own with Philip, but to do everything herself. I thought this very admirable of her (all the more admirable in that it was my idea of Hell), and never dreamt but that she would be delighted at the prospect of a fortnight's undiluted domesticity with Philip.

I told her quite casually that I had decided that this was the best thing to do, and was just going to ask her, more or less as a matter of form, whether she had any objection, when something interrupted us. Rene did not broach the subject again to me, and I took it that that was all settled.

I was wrong, very wrong. I did not see it for myself. Barry had to tell me.

Rather to my surprise he asked me, a little formally, to come out for a walk with him on the following Sunday afternoon. Recently it had been Barry and Rene who had usually been out together for walks then, accompanied by Philip in his pram. Barry seemed to have none of the conventional man's distaste for being seen walking with a pram. Considering that he was, after all, a headmaster, I found this rather sweet and endearing of him. I had usually either taken out Antonia in a different direction (two children were, I felt, really rather too much for Barry!) or, on the alternate Sundays when Blakey was on duty, stayed in and enjoyed having the house to myself for once. However, since on this occasion Barry gave a direct personal invitation to myself, and since it was Blakey's Sunday on duty, I accepted, with outward calm and with some inward surprise and speculation.

I had not to wait very long before I discovered the meaning behind all this.

"Vicky, I won't beat about the bush," said Barry, when a pause in our conversation occurred shortly after we had started out. "Rene doesn't like to tell you something herself—she thinks you'll think her so silly, although I assured her you wouldn't—so *I* said I'd explain to you."

"Good gracious!" I said, surprised. "Whatever is it?"

I forbore to add, "And however did Rene come to tell *you* about it?" although the words were certainly on the tip of my tongue. Now that my attention was drawn to the matter, however, I suddenly realized that Barry and Rene had been seeing quite a bit of each other recently and that it had occurred to me in a vague way that really those two seemed always to find quite a lot to say to each other.

Barry paused. "I don't want you to think Rene has been sort of going behind your back and in any way confiding to me things that she would do better to say straight out to you," he said gravely.

It seemed to me that this was precisely what Rene had been doing. However, I really didn't mind if she had. I made reassuring sounds.

"Rene is the most loyal person on earth and has the greatest admiration for you," continued Barry punctiliously. "She didn't want in the first place to tell me what the trouble was. I just saw something was the matter and made her tell me. In the second place she didn't really want me to tell you—but when she said she simply couldn't herself, I said I was just going to."

"All right, all right," I said kindly. "Let's get to the point and hear what the trouble *is*."

"It's just this. Rene is absolutely dreading the prospect of being alone while you're away."

"Good Lord!" I said amazed. "I quite thought she'd like it."

"It isn't the work, of course," explained Barry. "It's the being alone at nights."

"Whatever is she afraid of? Burglars? Bombs? Being ill?"

"Nothing, I think, that she can precisely put a name to, Vicky. She knows it's silly herself. These irrational fears are the hardest of all to conquer."

"She doesn't even want to try to do it?" I said, possibly a little scornfully.

Barry looked at me, and I felt a mild reproach in his gaze.

"It isn't so very silly to be nervous in the circumstances, Vicky. Remember Rene's a lot younger than you and never has lived on her own at all. It's quite natural I think, not to like the idea."

"Well, natural or not, Barry, it seems to me a problem that Rene's got to face *some* time," I said. "After all, she is a married woman more or less on her own, not a helpless dependent. I can't guarantee never in my whole life to leave her alone. We might so easily be reduced to a daily instead of a sleeping-in maid and would that then mean I could never go away with Antonia, even for a night, to see Mother or someone?"

I sounded perhaps more indignant than I should have liked to, but I really felt quite hysterical at the vista of future difficulties Rene's objection to being left alone opened up. Whatever I had bargained for, I had not bargained for *that*.

"Vicky . . ." said Barry pleadingly.

"What?" I snapped.

"Well . . . you see, why Rene was nervous of telling you herself?"

I sighed. I did.

"The whole situation's complicated, Barry, by the fact that, not realizing I was letting myself in for *this*, I rather firmly refused to let her have Mrs. Dabchick come while I was away. Did she tell you about *that*?"

Barry shook his head.

"Well, that's decent of her, considering I really was rather foul. It was like this." Briefly I recounted to him the course of the argument in question. I think I made my point—still, I was convinced, a perfectly sound and genuine one—without sounding offensive. Barry, at any rate, seemed to comprehend perfectly my attitude and to sympathize with it. I ended up, in a burst of candour, "And of course, Barry, even though I still agree with myself over the whole situation, I do see that I ought not to have said it was my house. The trouble was I had had a very harassing day at the office and wasn't in the mood to discuss things to start with."

"Oh, I quite understand, Vicky. Believe me, I do see your point there perfectly, and just how difficult it was for you to insist—quite rightly—without sounding nasty."

"It seems to me you're wonderful at understanding both Rene and me," I said, and then added, a little bitterly, "The only trouble is Rene and I never seem to understand each other at all."

"Vicky. Will you be offended if I suggest something?"

"No, no, I'm past being offended. No one realizes better than myself that I've made a pretty good hash of having Rene to live with me. I think it slightly odd and awful that we should talk *to you* about our domestic bothers, but if *you* don't mind, I certainly don't."

"Minor domestic bothers are only a symptom of something rather more fundamental," suggested Barry, "and, since I'm your friend and Rene's friend too now, I hope, I'm naturally interested in things that concern you both."

"Thank you, Barry. That makes it sound rather less trivial and squabbling. Well—what *were* you going to suggest?"

"Simply this. You say you'd had a tiring and harassing day at the office when Rene brought the subject up. Well—why on earth not *tell* her that as soon as you come in, if you like? Rene would be most awfully pleased if you would sometimes confide that sort of thing to her, and I'm sure that, if you did, no one could be more thoughtful and sweet about it. She can't be tactful if you keep her at arm's length always, now can she? Rene has never, of course, expressed any of this to me. She wouldn't. She's too loyal, and besides, she admires you tremendously, Vicky, as I said before. I'm only speaking from what I can see for myself without much difficulty."

"Barry." I paused and made up my mind. "Barry, that's a perfectly true and honest observation, and I'll give you a perfectly true and honest answer, shall I, even though you won't like me for it?"

"Please. I'm sure I couldn't dislike you for anything you say in all honesty, Vicky."

I accepted the compliment with a smile and (also with a smile) the implied rebuke.

"Well, it's like this, Barry. Rene, I am sure, *would* be sweet if I told her I was tired and worried. She'd fetch me cups of tea and tell me to put my feet up and love fussing round me. The trouble is, I just don't *want* that sort of cosy, feminine atmosphere around me. I don't much care for sympathy and cups of tea and girlish confidences in front of the fire. In fact, I'd go so far as to say I hate it. I *liked* Blakey's rather standoffish attitude, not out of snobbery but because I didn't have to worry about her. She was, for all her devotion to me, a self-sufficient sort of person—like myself. I *like* the unsentimental atmosphere of an office. I like, in the midst of people—I'm not hermit—to preserve my own independence. I don't want to 'serve' other people particularly—except Antonia, she doesn't count in all that I've been saying; the maternal instinct's very strong in me, I assure you, but a rather unrelated part of my character—and perhaps it's very reprehensible that I haven't much impulse to 'serve' people, but at least I don't want it both ways. I definitely dislike other people ministering to me, ministering spiritually, I mean."

Barry nodded. My words, I am sure, carried conviction.

"What exactly made you offer Rene a home, if I may ask?" he enquired.

"Oh—a sense of duty, more or less. A desire to take her off Mother's hands. The fact that I don't feel for other people as perhaps I should, and don't even want to feel, doesn't mean I haven't quite a strong sense of what I ought to do."

"You didn't think it would be nice to have her company or anything like that?"

"Good God, no! That was absolutely the last thing I wanted. Believe it or not, Barry, I was perfectly contented with my circumstances before Rene came. Frankly, Barry, Rene whatever she was going to be like, was going to be dead loss to me. She was something I just hoped to make a reasonably good job of because I had to."

Barry took me up rather quickly. I suppose I did sound a perfect brute.

"But surely you *like* her, Vicky? I can't imagine anyone not *liking* Rene. She has such a very sweet nature."

"I don't dislike her," I said cautiously (for, after all, I supposed rather drearily that I didn't), "but she's just so hopelessly—not my sort of person, Barry. Just as, I readily admit, I'm not her sort."

There was a rather horrid pause. All that I had said was so true and therefore so hopeless. I think Barry felt this too.

"I know I sound awful, Barry," I said apologetically. "And believe me I do see Rene's point of view very clearly. Just because things aren't right between us I see it all the more passionately. I think it's the most frightful waste that all her many good qualities happen to be ones I personally don't appreciate. She'd be a splendid companion to many people, I do see that."

"You see it—but you don't *feel* it," suggested Barry.

"Yes, I dare say you're right there. Only, in order to remedy that you've got to take me to bits and make me up again into a totally different person, haven't you? I think I had at first some faint hopes that Rene would perform a miracle of the sort on herself—and suddenly become independent and self-sufficient like me. We might have got on fine then. Only obviously she couldn't and wouldn't—and indeed, why should she?"

"You're very clear-headed about all this, Vicky. I'm glad to understand—even if it's only understanding that the situation really is rather at a deadlock."

"I'm afraid so. I only hope Rene doesn't see things as clearly as I do."

"No, I'm sure she doesn't," said Barry quickly.

"Oh well! There's nothing to be done about it," I said, thinking that really Barry must be spared further outpourings of the sort. "I think I can trust myself always to behave fairly well on the surface, you know. Better indeed than I would do if our relationship was on firmer foundations. I'll certainly, for instance, arrange that Rene *isn't* left alone while I'm on holiday."

"What will you do? Ask Blakey to stay on?"

"Well, if I was Rene, which, of course, I'm not, I should feel too awful if *that* was arranged for me. No, I'll try to get Mother to come here. It's only for ten days, after all."

"Good. That's a splendid idea," said Barry heartily.

We changed the conversation. Just as we were approaching the house, half an hour later, Barry referred to the topic once more. He thanked me for having spoken so frankly and fully.

"It was very nice of you to listen, Barry, It was a relief, telling you all that. Won't you come in and have tea now?" We had halted on the doorstep.

"No, thank you, not to-day. I must be getting back now, I've got some work to do. Good-bye, Vicky, and many thanks—for the walk and everything."

We shook hands, I don't know quite why. It seemed an appropriate gesture.

I lingered on the doorstep a minute, idly watching Barry's broad back disappear down the drive. I suddenly had the strangest sensation that he had, on this occasion, said good-bye to me in a way that was as final as it was intangible. Why should this be?

I knew. I had known really while he was listening to my long outburst about myself that afternoon. Sympathetically as he had received it, I had felt at the time that he was at last seeing me, by my own wish, for what I was, and understanding completely, sadly perhaps, but finally, that he and I would never have been happy, had I consented to marry him.

I had tried before, and failed, to make him see the sort of person I was. Now, I felt, he was at last convinced of the truth and, being Barry, the truth would shock him deeply in a fundamental way. The blood of his Quaker ancestors, all of whom had in their various ways lived to serve humanity and practise the principles of Christianity throughout their lives, had, I felt sure, risen in his veins to proclaim that this girl who spoke of 'independence' and 'self-sufficiency' as the breath of life to her, was no spiritual mate for him. Not only did I admit that I did not love my neighbour as myself, I asserted that I did not even want to. Indeed, my heart would have to be broken into small bits and refashioned anew before Barry and I would, in the deepest sense, speak the same language. And then—as perhaps he saw—I would not be Vicky any more.

Personality. The most fascinating unsolved puzzle in the world. How many thousands of times over as many thousands of years had two people mutually, tacitly, agreed to leave the riddle yet once again unsolved—and summed up the fascination and the insolubility of it all with the equivalent of a quick handshake and a casual, "Thanks for everything. Good-bye"?

Chapter 14

MY HOLIDAY was to last for a fortnight, and I could only have the bungalow for ten days—a week and two week-ends. I decided that the *odd* four days had really better be spent at home settling Mrs. Dabchick in. I wrote to her, accordingly, again, to ask her to come on the day after I returned home.

I did not want Mother to feel that I was "using" her too much, and I did genuinely want to see her again and for her to see Antonia, so I pressed her to stay the full fortnight with us. The question of room-space of course arose, for, since Rene had come to stay with me I had had no spare bedroom, but I assured Mother that we could manage perfectly well after my return; she could keep on in my room and I could easily park myself on a camp-bed in Antonia's room. Rather to my relief Mother wrote back to say she would really prefer to move out to the small private hotel close by when I returned. She would love to stay on and see something of me and Antonia, but she thought visitors in the house were a mistake when one was settling in a new maid.

I rather agreed with her, and felt infinitely relieved that she had seen this for herself.

It was funny, I mused. An outsider would have said that of the two of us, Rene and myself, I was undoubtedly the stronger character. And yet, for Rene's sake, I had done all sorts of things I would probably never have done otherwise—sacked Blakey, let down the office, shocked Barry, "used" Mother, and engaged a woman I would probably have turned down at sight myself. Even the fact that I was having a holiday now was indirectly due to Rene. I did not think it too far-fetched to say that if there had never been the "two doctors" upset over Rene, I would not have pressed Dr. Lambert so passionately for her advice as to whether there wasn't something more I could "do" for Antonia.

Funny. I dismissed this unprofitable line of thought with a mental shrug of the shoulders. Probably I had done all these things because I had a bad conscience about Rene, owing to the fact that I really could not like her. Or I might sound a bit more modern and call it a guilt complex. Same thing.

The last week before my holiday passed very quickly. On the afternoon of the day before I went Blakey left.

She was not going to another job, at least not for a month or two. She was going to stay with her recently-widowed sister in Cornwall. When I referred to this injudiciously as "a holiday" Blakey gave me to understand that, on the contrary, she was obeying the voice of duty. Her sister was, she said scornfully, a "poor manager," and had been "quite knocked over" by her husband's death. *Someone* had got to go down there to "see to things."

Saying good-bye to Blakey was something I had dreaded, and when it came it was just as unpleasant as I had thought it would be. Things often are, I have noticed, in spite of a prevalent popular belief to the contrary. I suppose Blakey got some grim satisfaction out of leaving the whole house more exquisitely clean and tidy than it had ever been before, but naturally I looked at the piles of Antonia's freshly-darned, freshly-ironed clothes in the linen cupboard and felt awful, and more awful still when I found that Blakey had left a complete three-course supper for that evening ready in the larder. When Blakey, as a finishing touch, produced a very old torn feeder of Antonia's—one that had been long more or less discarded—and apologized for leaving it unmended only we had just run out of tape, I wanted badly to smack her as a preliminary to an emotional reconciliation.

"Oh Blakey!" I exclaimed. "*Do* stop it. Put that feeder down and stop making me feel awful for goodness sake."

But Blakey was not having any. She just wouldn't play, and our final good-byes were just as miserable and constrained as Blakey apparently wanted. A frightful scene on the lines of "I have your address, haven't I?" (twice over from me out of nervousness) and, "I'm sure I hope the new person will prove satisfactory, Miss Vicky" (with a strong relish of grim foreboding), from Blakey.

When she was gone I could only feel heartily thankful that I myself was going away the next day, and, when the next day came, a sudden mood of holiday-making and frivolity descended on me as a delightful unexpected present from the gods. This lightening of the atmosphere was much appreciated by Antonia, and our journey down to Sussex was quite a riot of merriment, with bars of chocolate produced at unconventional times, games played out of the carriage window and altogether never a dull or peaceful moment. Such was my mood that I actually enjoyed it.

* * * * *

Harry and Margaret Smith, the married couple who ran the hotel, were not intimate friends of mine, but I had known them for some years, on and off (off while I was married to Raymond, whom they had never met), and I liked them both very well in a cool way. Harry was very good-looking, very amiable and easy-going, and possibly a little weak in character. He had a game leg which had so far debarred him from military service, although it was possible he would be called up in the future. Margaret was about my own age, very capable, very straightforward and outspoken, and a trifle domineering in a way that was still amusing rather than offensive, but might quite well become the latter one day. I had always considered them an excellent couple to run a hotel between them. Harry supplied the charm and the air of easy Welcome, Margaret the efficiency, and, I believe, the original capital.

The bungalow in the grounds of the hotel was really charming. It consisted of a big sitting-room, two bedrooms, and a bathroom, all very decorative and gay. I felt like a child playing at houses and loved it instantly. I had seen both hotel and bungalow, but never stayed there. It was an encouraging start to find it all nicer than I had remembered.

Margaret, who came over with me, to unlock the door, explained very apologetically that only the day before an unfortunate accident had occurred to the window of the smaller bedroom. One of the children staying in the hotel had thrown a stone and broken it badly, and they had not been able to get it mended yet.

"The mother was awfully apologetic, but all the same I could have smacked the little beast," ended up Margaret, and then looked at me a trifle aghast, suddenly realizing, I suppose, that my own potential "little beast" was tripping along beside me, and also perhaps that she had previously assured me that children were heartily welcome. "I mean it's an awful nuisance for you," she added quickly. "Because I suppose you meant to put Antonia in the smaller bedroom, didn't you? And I'm afraid it's now a choice between leaving the black-out screen up to cover the hole and getting no fresh air at all or else taking it down and getting too much. The other bedroom—the bigger one with a double bed in it—has plenty of room for another bed for Antonia as well until the window's mended, if you'd prefer to do that? Come and see, anyway."

I inspected the damage, and decided that it would certainly be the best plan for Antonia and me to share the big room. I did not really mind, and Antonia was delighted at the prospect—so delighted that (while slightly touched by her joy) I was obliged to remind her sternly that I was not going to permit any conversation at all until half-past seven in the morning.

I saw Margaret give me an approving glance. She had no children of her own, and evidently liked to hear the law being laid down to other people's. She was altogether rather a "no nonsense" person.

We moved the divan bed from the smaller room into the bigger one, and then all went back to the hotel to tea. Antonia, I was glad to see, still giving her best impersonation of a friendly but well-conducted child.

It was arranged that breakfast and supper should be brought across to the bungalow, and Antonia and I should have lunch and tea in the hotel.

That evening after I had bathed Antonia and was just preparing to turn down the divan bed for her, Antonia stopped in mid-act of taking off her slippers and said suddenly, "Mummy!"

"What?" I said. I knew that pregnant tone of passionate enquiry. Something terrifically important was coming.

"Mummy. COULD I sleep in the big bed. COULD I—*please.*" ('Please' was an obvious afterthought, thrown in for a makeweight.)

"Darling! Do you really want to?" I looked dubiously as the vastness of the double bed and the comparative smallness of Antonia's night-gowned figure.

"Yes, I do. I do *really*. I want it—more than anything else in the world!"

I laughed. Bless her! I could see by her face that she was not exaggerating.

There is still enough of the child in me to want small things passionately myself. There is not enough of the disciplinarian not to feel strongly tempted to grant ridiculous requests of the sort.

"And me sleep in the little one, you mean?"

A shade of half-doubtful apology crossed Antonia's face, but she nodded vigorously.

"Darling, you *are* a ridiculous sausage. Well, I tell you what." (Appealing as she was, I still felt I ought not for the sake of principle, to give in unconditionally.) "You shall sleep in the double bed until I come to bed if you want to so much, and then it will be *my* turn and you must move over."

At least the thing had now been established on a basis of "turns." It was the best the mother of an only child could do, artificial pretence as it was in this case. I did not really mind for myself in the slightest which bed I slept in.

Antonia's rapture as she clambered with some difficulty into the enormous bed and settled herself precisely in the middle, was amusing to watch.

"It feels perfectly *lovely*," she volunteered enthusiastically.

I kissed her affectionately. She looked so utterly ridiculous and so utterly sweet.

"Mummy?"

"Yes?"

"Are my slippers put properly. I can't see."

Antonia's habits with her slippers are one of the things that slightly appal me. Apparently they have to be ranged meticulously side by side before she can compose herself for slumber. This is her rule, not mine or Blakey's—*that* is what appals me. The rest of the room, I am both glad and sorry to say, can be in as much disorder as it likes.

"No, they're not. They're all over the place," I said, teasingly.

"Oh!" Antonia, concerned, began immediately to scramble out of bed again.

"No, don't get out. There! I've done it. Look!"

Antonia peered over the edge of the bed and heaved a sigh of relief.

"I was so excited I forgot," she explained guilelessly.

"Well, no more excitement now, and straight off to sleep," I admonished, with a final kiss.

Back in the sitting-room I grinned, in retrospective amusement, at the little scene that had just taken place between us. If Antonia had had six brothers and sisters, would the relationship between her and me be rather different?

Yes, I admitted with a sigh, undoubtedly it would be. The bond between mother and child would still be there, of course, but it would be more diffused. I would be so busy tucking them all up in their cots and beds that I should have no time to consider one child's whims over its slippers. Probably, I admitted with another sigh, that would be much healthier for Antonia.

I had to comfort myself once again with the reflection that I always comfort myself with on the occasions when I feel a little apprehensive about the effects on Antonia's character of being an only child. My consolation is this—that I personally have always found members of a really large family a little unsatisfactory as friends. So often they carry over into adulthood too much of the super-hearty atmosphere of their childhood. If "only children" grow up old for their age and precocious in intelligence, "big family" children seem, contrariwise, to suffer a little from arrested development. The corners have been *too* thoroughly rubbed off them in youth; and personally my preference is all for slightly "cornery" and individual adults.

* * * * *

My beautiful dream of the "children in the sandpit" and the bevy of mothers in the hotel all thanking me, did not precisely materialize. I did not mind as I was enjoying myself anyway. As a matter of fact, there were only two other children in the hotel, one a little boy of eight (he it was who had thrown the stone), and one a baby girl of a year old. There was practically no game Antonia and these two could co-operate in playing, and any half-hearted attempts to make them resulted in a far greater expenditure of effort than simply leaving them alone, as all we mothers quickly realized. However, I was not going to be baulked altogether of my desire to play the gracious hostess, and therefore, early in the first week, invited the eight-year-old to tea on the second Saturday of my visit. His mother accepted gratefully for him, but said would I mind if she did not come herself? She had been invited out to tea with friends in the neighbourhood that day, and had accepted, thinking she would have to take Richard with her—but naturally it would be much nicer for him to go to me and play with my little girl. I could see by Richard's face that his eight-year-old dignity was a trifle affronted by being offered the much younger Antonia as an entirely suitable companion, but he made no demur, and I was quite agreeable to having him without escort. A sandpit surely still pleased an eight-year-old?

I debated whether to ask the year-old girl and her mother as well, but eventually decided against it. I did not care for Mrs. Massingham (such was her name), who struck me as querulous and fretful. Smugly I decided that she did not deserve such a lovely treat as I could offer. The withheld invitation would be my private punishment to her for complaining so boringly to me one afternoon about the hotel and all its inhabitants.

Antonia showed no great enthusiasm for the sandpit during the first week of our visit. She had, after all, one at home, so it was no great novelty. The hotel itself was something really new however, and actually she much preferred it to the peace and privacy of the bungalow. The number of rooms, the several staircases, the waitresses all fascinated her. On the only really wet day she was extremely languid about the new painting book I competently produced, and only really cheered up when I suggested going across early to the hotel to tea. At her own request I walked her all over the public part of the building. It was agony to her that she could not look into the bedrooms, but she did quite well with "exploring" every bathroom and lavatory. After tea she demanded a repeat performance, and when I struck she settled me firmly in a chair in the lounge and then said could she *please* explore by herself? I knew I could trust her to be quiet and discreet in her bearing, and so, somewhat rashly I gave her permission, and then spent a rather agonized moment, immediately after she had run off, thinking that she would now certainly get shut by accident into some bathroom and be unable to get out. However, in five minutes she reappeared, whispered importantly, "Mummy! there are seven bedrooms up the first staircase, three bathrooms and two lavatories—now I'm going up to the next to count," and trotted off again. A little later she returned with a further batch of staggering statistics, including the information that on the top floor was a sort of cupboard room with a sink and brooms. *Would* I call it a scullery?

"No, a housemaid's cupboard," said Richard's mother (with whom I had meanwhile started a conversation.) "How many cans had it got in it, Antonia? Did you count?"

I recognized her as the best sort of fellow-mother—one who, when wanting to talk to me would never show by word or look that my child was in the way, but would, with an air of complete interest, suggest some occupation for Antonia to send her off., Thereafter I firmly squashed in my mind the mental vision of an imprisoned Antonia, and enjoyed an interesting chat with Richard's mother about children, happily undistracted by their actual presence. We both of us agreeably suggested further variants on this evidently fascinating game of counting and reporting whenever Antonia appeared again, and finally Richard arrived and, as a culminating glory, took Antonia to see his bedroom. Antonia, who had received with extreme incredulity my earlier assurances that hotel bedrooms were "just like any other bedrooms, darling, just like ours in the bungalow" ran off delighted at the prospect; and, oddly enough, did not seem at all disappointed when she came back again, having viewed thoroughly the reality.

That was Thursday. On Thursday evening, shortly after supper, when I was sitting in my bungalow talking to Harry and Margaret (who often dropped in to coffee with me, knowing that I would not leave Antonia alone in the bungalow after she was in bed) the telephone rang and the operator from the hotel told me that she was about to switch a trunk-call over to my extension.

During the few minutes, that I waited, receiver to ear, I had time to imagine quite a lot of disturbing possibilities. My mind I am afraid, works that way. A trunk-call could only be from Harminster, I thought, and, if so, could only be to announce calamity of some sort necessitating probably my instant return. Rene was ill? Mother had broken her leg? A stray bomb had fallen on the house?

"Hello? Vicky?" said Raymond's well-known voice.

The relief was considerable.

"Raymond!" I cried joyfully. "How ever did you know I was here?"

"Rang you up at home and they gave me your number."

"Did they sound all right at home?" I asked a little absurdly. "Whom did you speak to, Rene or Mother?"

"Your mother. Of course I was enormously interested in the situation, Vicky, but I could hardly ask them how they were getting on together, or what had driven you to this step. I was quite relieved to hear you had only gone for a holiday. For a moment I feared that you had abandoned the field of battle for good and left Rene in possession." His tone changed as he added, "I'm awfully sorry to hear Antonia has been ill. It must have been horrid for you."

"Oh, Mother told you that, did she?"

I did not altogether like the idea of Mother and Raymond chatting together. Raymond, of course, guessed as much from my tone.

"Your mother recognized my voice at once. Obviously a pleasant chat together was inevitable. She was very nice—not dramatic at all. It doesn't matter, does it?"

"No, no, of course it doesn't," I said hastily.

"You didn't tell me you were going away, Vicky. I rang you up in the first place to propose next Saturday for our outing together. But of course I suppose that's off now?"

"Oh Raymond! I'm so sorry, I'm afraid it is. I'm here till Monday, and can't very well leave Antonia."

"That's all right. It was very short notice in any case. The invitation still holds good for later on, does it?"

There was only good humour and politeness in Raymond's voice, and this had the effect of making me feel something of a cur. I had, after all, known about my holiday, when Raymond had first proposed this outing, and had not mentioned it. I had accepted gratefully his very kind proposal to devote a Saturday to me, and yet held him off to the extent of not telling him even about Antonia's illness.

"Oh Raymond! I *am* sorry," I repeated, and then added impulsively, as a sudden thought struck me, "Look here, though. If you *are* free next Saturday couldn't you come down here for the day instead? It's only just over an hour from London. Do!"

I could feel a slight hesitation over the wire, and added, with the strongest desire not to press him to do anything he did not want to, "Although of course I think it only fair to warn you that the only entertainment offered is a mild children's tea-party in the afternoon and the rather humorous spectacle of me playing the competent mother to Antonia."

I wanted to reassure him that the atmosphere would be in no way sentimental or intense. I had become a little conscious of the presence of Harry and Margaret, who had meanwhile been behaving as we are all forced to behave while obliged to listen in to a private telephone conversation—that is keeping up a polite pretence of chatting in subdued voices to each other—and thought it as well at this point to apprise Raymond of their presence. "Harry and Margaret, who run the hotel, are friends of mine you know. They're in the bungalow with me now, as a matter of fact. We might all have a slight party together at some point."

"Well I don't think I can resist the splendid offer of a children's party *and* a grown-up's party on the same day," said Raymond, laughing. "Thank you, Vicky. I'd love to. Do you know anything about trains?"

"Oh—Harry will come and tell you all about those," I said, and held the instrument out to Harry. "Will you, Harry? I know you know them by heart. Thanks awfully."

I resumed my seat, slightly surprised at this sudden turn of events and yet not at all displeased. I would never have thought of asking Raymond down, had he not happened to ring up, and yet after all why not? Why shouldn't he see Antonia sometimes? And what better opportunity could there be thaw in the comparatively impersonal atmosphere of a hotel with no Rene to be embarrassingly present or as embarrassingly tactfully absent?

Harry concluded his conversation with Raymond and rang off. I suddenly realized that, by mentioning Harry and Margaret to Raymond and explaining them as friends of mine, I had let myself in for some sort of explanation to them as to his identity. Hitherto I had vaguely supposed that the question need not arise. Neither of them had ever met him, or I would have avoided the whole situation.

If anything was going to be said, obviously it had better be said at once.

"You may well be wondering if that *is* the Raymond I married," I said with a laugh. "And, as a matter of fact, it is. We're perfectly good friends and meet from time to time, and this seemed a good opportunity."

Harry and Margaret are by no means an unsophisticated couple. They agreed calmly that it was an excellent idea. Harry said that he had offered to motor Raymond to Hayward's Heath after dinner on Saturday so that he could catch a later train back to London than would otherwise be possible. I saw Margaret dart a slightly watchful glance at Harry when he said this (her line had always been that Harry put himself out too much for the hotel guests) and I thought it a tactful moment to invite them both to come over to the bungalow after dinner on Saturday and have drinks before Raymond went. It was rather awkward carrying glasses over from the hotel bar, so I would, I said, lay in a bottle or two of my own and it should be my party. On this suggestion, which pleased everybody, the evening concluded happily.

Why shouldn't Raymond see Antonia sometimes? The query, originated by myself during the course of my telephone conversation with Raymond that evening, recurred idly to me as I undressed. Many divorced couples shared the children—a violently unsatisfactory state of affairs—but, even though I was the "innocent" party, wasn't I extraordinarily lucky in having complete and utter possession of Antonia?

I stopped short, really amazed at having stumbled on such a new idea, and equally amazed at the reflection that never had I really seen the thing from the angle before. I had violently refused to accept any alimony from Raymond, but there again I had been lucky to be in a sufficiently secure financial position to behave so proudly. On my twenty-first birthday I had inherited a substantial legacy from my grandfather, and more money had come to me on my father's death. I could have supported Antonia and myself on my private means alone—at least until the war came. Now I was extremely glad to have my office earnings as well, but that was an irrelevant fact, nothing to do with my attitude at the time.

Supposing I had revealed to the courts that I was expecting a child? As far as I knew, that would have been no reason for not granting me a divorce, but would not the Judge have directed that the father was to "have access" to the child or something of that sort?

What had Raymond thought of it all? So obsessed had I been at the time with my own defensive attitude—that the baby was *my* fault and therefore entirely *my* affair—that I had simply never given a thought to Raymond's possible rights. Like a wounded animal I had, figuratively speaking, crept away into a corner, and snarled at anyone who approached me. Pride and misery had combined to make me absolutely impervious to Raymond's possible sufferings. He might well, I saw now, have reproached me bitterly, even abused me—had I ever given him the chance, which I had denied him. At the time I believe I thought he ought to be, if not grateful, at least relieved. But then at the time I thought he was going to marry Sandra. At the time I regarded the coming baby purely as an encumbrance.

I passed from this reflection which now, in view of my devotion to Antonia, seemed almost fantastic, to another thought. How would Raymond and Antonia get on together when they met or Saturday?

I found, rather to my amusement, that I had absolutely no idea. They would each, I thought, be a complete novelty to the other. Men of Raymond's age were hardly a familiar feature in Antonia's life. Children were as far as I knew an unknown quantity to Raymond.

It was a curious thought.

Chapter 15

I HAVE OFTEN heard it stated that children do not like to be "talked down to," and I consider the statement absolute nonsense. All the children I have known like adults to descend to their conversation level very much, to talk about things that they, as children, find sensible and interesting, rather than the silly topics that grown-ups ordinarily discuss. If this is not "talking-down" to them I do not know what is. But of course to be well-done it must be done directly and simply without too much of a show of condescension.

How Raymond knew this I do not know, but his manner with Antonia was, right from the beginning, excellent. He paid her the compliment of treating her as a person, and spoke to her directly without shyness or facetiousness, while at the same time remembering that she was a child with a child's simple concrete interests. Antonia and I took a bus down to the village to meet Raymond's train, as I wanted also to do a little shopping. Raymond seemed to understand instantly Antonia's housewifely preoccupations over the cakes we went to buy for the tea-party that afternoon. Eventually I left them together in the shop, debating seriously the question of a Swiss roll versus rock-buns. Raymond took up the very satisfying attitude that the whole question needed thorough consideration. Who was coming and what did each person personally prefer? Antonia was only too ready to tell him. It all took rather a long time but fortunately the woman in the cake-shop seemed to be amused, and I was able to get the rest of the shopping done expeditiously and by myself.

When we got back it was time for Antonia's mid-morning rest. Raymond, whom Antonia invited cheerfully into the bedroom, was amused at the spectacle of the small child in the vast bed.

"At night we take it in turns," explained Antonia. "But I can always have the nice bed at this time because grown-ups don't rest before lunch you see."

When we got back into the sitting-room Raymond asked me, with amusement, whether there was anything correspondingly "nasty" about the other bed.

"Oh no! It's very comfortable. It's merely that Antonia has conceived a passion for that ridiculously unsuitable double bed. It's the high spot of the holiday for her, I assure you."

"Do you set an alarm clock and change over once an hour during the night?"

"No. She just sleeps in it till I come to bed and then has to move over. 'Night' for a child means two big stretches you know—one before the grown-ups come to bed, one after."

"So it does," said Raymond thoughtfully. "I'd quite forgotten, but of course I remember now it does."

"It's probably awfully spoiling letting her have her way about things like that," I said. "But this absurd system of 'turns' in very easily arranged. Anyway, I'm afraid I'm a pretty indulgent Mother, and it amuses me so much to see her in that vast bed . . ."

"Good heavens, yes!" said Raymond easily. "Surely one's permitted to enjoy one's child—one doesn't need to act on principle the whole time?"

"Well in practice one feels one ought to act mostly on principle but often can't be bothered," I explained.

"Well, the results seem very nice anyway," said Raymond.

I felt a pleasant glow, such as every mother feels on receiving even the mildest compliment about her child, but, with great restraint, forebore to angle for further praise, and turned the conversation.

Presently we all went across to the hotel for lunch. I introduced Raymond to Harry and Margaret, who promptly invited us to share their table. They seemed to get on well with Raymond, and I had the comfortable feeling that we were all very friendly and civilized people. No precise introductions between Raymond and Antonia had been performed—I had quite simply funked explaining to her that he was her father—and during the course of lunch, Antonia began guilelessly to call him "Raymond." I do not personally care for children calling their parents by their Christian names, but in the circumstances I thought it a good solution.

After lunch we all had coffee in the garden, and Richard's mother tactfully sent Richard over with a message asking Antonia to join her and Richard's coffee-party which was taking place a little distance away. Antonia, who was enjoying' herself very well with us, looked a little reluctant, but I quickly succeeded in fooling her into thinking it a lovely special invitation. I saw Raymond shoot a glance of amusement at me, and I suddenly realized that I, as a mother, was as much of a novelty to him as Antonia as a child. I returned his look with a slightly triumphant grin as Antonia ran off with Richard.

We all stayed on the lawn talking and drinking coffee until it was time to go back to the bungalow and begin getting the cakes out and the table ready for tea. The bungalow had a gas-ring and a little china of its own, so we were independent of the hotel for this tea-party except for milk and bread and butter, which Margaret had promised to send across.

Richard and Antonia got down to things in the sandpit. Richard, it seemed, was scornful of more sand-castles or simply paddling in the adjacent paddling-pool. He took charge of the proceedings and promptly began to develop a quite complicated scheme for building a seaside town in the sandpit. The sea, I need hardly say, consisted of water fetched in buckets from the paddling-pool, and naturally needed constant replenishment. When I had first noticed the extreme proximity of the sandpit and the paddling pool I had thought that inevitably any child of spirit would instantly set about thoroughly mixing the two elements, and had tentatively asked Margaret if there was a local rule that water was not allowed in the sandpit. She had assured me that indeed there was not. All the children always wanted to make mud-pies, and if their parents didn't mind she didn't.

I certainly didn't mind. I liked to see Richard and Antonia bare-legged, filthy, happy and absorbed. I saw them started, and then went in to lay the table. Raymond, I offered a deckchair and a newspaper in the front garden (the children were in the back. He accepted, but presently, as I glanced out of one of the front windows, I saw that he had disappeared, and, a few minutes later, saw him in the sandpit with the children. He was evidently playing the role of consulting engineer for a pier that was now being constructed, and seemed to be about as absorbed as the other two.

I had just finished laying the tea when I saw Mrs. Massingham wheeling her baby and also a large parcel in a pram past the bungalow front door. Because I was feeling vaguely pleased with myself for playing so competently at Mummies and Daddies and houses and hostesses, I spoke to her through the open window and asked her if she was going down to the village to the post, as the parcel seemed to suggest.

"Yes," Mrs. Massingham said, fretfully. "And it's a horrible long way on such a hot afternoon and I'm very late in getting off but I must get this parcel off so that it gets there first post on Monday."

"Wouldn't you like to leave Susan with me, and catch the bus by yourself?" I suggested. "It's such a push up the hill with a pram, isn't it? Susan wouldn't mind would she? She could sit in her pram and watch the others or crawl about on the grass."

Mrs. Massingham's long rather anxious face brightened at this suggestion.

"Well, thank you very much. That *would* save me a lot of trouble, if you really don't mind. Susan will be as good as gold, I'm sure. She's a marvellously friendly little soul. She'll go to *anyone*."

The emphasis on the last word was not precisely flattering to me. With an inward grin I put Susan's vaunted friendliness to the test by taking the handle of the pram and preparing to wheel it round the corner of the house, remarking to the child that I was going to take her to see my little girl now and that Mummy would be coming back soon for her. As I spoke we heard what sounded like the bus-coming down the road, and Mrs. Massingham hurried off, shouting over her shoulder to me that Susan would love to get out and crawl on the grass a little. I took the pram round the corner of the house and introduced Susan to Richard and Antonia, who, in the manner of children already completely occupied, showed not the faintest interest. Susan's face registered no expression whatsoever. She seemed to be an easy guest, if perhaps a trifle stolid. Presently I remembered her mother's parting suggestion for her entertainment. I fetched a rug and deposited her upon it. She did not appear very mobile for a one-year-old, and therefore was very little responsibility.

I suddenly realized that it was nearly half-past four and that the promised bread and butter and jugs of milk had not arrived over from the hotel. This was distinctly tiresome for one who was playing the hostess with such smug enjoyment. I decided to run over to the hotel and enquire from Margaret personally what had happened. Ringing up seemed a little peremptory and too much like the usual complaining guest, I thought.

I decided that Susan had better go back into her pram and accompany me. However, when I picked her up and began to put her back it immediately became apparent that the child had been enjoying herself on the rug more than she had let on. She burst into tears and struggled fiercely. This was disconcerting. I stopped, perplexed, Mrs. Massingham was due back any minute, and the last thing I wanted was for her to find Susan screaming. Was she the sort of child to keep it up or not? She did not look a passionate nature, but her stolid appearance might conceal a fiery and not easily appeased temperament, for all I knew. Wildly I looked round for some object with which to distract her attention, but the lawn appeared devoid of anything but filthy buckets, and Susan was dressed irreproachably for an afternoon pram promenade.

"What's the trouble?" asked Raymond, coming up.

"She doesn't want to go back in her pram," I explained.

"Then why put her back?" queried Raymond with pleasant masculine lack of principle.

"I wouldn't, only I must dash over to the hotel to see why the tea hasn't come and I thought I'd better take her too."

As I spoke I put Susan back on the rug, the better to consider the situation. The screams stopped instantly. Susan clutched at a daisy and began intently pulling it to pieces.

"You'd better leave her here. She's perfectly all right," said Raymond easily. "I'd offer to go over to the hotel myself only I'd have to wash so much first."

"You would," I said, looking at his bare sand-caked feet and rolled-up trousers. "All right then—I won't be more than a few minutes. If Mrs. Massingham comes, explain what's happened, won't you, and don't let on the child howled. She's very much the 'anxious mother' type."

Hastily I erased all traces of tears from Susan's face, and hurried off.

I could not have been gone more than ten minutes, for I met the bread and butter just starting from the hotel, and returned straightway with it. I was all the more appalled at the sight that greeted my eyes on the bungalow lawn.

Mrs. Massingham was kneeling in horror beside Susan, holding up Susan's frock and dabbing at it angrily with a handkerchief. Raymond was standing apologetically beside them. The two older children were still absorbed in the sandpit.

"I'm terribly sorry," I heard Raymond say as I hurried up. "I'd really no idea Susan could move at all, or I'd have watched her more carefully."

"Not move at all! Why she's a year old and can crawl about all over the place when she wants to!" retorted Mrs. Massingham angrily.

Poor Raymond, usually so tactful, had not for once found the right thing to say, I reflected, torn between amusement and apprehension.

"I'm sorry. I ought to have foreseen then that she'd want to," said Raymond.

"You certainly ought!" snapped back Mrs. Massingham. "Who are you, anyway? I left Susan in the care of Mrs. Heron."

Too bad, I thought, hurrying up, too bad of me to have let Raymond in for this.

"I'm terribly sorry, Mrs. Massingham," I said, completing my entrance at a run. "Has Susan got into an awful mess?"

I did not think, examining the child myself, that the situation was very desperate. Evidently the trouble was that she had succeeded in reaching one of the discarded buckets, and had rubbed it, all wet and dirty as it was, over her frock. Even so, she was not as dirty as Antonia and Richard, or even Raymond. But they were dressed for it and Susan wasn't. I did feel apologetic, much as I resented Mrs. Massingham's tone.

"The whole lawn is sopping wet with filthy water!" exclaimed Mrs. Massingham, feeling the ground around her offspring furiously. "It won't be surprising if Susan catches a cold, will it?"

"Oh surely—in the summer—a little damp . . ." I said hopefully.

To say the whole lawn was sopping wet was an exaggeration. Susan's rug had been on a safe dry patch. It was peculiarly provoking of the child to have crawled towards the area between the paddling-pool and the sandpit, where undoubtedly a certain modicum of water had been spilt.

"Well, I don't know what you think you're doing to let your children make such a mess of the sandpit *and* of themselves," announced Mrs. Massingham. "Certainly when I entrusted Susan to you I had no idea what was going on here."

I began to lose my temper.

"I really don't think it's your business what I let *my* child do, Mrs. Massingham," I retorted tartly. "Personally I've no objection to sand and water at all. I quite see, however, that it's very annoying for you about Susan's frock. Will you let me have it washed for you?"

"Certainly not. Those grass-stains need the greatest care to get out without ruining the fabric. What I really object to, Mrs. Heron, is the way you calmly go off and leave my child, as well as yours, in the charge of a casual stranger."

"Yes, I heard you attacking him as I came up," I said, really angry now, for, genuinely sorry as I was about Susan's beastly frock, Mrs. Massingham in a maternal rage was really unbearable. "Casual I may be, according to your standards, but not quite as casual as that. As a matter of fact—"

I do not know quite what I was going to say, but Mrs. Massingham decided me by interrupting with a sharp, "Who is he, anyway?"

"He's my husband," I said simply.

I did not dare look at Raymond, but I felt silent support for this outrageous statement flowing from him. The children, I am glad to say, were some distance away and paying no attention to us.

"Oh!" said Mrs. Massingham, nonplussed. "I'm—I'm sorry. He isn't staying here with you, is he? I've never seen him before. You never *said* anything about him. I rather took it you were a widow."

Even in her semi-apology she sounded accusing.

"Naturally he can't leave his work to take an extra holiday with me," I said, lying so convincingly and with such an appearance of common sense that I almost felt I was speaking the truth.

"Well, even if he is your husband he ought to have been more careful."

What a shrew! I thought. Is anything ever going to end this scene? To my relief, Raymond did.

"Yes, I ought to have been. I've apologized before and I apologize again now," he said politely and yet with a certain finality in his tone. "As you see it really wasn't my wife's fault."

Again I did not dare to catch Raymond's eye. "My wife," indeed!

Mrs. Massingham accepted from Raymond this dismissal of the subject better than, I suspected, she would have taken it from me. Without further accusations or reproaches she dumped Susan in the pram and prepared to quit the field of battle. Susan, I take great pleasure in recording, cried again on being put into her pram and Mrs. Massingham's exit was accompanied by shrieks.

"Actually we were both considerably in the wrong," I remarked, as the pram with its wailing occupant, disappeared from sight. "But my God! I feel as if we were entirely in the right. Don't you?"

"Anybody would feel passionately in the right after talking to that woman for a little," rejoined Raymond.

"Oh well! We'd better have tea," I said.

* * * * *

Although I am quite capable of losing my temper and not disliking doing so at the time, I always pay for it in retrospect. I know people who assert that "a good row clears the air." This has never been my experience. "Rows" are never "good" to me, but always leave a nasty taste in my mouth.

Although tea with the children was a cheerful talkative meal, and although I was busy after tea clearing away and then putting Antonia to bed, I could not altogether forget the unpleasantness with Mrs. Massingham. It rankled vaguely at the back of my mind. After Antonia was tucked up, and I had the opportunity of a little quiet conversation with Raymond, I reverted to the subject, knowing perhaps that I was being tiresome in doing so, but unable to help myself.

"I must warn Harry and Margaret that, if Mrs. Massingham says anything to them, they mustn't divulge that you're my divorced husband," I said, with a slightly forced laugh. "That *would* finish me in her eyes."

A shade crossed Raymond's face.

"Surely you don't care what a woman like that thinks of you?" he suggested.

"Raymond, you didn't *mind* me calling you 'my husband' to her, did you?" I said tentatively. "I know I oughtn't to have done it—but I just *had* to. And you backed me up splendidly. I was so grateful to you."

"No, Vicky, at the time I heartily supported you. I nearly cheered when you said it. Only—why not let the whole thing drop now? Why tell Harry and Margaret?"

"Oh, just because Mrs. Massingham *might* start complaining to them about me—she's just that sort of woman." I paused, examining Raymond's rather reticent expression with some lack of comprehension. "I'll just make a joke of it all, you know," I ended up reassuringly.

"An excellent joke," said Raymond grimly.

"Raymond! Whatever is the matter?"

"Nothing. Let's joke like anything. We've always been good at *that*, whatever else we failed at."

"I gather from your sardonic expression that nevertheless the joke doesn't appeal to you, and that you'd rather I didn't tell Harry and Margaret?" I hazarded.

"I think the joke, appropriate as it was at the time, might now be allowed to drop."

"All right," I said meekly.

I thought it curious of Raymond to mind about a little point like this, but everybody has his or her sensitive spots and everybody's are in different places.

"You don't feel at all that way yourself, Vicky?" said Raymond, shooting a sudden enquiring glance at me.

"What do you mean, exactly?"

"I meant it would be the easiest thing in the world for you to retail it all to Harry and Margaret as a joke? You think it funny yourself?"

"Well, Raymond . . ." Airiness died on my lips. Quite suddenly, as I looked at him, standing rather tall and haggard by the mantelpiece, a note of warning rang like a bell in my mind. I must not hurt Raymond's feelings, even though, I dimly apprehended, he was in some way asking for them to be hurt.

"It's like this, Raymond," I said. "Of course at the time—whatever I pretended—I didn't think our divorce in the slightest amusing. It hurt frightfully. I couldn't possibly have made a joke out of it."

"Oh, it did hurt you frightfully at the time, did it?" interjected Raymond. "Thank you, Vicky, for telling me. I was never quite sure. I take it that you're completely—'cured,' shall we say?—now?"

"Oh Raymond!" I sighed. "Isn't it a mistake to get on to this subject really?"

"You're right. It is. We ought to go on playing the good old game of 'gestures' *ad nauseam*. My only apology is that it was you who first put the idea of the how much we *did* play at 'gestures'—you and I—into my head, and now I can't leave the idea alone, curse it. I'm always wondering . . ." He swept a restless impatient hand over his head, as if to brush away the speculations that worried him.

"Yes, Raymond?" I said softly (I had to speak warily so as not to frighten away this new Raymond I was seeing now, a defenceless, confiding Raymond of whose very existence I had been unaware.)

"Always wondering how much *you're* playing a game of civilized divorce now, just as I am, and whether, frankly, the game's worth the candle. Wouldn't it be better to chuck it all up as too difficult and not meet again?"

"You do find the game difficult, do you Raymond? I hadn't realized."

I hadn't. I had often smugly congratulated myself on the ease of our newly established relationship. The game had not been difficult for me—but then I, as I suddenly and entirely for the first time realized, had been all along in the stronger position. Five years ago I had sent away Raymond of my own free will, and *that* agony had burnt itself out, furiously but utterly. Then Antonia had come into my life, and gradually filled a bigger and bigger part of it, and besides that I had my work and my own home. What had been Raymond's lot compared to mine? A broken "affair" with Sandra, no real home, a career disrupted by the war, tuberculosis.

"Oh Lord yes, I find the game difficult," Raymond was saying wearily, as all these thoughts flashed, startling in their novelty, through my head. "I thought you guessed that—that night at my flat. Didn't you realize that to have you actually staying there would be more than I could stand?"

"You mean you'd have wanted to make love to me?" I blurted out, amazed.

Raymond gave a faintly amused smile at my evident astonishment.

"Nothing quite so crude and direct as that, Vicky. Making love isn't the only thing one misses, surely? No, the position is just that every step seems so simple and obvious—why not meet for lunch, why not meet for dinner, why not come down here for the day; why not get to know Antonia? All incredibly sensible and all most frightfully mistaken. Why should I tantalize myself at this so obviously too late hour? Where's it leading us to? Nowhere. It's not worth it, Vicky. Let's chuck it."

"Oh *no*, Raymond!" I cried impulsively.

It was not that the thought of a future without Raymond appalled me. It did not, much as I should miss our occasional outings. It was just that I felt that I could not bear things to end on such a miserable note.

"My dear," said Raymond gently, "I'm being entirely selfish over this, you know. You didn't answer my question as to whether you consider yourself 'cured' of me now, but you needn't. I can see for myself you are. The game's easy for you, and therefore you've no objection to going on meeting me. Unfortunately I'm not as 'cured' as you are. I thought I was, but it's becoming more and more apparent I'm not. So I think really I'd prefer to stop. I'm only sorry I've dragged all this up first, instead *of* just quietly stopping."

"Oh no Raymond! It's much better surely to have things out. We never did before, did we? Not properly, Raymond, if we must part we must, but there is something I want to say to you first . . ."

Raymond had just paid me the compliment of being at last honest with me about his feelings towards me now. I wanted badly in return to tell him something of my feelings towards him at the time of my divorce—how I had been by no means as hardboiled about it all as I had appeared, how I had genuinely believed that he did not want "forgiveness" from me but freedom to marry Sandra instead, how clearly I now saw that I had been wrong in concealing, out of pride, the fact that I was going to have a baby, and finally how, although it was true I was "cured" now, I was not at all sure that the "cure" had been on sound foundations of real comprehension and sympathy but father a bogus affair of a gesture so long practised that it had in the end hardened into reality. I was "cured," yes. But perhaps in the process I had twisted my own personality considerably for the worse—and none of this was Raymond's fault, but entirely my own.

All this I wanted passionately to say, but none of it got said. There was a cheerful knocking on the front door, and Harry's voice called, "I say you two, what are you going to do about dinner. It's on now. Is Raymond going to come over and have it with us, Vicky, or what? May I come in?" He came, as he spoke.

The spell was broken. There is nothing so putting-off as an interruption at the wrong moment. No, I would not suggest Raymond having supper with me in the bungalow.

"Yes, you'd better, Raymond," I said flatly, suddenly feeling rather tired, and by no means disliking the thought of a quiet hour to myself before Harry and Margaret came back for the after-dinner party I had invited them to.

"What about you, Vicky? What are you going to do?" asked Raymond.

"Me? Oh, I always have sandwiches and coffee sent over on a tray. I don't like to leave Antonia alone in the bungalow, you see, even though she is in bed. And besides one full-size hot meal is as much as I can ever manage. But you'd much better go with Harry, Raymond, and have a proper dinner."

"Really?"

"Yes, really Raymond," I answered firmly.

"Come on then," said Harry, cheerful and obliging as ever.

They went.

So that's that, I thought, as the door closed behind them. I shan't have any more chance of private conversation with Raymond this evening and after this evening—the end.

I went, rather wearily, to the bathroom, to wash and tidy up. Suddenly, to my own astonishment, I felt a sudden lump rising in my throat and tears stinging my eyes.

Why was I crying? I honestly was not at all sure. Because a day that had promised to be such fun—and indeed had been for the most part great fun—was ending miserably? Or because our marriage had smashed up five years ago? Or because I wasn't now and never could be again the girl who had been "in love" with Raymond? A bit of all perhaps.

* * * * *

I very rarely suffer from insomnia. But that night I found I could not sleep.

Earlier on I had pulled myself together with, I thought, total success. I had stopped crying, eaten my supper, entertained Harry and Margaret and Raymond when they arrived, said goodbye to Raymond in public with complete composure, and retired calmly to bed, confidently expecting to fall asleep quickly.

No such thing. I became instead wider and wider awake. It was not unlike that night at Betty's when my thoughts had got so badly out of control and whirled me, against my will, into a maze of fruitless speculation. The sensation was the same, and yet the trend of thought, on which I found myself ruthlessly carried away, was different. Then I had dwelt on the five-years dead past. Now it was the recent past, the meetings between Raymond and myself during the last few months, that forced themselves into the forefront of my mind.

I felt that somewhere I must have behaved badly, or at least foolishly, I felt that things ought never to have come to such a crisis as they had reached that evening. I felt that I had in the good old phrase "led Raymond on" without ever thinking about his feelings. I felt that when at last I had (unwittingly) driven him to break down into honesty, I had given him no word of comfort or even comprehension. I had, it was true, been interrupted. But—as a sudden flash of insight revealed to me—what man who has just admitted to a girl that he is unhappy about her wants, in return, a priggish set speech about how *she* once had been unhappy over him and had cured herself? No comfort at all, of course—merely superior and irritating—it was lucky, after all that Harry had interrupted us when he did. Emotion should call forth a reciprocating emotion—not a burst of self-analysis. Post-mortems on the past are insufferable unless the present is so gloriously right that dissecting dead griefs and misunderstandings becomes a luxury.

Yes, but surely I wasn't arguing myself into thinking I ought to have burst into tears on Raymond's shoulder? Quite honestly

I hadn't wanted to. (Ah, but later in the bathroom I had found tears running down my cheeks.)

Raymond would never know that. Raymond, I did not think, had ever seen me cry. No lovers' quarrels between us ever, no husband and wife tiffs. Much laughter, much passion, there had been in our relationship, curiously little else. For a long time we had been such "spoilt darlings" of life that there had been no occasion to learn, through experience, what the marriage service so continually hinted at in its antithetical cadences—"for better for worse, for richer for poorer, in sickness and in health, to love and to cherish." No, we had not learnt. When the smash came we were caught unpractised, defenceless, with only pride to carry us, with heads high, through the shipwreck.

Poor Raymond! How bitterly he must now be regretting that I had ever come into his life again. How much better for things to have been left as they were without this strange and bitter corollary to our ruined marriage.

He would forget me again, of course. Everybody forgot everybody in time. Probably some day he would marry again—or would he, in view of his medical history, hesitate to do so? Surely if he was, as he said, cured, it would not matter that he had had T.B.?

And what about me? Betty's attempts to probe my feelings towards marrying again occurred to me. What did I honestly feel about it, supposing the chance ever occurred?

I could not imagine falling "in love" again—not in love as I had been at twenty. That was, after all, only natural. I could imagine being strongly attracted physically by someone. I could imagine liking someone very much, thinking him "my sort," enjoying his company. If I was lucky these two "some-ones" might be the same person, and, if I was even luckier, I should consider him a nice stepfather for Antonia. Even granted all this—what should I say?

I must, by this time, have been in a ridiculously worked-up state of mind, for I found I could not fling the whole question aside as absurdly hypothetical. Somehow I felt that if only I could decide in my own mind under precisely what circumstances I *would* contemplate marrying again, I could succeed in slowing down my racing thoughts and getting at last within measurable distance of going to sleep. The idiocy of such mental gymnastics in the void at two o'clock in the morning fretted me horribly, and yet, try as I would to rid myself of such nonsense, I could not. Eventually, failing miserably either to reach any conclusion to my ridiculous self-imposed problem, or to put the whole thing out of my head, I decided that the one thing I really needed was a cigarette. I did not want to smoke in the bedroom where Antonia lay, all this time most peacefully asleep, so I got up and went into the sitting-room. There, with a sigh of relief at having escaped, at least for a few minutes, from my hot tumbled bed and from the thoughts which harried me there, I switched on the lights, gave a quick look round as one does involuntarily look round a room when one visits it unexpectedly in the middle of the night, decided a drink of water before my cigarette would be refreshing and went out of the door again leaving the lights on to go to the bathroom to fill a glass.

Just as I was crossing the tiny hall the letter-box on the front door rattled gently.

I stopped short, amazed, and, underneath my amazement, I am ashamed to say—frightened. Who was it? It could not be the wind. It was a perfectly still night. It must be someone. What could they want? Who stood outside there in the dark rattling the letter-box? Oh, why hadn't I stayed in bed and gone to sleep arid not heard it?

I am not frightened of burglars, and in any case a burglar would hardly rattle the letter-box. It is the supernatural, the mysterious, which, in stories or films, can easily set my nerves on the rack. As a child I used to read quantities of ghost stories and literally terrify myself. As an adult, with no psychic experience whatsoever, I can dismiss the whole thing as nonsense until a strange shadow on the wall, a dimly-lighted mirror in an empty room, or a mysterious sound in the middle of the night can suddenly light up again in one nightmare flash the whole eerie realm of these childish terrors, buried deep now in my consciousness, but never forgotten. I suffered now a sudden awful vision of a skeleton hand, unattached to any body, climbing up the door and poking bonily about the letter-box. Night-gowned and barefooted in the semi-dark I flinched, shuddering hastily away from my own imagination.

The letter-box rattled again.

"Vicky?" said Raymond's voice.

"Raymond!" Relief, warm human relief, came flooding back on full tide. I opened the door and almost pulled him in. "I thought you were a ghost!" I exclaimed, hovering between tears and laughter.

"I'm no ghost, Vicky. Vicky—darling!"

I do not know quite how it had happened. It was my doing I am sure—but somehow I was clinging to Raymond, trembling, holding up my face to be kissed, and whether tears or laughter had finally won, I have no idea.

"Oh Raymond! I'm so glad you're not a ghost," I murmured incoherently.

"Darling! I didn't mean to frighten you. It was only that I looked back just as Harry and I had passed your bungalow and saw a chink of light appear in the sitting-room—black-out rather poor, Vicky!—and thought I'd just tell you the car broke down and we missed our train and—"

"Never mind. Never mind as long as you're here. Never mind as long as everything isn't miserable and finished and me awake not being able to stop thinking about it."

"Vicky darling! *Are* you awake? Am *I* awake. What's happening to us? *Is* this us? Isn't it all a dream?"

I could feel his heart pounding painfully against his chest and knew that, while yet holding me in his arms, his mind was struggling to get free.

"No, it's not a dream. Raymond—don't let's be apart any more. Let's be together."

"Vicky—darling. I don't understand. What's come over you? Are you crying or laughing?" Gently he tilted up my head in an attempt to see my face clearly in the half-light.

"Were you frightened or were you miserable? How can I understand you?"

"You don't need to. Just say we'll be together."

"Vicky . . ."

"It's no good, Raymond. I don't understand myself. It's just that when you said like that 'I'm not a ghost' something sort of clicked in my mind. Oh Raymond, I've been awake for hours living with ghosts—ghosts of the past, you and me together, ghosts of the future, you and me again but separate. Why be separate? Why? Just say we can be together, Raymond, and I'll let you go in peace."

"Darling, that's the awful thing. I've *got* to go. Harry's waiting over at the hotel to let me in and lock up."

"Then just promise—"

"Promise *what*, Vicky? Oh, my darling, promise *what*?"

"Promise you won't go out of my life again, Raymond. I can't *stand* it twice over. Once was awful enough. Let's pretend we were never divorced."

"Oh Vicky—God knows I wish we never had been, but—"

"*Make* it as if it never had been then, Raymond. Marry me again if you like."

I could feel Raymond, like myself, trembling, but his voice when he finally spoke, was low and grave.

"Vicky! How can I . . . ? Oh, God you do make it difficult for me! Would you mind taking your arms away one minute?"

"No. I refuse to. How can you—what?"

"How can I take advantage of your mood to promise a thing I like that? To-morrow you'd be regretting it."

"Would you, Raymond—regret it to-morrow?"

There was no answer. No sound in the cottage but Raymond's heavy breathing. No sound from outside except a sudden half-drowsy chirp from a bird.

"*Would* you Raymond?"

Shameless in my utter confidence, I clung to him and repeated my question.

"You know damn well I wouldn't, Vicky," said Raymond at last in a voice so resolute that it was almost grim.

With a sigh of utter content, I released him.

"Very well. Good. Now you can go," I said.

"Vicky!" He made an involuntary move as if to take me in his arms again, and then, as quickly, checked himself. "I've promised nothing!" he declared.

"Haven't you? I think you have. Anyway, you will. You'll never be rid of me now, Raymond," I asserted, a little lightheaded with triumph and exhaustion.

"Vicky! Oh my shameless lovely woman, you know as well as I do that you've tricked me and that there are so many many things I ought to say—"

"—which you haven't time to now," I finished impudently, "because Harry's waiting."

"—Which I shall say to-morrow," corrected Raymond.

"I'll be here," I promised in a satisfied voice.

Chapter 16

AND SO, IN THE END, only a few of Raymond's "many, many things" got said.

We did talk together, of course, an enormous amount on and off the next day, but more in a happy light-hearted way about the future, the immediate future (for we decided we wanted to get married as quickly as possible) than about the past. Somethings, such as Raymond's reasons why he ought not to marry me, I flatly refused to discuss. When Raymond finally pinned me down with one definite question—would I ever have thought of wanting to marry him if he hadn't happened to come back at that particular time? I replied, as honestly as I could, that I had not asked him to marry me because I was in a hysterical mood—I admitted the hysteria—but that my wrought-up state had permitted me to say things which in cold blood I could never have said but which all the more came from the heart. I suggested that sooner or later something of the sort would have happened, anyway, and Raymond nodded and said that that was exactly what he had been afraid of, although, he added, he had thought I was the "safe" one and he the "dangerous." A little shyly, I said that he wasn't *ever* to tease me about my behaviour the evening before. I knew it was shocking, but I hadn't cared at the time and wasn't proposing to feel ashamed now.

It was a novel and sweet delight to be cosseted and told that, on the contrary, it was behaviour of which to be proud, and that my utter shamelessness had endeared me more to him than anything else I had ever done. It was not the sort of thing we had ever said to each other in earlier days. It made me see what a lot we had missed in our first marriage. We had loved each other and laughed with each other. We had not been mutually dependent on each other in the slightest. Henceforward, I felt, we might grow to be.

I, in my turn, did ask Raymond one definite question. I asked him whether he had ever thought of "proposing" formally to me? He answered, quite simply, that he had never allowed himself to think of such a thing. I had made a better life for myself out of the wreckage of our marriage than he had done, I seemed happy in my home, my child, my work. Why should a tubercular crock think he had any right to butt in and upset things again?

I would not listen to any talk about T.B. No talk at all, and told Raymond so quite firmly—(so *that* disposed of the chief of the "many many things").

I did not at any point say, and Raymond did not ask me to say, that I was once more "in love" with him. I think he realized that all I should be able to answer was that I was absolutely sure I wanted to marry him, and that, on this firm foundation the future could be left to take care of itself. We were both delighted at the prospect of sharing Antonia.

On the whole our conversation was not very coherent. Either one of us began to laugh out of sheer light-heartedness, or else Antonia interrupted us or else Harry or Margaret put in an appearance. (And what fun it was to play before them the game of "civilized divorce" knowing all the time of the secret that lay between us.) Neither of us did more than just brush the topic of what had happened between us five years ago. Some day, I thought, I would ask Raymond a little more about Sandra—but not yet. Some day I would find out if he had thought I wanted to marry Charles—but not yet.

I quite forgot to ask Raymond more about his adventures on the previous evening until Harry looked in and spoke as if I knew all about what had befallen them. I pretended, of course, that I did, and afterwards asked Raymond to coach me quickly in all that he was supposed to have already told me. It seemed that they had had a most difficult time—the car had broken down and, after spending a long time trying to get it going again they had finally abandoned it by the roadside and got a lift to within a mile of the hotel, completing the journey on foot. Harry had taken it for granted that Raymond would spend the night at the hotel, and Raymond had seen no way of avoiding the anti-climax of meeting me again. It was Harry who had suggested, when they had seen the bungalow light go on, that Raymond should stop and tell me what had happened, and again Raymond had acquiesced to avoid awkward explanations.

"Quite quite cold-blooded and cool-headed?" I mocked.

Raymond grinned.

"Not entirely," he admitted. "As a matter of fact the prospect of seeing you again—just for a minute or two—attracted me strongly. I thought if I allowed myself that one last agonizing treat I could make a better and quicker get-away in the morning, I thought, even if I did find myself most unwisely kissing you good-bye, it would be pretty 'safe' because I *had* to tear myself away again immediately because of Harry. All the same I was pretty wrought-up on the doorstep, I can tell you."

"So was I!" I said, and we laughed happily at the vision of ourselves quaking on either side of the bungalow front door in the middle of the night.

"It does seem the most extraordinary chain of events that's led to this equally extraordinary but very gratifying conclusion," I said. "That first accidental meeting, due to Philip beginning to be born and the telephone breaking down . . ."

"That meeting was a dead end. At least I meant it to be," interrupted Raymond.

"All right. Dead end. Start again at Betty's house. That was another accidental encounter."

"Yes and no."

"You mean Betty engineered it?" I said surprised.

"No. No. I only mean Betty treated us as we had led our friends to suppose we wanted to be treated—no need for tact to see we didn't meet or anything of the sort. Given those circumstances we were bound to run into each other sooner or later."

"All right. Perhaps. Anyway, our next meetings weren't accidental."

"You're right. They weren't."

"But the fact that you came down here yesterday (good Lord, it was really only yesterday!) and then the way things went *did* depend on all sorts of odd accidental happenings. Raymond," I urged, "if Antonia hadn't been ill, I shouldn't have been here, anyway. If Mrs. Massingham hadn't infuriated me to the point of making me refer to you as 'my husband,' I wouldn't have annoyed you by wanting to tell Harry and Margaret about it as a joke, and *then* you wouldn't have let me see quite so clearly how little of a joke it was to you. Even then nothing might have happened if Harry's car hadn't broken down. *Don't* you think it's all rather extraordinary, Raymond?"

But Raymond refused to appear impressed.

"It does seem rather peculiar, Vicky," he admitted coolly. "But I think that's all an illusion you know."

"What do you mean—an illusion?"

"I mean you can always make your head spin by arguing along those lines, but after all the slightest trivial encounter or happening anywhere in your life is just as much due to just as extraordinary a chain of circumstances. Isn't it?"

I thought a moment. "I suppose it is. How disappointing!" I said. "I was quite hoping Destiny had marked you and me out as specially interesting and much more important than other people and had thoughtfully managed all this for our benefit."

"A suggestion which takes us perilously near one of those splendid semi-philosophical talks on pre-destination," remarked Raymond. "No. Destiny can keep her hands off me, as far as I'm concerned. All the same I don't think it's all quite a toss-up, Vicky."

"No?"

"No. I mean given the characters:—you and me—and the scene, set by chance, I agree, but likely to *be* set sooner or later out of sheer probability—well then *some* drama is bound to take place, isn't it? And the lines along which it will develop depend more on your character and on mine than on Fate, don't you think?"

"I see what you mean. Brilliant exposition of the old 'Dear Brutus' theme in fact?"

"More or less."

"We two—if we meet at all—there's something between us that's *got* to be worked out," I said slowly.

"Yes. It looks like that anyway."

"It's not unlike what I was thinking about Rene once—only the other way round."

"What did you think about her?"

"Oh!—only that I seemed to have been so unlucky with her over all sorts of tiny things that had put us across one another, Then I saw it wasn't bad luck at all—it was incompatibility of character. Something unfortunate was bound to occur."

Raymond grinned.

"And what precisely is going to occur to Rene now?" he enquired.

I stared at him, aghast, and then burst out laughing.

"Raymond! *What* a problem! Honestly I've no idea."

* * * * *

Raymond went back to London early on that Sunday evening. On Monday morning Antonia and I set out for Harminster. I was not due back at the office until the following Friday. I had resolved that by that date I would have everything settled, including the date of our wedding—a staggering task, but I faced it blithely.

In the train I told Antonia that she and I were going to move from Harminster and live in another house with Raymond. I was going to be married to him, I explained.

"Why?" said Antonia.

Her tone was interested but entirely casual. I was intensely grateful for the innocence of extreme childhood. Had she been twelve or thirteen the news might have been much more disturbing for her.

"Because I like him, and because I think it will be fun you and me and him living all together, and him being your Daddy," I explained. "Don't *you* think it will be rather fun?"

"Yes," agreed Antonia readily. "What colour will the curtains in my new bedroom be?"

"I really don't know, darling. What colour would you like them?"

"Pink," said Antonia instantly. "Pink with little flowers."

Probably we should have to take a furnished house, at least to start with—Raymond and I had already discussed it and decided that it must be in a "safe" area and yet accessible for daily travel to London. Nevertheless, I recklessly promised Antonia that I would try to arrange "pink with little flowers" curtains for her. I felt grateful to her for being so amiable about it all. If I was to have such a big excitement and thrill why shouldn't she have a corresponding little one of her own? Even if it meant hunting for material and getting curtains specially made up.

"But don't say anything to Auntie Rene yet," I warned her. "Just for a little it's a secret."

I had already made up my mind that, just as I had once tackled Rene for Mother, so Mother should now tackle Rene for me, and break the news to her.

"You mean it's a secret about how they're going to be pink with little flowers?" said Antonia.

"Yes, darling. At least that's *your* secret. Mine is that I'm going to be married. Don't tell Auntie Rene either of those things just yet."

"No, I won't," promised Antonia, looking pleased and important.

I dare say my expression was much the same.

It was certainly fortunate that Mother was on the spot when I got home. My mood was such that I could not have borne delay and laborious explanations by letter. It was also fortunate that

Mother had, that morning, moved out to the little hotel round the corner. As soon as Antonia was in bed that evening I was able to leave Rene in charge of the house and pour out the news to Mother in privacy.

Mother had, I think, already got over her greatest shock, when she had recognized Raymond's voice on the telephone the previous Thursday evening. Mother had never comprehended the rules of the game of "civilized divorce" as played by myself and my friends. To her it seemed inconceivable that divorced couples should arrange to meet each other unless "something was up"—and she showed me very clearly (with a slight suggestion of patting herself on the back for her feminine intuition) that she *had* considered "something was up" when she had learnt the other night that Raymond and I already had a tentative agreement to meet and spend a day together.

I did not disillusion her. I simply told her that Raymond and I had talked over the whole question and decided to marry again—and make a proper go of it this time. The last bit I added for Mother's benefit and because she was so obviously expecting the sentence to end that way.

"Darling, I'm absolutely delighted!" said Mother warmly. "As you know I always liked Raymond" (I could almost see her swallowing the phrase 'however he behaved over that woman'), "and he's Antonia's father and it will be lovely for her to have a Daddy again, won't it?"

"Yes. She and Raymond took to each other at once too, which was nice. I've already told her we're going to move and live in a little house together. She seemed quite pleased."

"Have you told her he's her father?"

"I've said he's going to be her Daddy. That's as far as I'm going at the moment; it's all so utterly above her head. I'll have to ask Raymond how much more to tell her later on."

I saw Mother nod in a satisfied way, and guessed, amused, her thoughts. ("Ah! *this* sounds better! Vicky saying she must consult her husband! *That's* more like it!")

"Well, darling, I'm delighted," said Mother again. "Although, of course . . ." She checked herself and flashed me her 'No, I'm a well-trained Mother' glance.

"Although what?" I queried indulgently.

"Although of course you can't expect me not to think that all these years apart haven't been so—so unnecessary. Such a waste."

"I don't think so, Mother. I don't honestly. I think we have a much better chance of being really happy now than if we'd never got divorced. People say it's dangerous to marry your first love, and both Raymond and I did. Now we're not."

Mother looked a little scandalized.

"I don't mean anything very shocking, Mother," I said hastily. "I only mean that now we're both ten years older and both rather different people. It really hardly seems to me that it's the same Raymond marrying the same Vicky. It *isn't* so. It's a different Raymond marrying a different Vicky. That's all I mean. However, don't let's talk about the past," I added hastily. "It's the future that really interests me now."

"Will you give up your job, Vicky?"

"Oh no! You never could really believe, could you Mother, that that *wasn't* a bone of contention between us? Only, at least, in so far as it affected the question of having a child. Perhaps we'll have another one day now—not just at once but sometime."

"Will you and Raymond go on living here, Vicky?"

"No, definitely not. It's too far for Raymond to travel up every day. It would be frightfully tiring for him." (Again I saw a shade of satisfaction cross Mother's face—Vicky considering her husband's comfort. Splendid!) "Besides," I added, "personally I'd much rather start afresh in a new place. I can easily give the cottage up. I only have it on a three-monthly lease you know, which I've just been renewing all the time. There's one thing I *must* do to-morrow—write to Blakey, and ask her if she'll come back to me when I move. She will, I'm sure."

"I don't quite understand why she ever left you," said Mother. "I know she can be tiresome, but she was devoted to you, Vicky. Such a *very* faithful soul, I always thought."

"Oh very! I really want nothing better than to have her back again. She didn't exactly leave me, you know. I sacked her—because of Rene. It's a frightfully long story which I'll tell you one day. In the meantime we've got this Dabchick woman arriving to-morrow of course. Oh well! One thing, I really don't care in the circumstances *what* she's like. I just can't be bothered to train her."

Mother looked slightly shocked.

"It seems a pity you engaged her, Vicky. It's rather letting her down, isn't it? Not that you can help it, of course. I suppose it wouldn't be best to send her a telegram . . ."

"Oh no, surely I'd better have her for a month or two, anyway. I must have *someone* to help Rene while I'm at the office."

"I'd willingly stay and look after Antonia," proffered Mother.

"That's very sweet of you, Mother. I'd *love* you to stay, but I won't have you trying to do too much. Let's have the Dabchick and you as well if you will—if you wouldn't mind staying on in this hotel here and just helping with Antonia? She'll love it, and it will be a weight off my mind to know *you're* coping too."

"Very well, Vicky dear. If you really think that's a good plan, I'd love to. What's Mrs. Dabchick like?"

"Not the sort of person I wanted at all really," I answered promptly, and gave Mother a quick character sketch. "The one thing about her was that she was obviously a nice woman in her own style, so to speak, and that Rene and she got on together like a house on fire."

"She's a lady?" suggested Mother.

"Oh yes! Certainly. Not even a distressed gentlewoman. She's got a bungalow somewhere and a little money of her own. She told me she wanted a home more than a job. Why?"

"I was only thinking—if Rene and she took to each other so much—and really Rene's future *is* a problem Vicky, because I don't think I *can* offer her a home with Maud and me. I know Maud wouldn't care for the idea, and—"

"No, indeed. Why should she? Mother, whatever's decided about Rene, *you've* done your share over her and can't be expected to upset your life again. That's certain."

Mother frowned thoughtfully.

"*Some* provision must be made for Rene, Vicky. She has so very little money of her own. Of course, as far as *money* goes, I'll willingly contribute . . ."

"Oh Mother! Why should you?"

Mother gazed at me, shocked.

"Vicky! Of *course* I must! She was Philip's wife after all, and the baby—what a darling he is now, by the way, Vicky—is my own grandchild. Of *course*, I'll make Rene an allowance. I've helped her already, you know, and I've promised to pay for Philip's schooling and I'll help her more in the future—it will have to be rather more naturally if she isn't living with me or with you any more."

"I'll help too," I said, a little rebuked by Mother's utter and calm acceptance of family obligations.

"No, no. That's not necessary, darling." Hastily but firmly, Mother waved the suggestion aside. "I've plenty—really I have—and nothing much to spend it on now except my grandchildren. Rene and Philip won't get anything that Antonia ought to have, Vicky, I can promise you *that*."

"Mother!" I cried, shocked in my turn. "As if such a thought entered my head!"

"No, no. I wasn't suggesting it had," returned Mother unruffled. "I'm only just telling you, so that you may know it. Well—where was I?"

"Something about Mrs. Dabchick and Rene some way back."

"Oh yes! I wondered if just possibly you could hand over the lease of the cottage to Rene—*I'll* pay the rent—and let Mrs. Dabchick stay on with her—more as a companion than as anything else. I'm not suggesting Rene should employ her—more of a 'sharing' arrangement,"

I goggled at Mother, trying quickly to adjust my mind to such an altered view of the circumstances.

"Well! that's an idea!" I exclaimed.

"Yes. It's only the merest suggestion, of course but if she is, as you say, a lady with a little money of her own, and if she really wants a home more than a job, as you told me she said, and if she and Rene *do* like each other as much when they know each other better... Why did Mrs. Dabchick want to take a job, anyway?"

"Oh, because she got lonely, living alone."

"So would Rene," said Mother. "In fact, I don't think she *could*, not if she's so nervous about being alone at night. And yet it would be absurd for her to have a maid, Vicky, even if she could afford one. She's awfully capable in the house you know."

"And Mrs. Dabchick would love Philip," I put in.

We gazed at each other round-eyed, and then burst out laughing.

"Well! We've certainly arranged Rene's future between us!" I said. "It only remains to explain this splendid scheme to Rene and Mrs. Dabchick."

"Oh, of course we must see, a little more of Mrs. Dabchick first," said Mother cheerfully.

"One minute we're going to send her a telegram telling her not to come," I giggled, "the next—"

"Yes, but it was after you explained to me what Mrs. Dabchick was like that the idea suddenly occurred to me," explained Mother, laughing defensively.

"Won't it be rather awkward first of all giving Mrs. Dabchick orders and then suddenly transforming her into Rene's bosom chum, who's going to share, not be employed at all?" I suggested.

"Well, I don't imagine it will be Rene who gives her many orders," said Mother. "Rene wouldn't know how—she's never been accustomed to that sort of situation. Now *don't* look at *me* like that, Vicky! I'm not being snobbish. I'm merely stating a feet."

"Quite, darling." I grinned, "It's just the *way* you state it you know. However... I don't think *I* shall give Mrs. Dabchick any 'orders' either then. It will save a lot of trouble."

"Just treat her as a sort of friend," assented Mother cheerfully.

"Quite. Rene wins in the end, so all the fuss was about nothing." I could not help bursting out laughing.

"What fuss, Vicky?" asked Mother suspiciously.

"Oh—another long story. I'll tell you one day."

"Has there been more going on between Rene and you than you ever let me guess?"

"Yes, much more," I answered frankly. "However *nothing* to what's going on now between you and me. Oh, I do hope our lovely schemes come off! I shall be so disappointed if they don't."

"We mustn't set our hearts *too* much on it, Vicky," said Mother. "We must just keep it in mind and wait and see—if it does seem possible I'll put the idea into Rene's head and then she can suggest it tactfully to Mrs. Dabchick in due course. Leave it all to me. I don't want anybody to get the impression they're being forced into anything," concluded Mother conscientiously.

"Of course not. Still, if I was Rene I'd jump at any scheme which meant I didn't have to uproot myself again."

"Yes. Moving round with a small baby can be very tiresome. And also Rene's got some nice friends here—"

"Has she?" I interrupted, surprised. "Who?"

"Well, I was thinking chiefly of that nice schoolmaster who lives near. We've seen him several times while you were away, Vicky."

"Oh—Barry! Yes. He and Rene are quite chums, that's true."

"You never mentioned anything about him in your letters, Vicky," said Mother, a trifle reproachfully. "I had no idea he and Rene . . ." She paused delicately.

"Good heavens, Mother! What are you hinting at now?" I exclaimed.

"I'm not hinting at anything, darling. How could there be anything to hint at—yet?"

"Well, you've certainly put an idea into my mind which wasn't there before," I said.

Mother certainly had. My first impulse was to tell her flatly that she was wrong—that it was *me* Barry had been "paying attention" to, or whatever was the correct phrase. I did not, however, want to tell Mother that Barry had once proposed to me. I had told her nothing about it at the time, I had never even hinted of it to Rene, and I had an idea that Barry now considered that episode as finally closed as I did. It seemed unfair on him to rake up old history.

Particular unfair, of course, if there was anything in Mother's hints about him and Rene now. I could hardly believe there was, and yet . . . I remembered how Rene's face always lighted up as she talked to him. I remembered Barry saying to me in his grave voice, 'She has such a *very* sweet nature.' Even if one discounted the fact that Mother was incurably romantic, she might yet have stumbled on a possibility to which I had been blind just because of what lay in the past between Barry and me. And yet—as I had just reflected—that bit of past *was* over, and therefore Mother, coming in fresh as an outsider, might be seeing future possibilities more clearly than I, Or even Barry or Rene, could yet.

"I don't say the idea's definitely in *anyone's* mind yet," said Mother. "I only say Rene and he seem to get on very well together, and it's nice for her to have a friend so close. I'm not suggesting for a moment that Rene's beginning to forget Philip or anything of the sort. How could she in so short a time?"

"But you wouldn't feel—hurt or anything—if she married somebody else one day?" I hazarded.

I could not imagine myself feeling hurt in the circumstances, but, knowing how Mother had felt about Philip, it seemed just possible that she might.

Mother however shook her head.

"Oh no, Vicky. Some day—not just yet of course—but some day, I should like her to marry again. I know Rene's not exactly your type, Vicky, but nevertheless she's a very sweet girl in her own way and would make a very good wife to some man. It would be much the happiest permanent—solution—for her."

"Yes. I agree with you. And in that case the very best thing I can do is to remove myself from her, and let her work out her own destiny."

I was thinking, as I spoke, of Barry and of how my presence might so easily have proved a deterrent to a budding romance between those two. It might turn out to be the happiest possible thing for Rene that I was going out of her life again as suddenly as I had come in.

I chuckled silently, amused at this novel point of view.

* * * * *

Two months later I married Raymond.

Extraordinary to relate, everything concerning Rene and Mrs. Dabchick fell out according to Mother's plan, and was settled just as we had arranged. One could never quite tell, of course, but Mother and I both agreed that there seemed every chance of the scheme succeeding. It was perfectly clear to me, after a little of Mrs. Dabchick's society, that the original plan of employing her as Mother's Help would have been foredoomed to failure. She was not precisely incompetent—but a *home* was certainly what she wanted rather than a job. I quite liked the woman, but could not help being heartily glad that it was Rene who was to offer her the home, not me.

Raymond and I found a furnished house near Elstree. It was by no means a dream cottage and compared highly unfavourably with our miniature but carefully furnished first home in Chelsea, but neither of us cared a rap.

Blakey agreed to come back to us. She did not express much pleasure at the prospect, but, when I saw her, I knew she was secretly much gratified. The thought of being reunited with Antonia (even though Antonia would henceforward be a schoolchild) was enough to make her swallow her scruples over my recklessness in marrying the same man again. Mother, I believe, had a short talk with her and tried to hint to her that Raymond had never been the unworthy traitor she had so firmly believed. I doubt if Mother made much impression, but I did not worry. The future would, I confidently felt, show her that she had been wrong, and, until Raymond himself won her allegiance, she would, I knew, serve him dourly as a 'gentleman'—however much of a swine—should be served. Best of all, Raymond and I could laugh over it all together.

On the night before I married Raymond I thought, as I got into bed, of the contrast between my first wedding-day and what lay before me on the morrow.

No trousseau this time. No orange-blossom and bridesmaids and reception. No honeymoon to the Italian lakes. Simply a short ceremony at a registrar's office, a long week-end in a hotel in the Cotswolds, and then back to the rather ugly Elstree house and straightway into ordinary married life in the middle of the worst war ever known to history.

I smiled cheerfully, turned out the light, and went quickly to sleep.

THE END

FURROWED MIDDLEBROW

FM1. *A Footman for the Peacock* (1940) . . . . RACHEL FERGUSON
FM2. *Evenfield* (1942) . . . . RACHEL FERGUSON
FM3. *A Harp in Lowndes Square* (1936) . . . . RACHEL FERGUSON
FM4. *A Chelsea Concerto* (1959) . . . . FRANCES FAVIELL
FM5. *The Dancing Bear* (1954) . . . . FRANCES FAVIELL
FM6. *A House on the Rhine* (1955) . . . . FRANCES FAVIELL
FM7. *Thalia* (1957) . . . . FRANCES FAVIELL
FM8. *The Fledgeling* (1958) . . . . FRANCES FAVIELL
FM9. *Bewildering Cares* (1940) . . . . WINIFRED PECK
FM10. *Tom Tiddler's Ground* (1941) . . . . URSULA ORANGE
FM11. *Begin Again* (1936) . . . . URSULA ORANGE
FM12. *Company in the Evening* (1944) . . . . URSULA ORANGE
FM13. *The Late Mrs. Prioleau* (1946) . . . . MONICA TINDALL
FM14. *Bramton Wick* (1952) . . . . ELIZABETH FAIR
FM15. *Landscape in Sunlight* (1953) . . . . ELIZABETH FAIR
FM16. *The Native Heath* (1954) . . . . ELIZABETH FAIR
FM17. *Seaview House* (1955) . . . . ELIZABETH FAIR
FM18. *A Winter Away* (1957) . . . . ELIZABETH FAIR
FM19. *The Mingham Air* (1960) . . . . ELIZABETH FAIR
FM20. *The Lark* (1922) . . . . E. NESBIT